D0952343

ARCHIBALD FINCH
AND THE Lost Witches

≈ ≈ ≈

MICHEL GUYON

Illustrated by Zina Kostich

To my mother,
for showing me the way . . .
And to Daniella, for guiding me
through the birth of Archibald
with extraordinary wisdom,
unique insight,
and the most inspiring stories.

Much about this story is truer than you may think.
As a matter of fact,
any resemblance to persons, living or dead—
but especially dead—
is definitely NOT coincidental.

CONTENTS

• • •

PROLOGUE

Three young girls are wandering through dark woodland.
They've just heard something.
Was that a scream, rising from beyond that ridge?
They are not aware of it yet, but life as they know it—
and as they've known it for the last 498 years—is about
to be turned upside down . . .

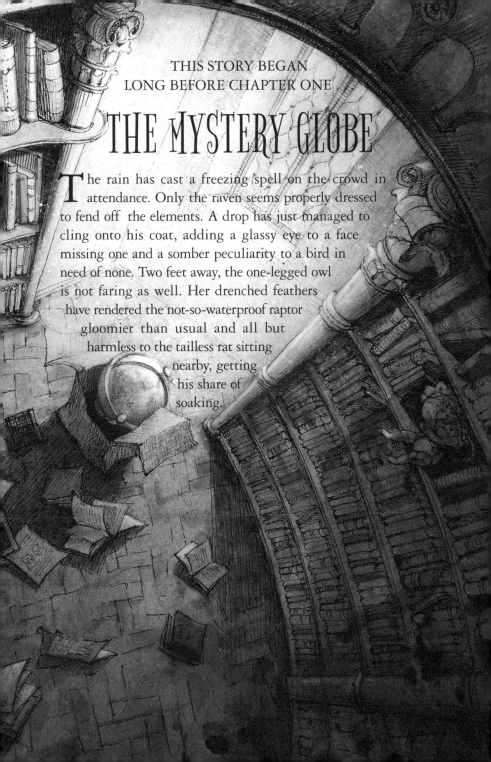

THIS STORY BEGAN
LONG BEFORE CHAPTER ONE

THE MYSTERY GLOBE

T he rain has cast a freezing spell on the crowd in
attendance. Only the raven seems properly dressed
to fend off the elements. A drop has just managed to
cling onto his coat, adding a glassy eye to a face
missing one and a somber peculiarity to a bird in
need of none. Two feet away, the one-legged owl
is not faring as well. Her drenched feathers
have rendered the not-so-waterproof raptor
gloomier than usual and all but
harmless to the tailless rat sitting
nearby, getting
his share of
soaking.

Even more ill-suited is the nearly bald moth struggling to hang onto the tree.

Slowly blending with the gray bark, he will probably never fly again, having lost most of his scant, powdery fur.

A few branches below, a ceremony has just begun: the burial of Celestine Finch. Despite the weather, her son, Stuart, is not rushing his words, now partially smeared and streaming off the paper.

"My mother's life has ended. An incredible life, if I may add. She was said to be ninety years old. Perhaps a bit more. Nobody really knows. Her birth certificate was lost a long time ago."

Sitting in a circle, two dozen friends and relatives have joined hands, frozen in silence. Standing out among a dark cluster of umbrellas, a light-brown casket is ready for its final journey—a grand, vertical six-foot trip.

Perhaps to better navigate the waters of the afterlife, the pine vessel has been adorned with a strange fishlike symbol—quite lonely in the sea of stars, crescents, and crosses carved on nearby tombstones. Consisting of a simple loop, like a half-tied shoelace, such a naive drawing would seem better suited for the coloring book of a two-year-old.

Right below, a no less unusual inscription confirms Stuart's story:

Celestine Finch
????-2021

He goes on to talk about her career as a writer. "Her unique prose brought Celestine more success than she ever dreamed of or sought. In fact, despite the bestsellers and the prizes, she always remained humble. You will never see a picture of my mother on any of her books—or anywhere else, for that matter, except right here."

On top of a chair next to Stuart sits a picture of Celestine, looking sixty rather than ninety, with her sweet almond eyes, long salt-and-pepper hair parted in the middle, and a thin mouth set in an almost childish smirk.

"To fame and distinction, she preferred the solitude of her home, often disappearing for years at a time," continues Stuart. "Most known for the lost words she nursed back to life, she did the same with children affected by war, famine, and other tragedies. Her legacy speaks for itself, as she leaves behind nearly fifty orphanages around the world."

Three people are seated slightly closer to the casket and the gaping hole in the ground. Two have their heads down: Stuart's wife, Kate, and their teenage daughter, Hailee. One has his head up. This is Archibald. Gazing at the busy branches above, the young boy is slurping rain, his long hair channeling drops directly into his mouth. Could he be the one who drew that fish on the casket? It's very possible. In all of his eleven years, Archibald has never been fond of Celestine.

"Why did you let Grandma give me this stupid name?" he often asks at dinnertime. A name he blames for all the teasing he gets at school, although, in all fairness, he owes most of that treatment to his reputation—as a teacher's pet. A status he's gained rather reluctantly. Please don't get him wrong. By all accounts and by far, Archibald is way smarter than any other student at Amesbury Academy, and it's nothing new. As far as he can remember, he has always known everything about everything. But that's not really his fault, you see. For one, Archibald never studies particularly hard. In fact, he hardly studies at all. For some reason, he just happens to know a lot, from mathematics to history and pretty much everything in between. Should he want to be a millionaire, he could make the rounds of a few game shows and never have to work a day in his life.

The only thing that still eludes him, though, is *why* he knows so much. Teachers don't care about the why, how come, or by what means. They just love him—too much, apparently. Archibald has tried everything to reverse that curse—lie, cheat, play dumb—all of which he is really good at. Unfortunately, it has made no difference. At the end of the day, when a question is asked and no one else has the answer, Archibald can't help it; he has to raise his hand.

It doesn't help that his favorite way to express shock or surprise is to shout, "Holy bejabbles!" Not quite the best habit for fitting in and making friends. Nobody knows where the expression comes from or what it even means. Some say those were the first two words Archibald ever uttered. The ones he hears most often, though, are "dweeb" and "brownnoser," from many of his classmates. But, again, they're just telling him the truth, sort of. Except for William Tanner—*he* is a bully. Last week, that brute even tried to kiss Archibald's sister. On the mouth. Twice. What did Archibald do to stop him? Nothing. He was far too afraid. That's the other thing about him: while he dreams of blending in like a chameleon, his default move is to play possum. To put it plainly, our hero is a bit of a wimp.

A few days after the funeral, Archibald and his family arrive at 8 Culpeper Lane. Why the address doesn't just read 1 Culpeper Lane is a mystery, since there seems to be only one house on this obscure road. Not just a house, though: a grand, majestic, three-story manor—a big, fat mansion for short.

Rising at the end of a long driveway, the humble dwelling boasts twenty-seven windows on its façade alone. This is the place they inherited from Grandma Celestine, in the town of Cuffley, in Hertfordshire County. Their small car is followed by a not-so-big-either moving truck. Archibald's family obviously didn't own much—until now.

"How could she hide this from us all these years?" asks Kate, taking in the endless grounds of the property, formal gardens with short hedges planted in the most intricate patterns—swirls, commas, zigzags, but rarely a straight line.

Whoever did this drank way too much beer, thinks Archibald, making himself chuckle.

For his part, Stuart just wonders why his mother would have needed such a big place. His best guess: "Maybe this was also an orphanage at one point."

"You think so?" asks Kate.

"You know my mother," he says. "She was so secretive."

"And so mean," adds Archibald from the back seat. "What kind of name is that, anyway? Archibald?" he asks for the nine-hundredth time.

"She was not that bad," says Stuart. "You should read her books. You never know; you could learn something. You, too, Hailee."

Learn something? Archibald doubts it. That would imply there's something out there he doesn't already know, hence the frown. As for Hailee, she barely strays from her frenetic texting rhythm.

"Why couldn't we stay in London?" she questions.

"Oh, please," sighs Kate. "Thirty minutes by train to the city—in a way it's still London. Can't you focus on the bright side of things? We're so close. You'll both keep your school and your friends."

"I have no friends," mumbles Archibald. "I wouldn't mind a different school."

5

"Are you crazy?" Hailee thunders at him.

"Hailee, please don't start," demands Stuart. "We haven't even moved in yet."

"Holy bejabbles! Look at those topiaries!" exclaims Archibald, seeing two trees trimmed to the shape of animals—a horse and an elephant.

"How you know these are called topiaries, I have no idea," says Kate.

"Me neither," he replies. "I thought everybody knew that."

"Why would we want to know that?" asks Hailee.

Archibald shrugs her off, focused on those weird sculpted trees, which remind him of something. "This yard's so big I can finally get a dog, eh, Dad?"

"I'm not sure you're ready for that, Arch," cringes Stuart.

"I'll call him Paws," says Archibald.

"Now that's original!" mocks his sister.

"A small dog maybe, like *this* big?" says Archibald, suggesting a lap-sized pup. Verdict: still too big. Stuart shakes his head in the rearview mirror as he parks by a dried-up fountain.

The Finches have arrived but won't quite grasp the full scale of their new home until they stand by the entrance, dwarfed by the colossal double front door.

"Giants must have lived here once," Archibald says to himself, staring at the huge door knockers that even his dad has a hard time lifting.

"Clang, clang." The metallic knock reverberates through every corridor, every cracked stone, every soot-filled chimney, every wobbly pipe and chandelier in the house.

While they wait, Archibald strokes one of the two winged lion statues flanking the entryway.

"Flying cats! These would make great pets," he mutters.

He is not as excited, to say the least, about the other stone creatures projecting from the roof above: ivy-clad monsters—part dog, part pig, part bat—lurking at either end of the gutters.

"Gargoyles," he whispers to himself.

The door eventually creaks open. Or was it the skinny old man greeting them who was creaking? Presumably tall but mostly extremely bent, Bartholomeo was Celestine's butler. He came with the house, in charge of a grand staff of one: himself—as cook, handyman, housekeeper, beekeeper, keykeeper, and apparently gatekeeper as well—definitely a keeper.

"So nice to see you again, Bartholomeo," says Kate. "You did such a marvelous job planning the funeral."

"Thank you for taking care of my mother all these years. You're one of her best-kept secrets," says Stuart, his hand disappearing into Bartholomeo's large mitt.

"Yes," the servant replies with a strong Italian accent and a surprisingly sweet voice that offsets his dreary appearance—to a degree. A man of few words, that Bartholomeo. He uses about fourteen, including "maybe," "okay," "huh," and "no, I'm not a hunchback," in response to Archibald's question starting with "if you don't mind me asking," which sounded like one of Grandpa Harvey's slipups. But Bartholomeo does not mind, and he goes on showing his new manor-mates around, room after room, after room, after room—fifty-six in total.

"No doubt," whispers Kate. "It does look like an orphanage." The creepy kind, if you ask Archibald. The maze of drafty hallways sends chills down his still quite mushy spine. His hand freezes on every knob, for he fears that every door conceals a ghost—or a monster. The squeaky floors paralyze his almost comically cautious steps. The clanging of Bartholomeo's huge key ring shakes him to his rather easily shakable core. The hairless dolls in the library seem to always keep their eyes on him—no matter where he stands. Not to mention the countless spiders that reveal their size—ginormous—as they slide down stalactites of cobwebs hanging from the highest of ceilings.

And then there's his fear of the paintings. It's not so much the ones lining the walls that scare the bejabbles out of Archibald. The landscape masterpieces are boringly peaceful. Same thing with the rugs hanging around the house. Yes, hanging *on* the walls, if you can believe it. Archibald knows the culprits: *Probably the same drunk guys who planted those hedges all crooked.* He is only joking. Of course he knows what these are, and, just like the topiaries, they have a special name: tapestries. Did he read about that somewhere? No, he just knows. These wall carpets might actually harbor something spooky in their handwoven threads. But they are so old, with colors so faded, that each scene is essentially a blur—a welcome, nonthreatening blur.

What Archibald is worried about, though, are the paintings that are missing—the ones that once decorated the wall alongside the grand staircase. Clearly there for a long time, as two rectangles of unfaded wallpaper can attest, they are now reduced to ghostly silhouettes haunting the foyer. When and why those paintings were removed, where they could possibly be now, and, more importantly, what or whom they depicted, are all matters that torment the newcomer each time he goes up or down the stairs.

Should his parents decide to sell this house, Archibald would certainly not mind. In fact, he'd gladly volunteer to write the ad himself: "For sale (ASAP): dumpy mansion, ideal as horror movie set, creaky throughout, ~~probably haunted,~~ haunted for sure, smells funny, will trade butler for puppy or kitten. Did I mention ASAP?"

In the meantime, he insists on sharing a room with his sister, an idea Hailee reluctantly agrees to at dinner on their first night.

"I can't believe this," she seethes. "There's a million bedrooms in this house and we've gotta—"

"Twenty," corrects Bartholomeo as he brings pudding to the long table lined with many empty chairs.

"I beg your pardon?" asks Hailee.

"Twenty, not million," he says.

8

"It's just an expression," says Hailee, shaking her head but unable to shake the stone-cold look off Bartholomeo's face. "Okay, fine, *twenty* bedrooms," she concedes. "So why should we have to share one?"

"No biggie, you guys were already sharing a room," says Stuart.

"He keeps his light on all night! I can't sleep!" snaps Hailee.

"Okay, he's scared of the dark, like most kids," explains Kate.

"Most kids, yes, but not after they turn three!" says Hailee.

"Maybe he can use a flashlight instead—right, Arch? Under the blankets?" suggests Stuart.

Archibald shrugs a "why not?"

"It will be fine. Bedrooms here are twice as big," adds Kate.

"That's the point!" fumes Hailee. "I wanted a bigger room and privacy. We're not kids anymore! We already share everything. Do you know what it's like to be in the same class as your brother, even though I'm two years older than him?"

"I never asked to skip grades."

"I know, right? It just happened. You're just too smart! And I'm the dumb one," she says with a fake grin.

"Hailee, no one called you dumb," says Kate.

"You don't need to, Mum."

"Look, it's only for a couple of months," says Stuart, "until Arch gets used to this new house." That's if he ever gets used to it—and that's a big if.

Archibald is most fascinated—meaning scared—by the living room fireplace. Some people have a walk-in closet. This is a walk-in fireplace, under which one can literally stand. More than one, in fact. As Stuart said when they arrived, "You could easily fit ten people in there." Or wood logs as big as entire tree trunks.

It takes Archibald a week to get close enough to the stone mantelpiece to make out the carvings: three women, their heads shaved, faces distorted by screams, hands tied to poles, tongues of infernal flames licking at their dresses, and all around them a mob of crazy folks dancing and waving pitchforks. Archibald immediately regrets laying eyes on this dark spectacle.

What did they do to deserve that? he asks himself. But more importantly, *Who would put such a horrible thing in their house? Grandma, that's who!* Archibald already knew she was a bad person for giving him that stupid name. Now he is also convinced that Grandma, behind her innocent little smirk, was a monster.

What if this fireplace was used for something other than melting marshmallows? Archibald wonders suddenly, *Didn't Dad say, "You could easily fit ten people in there"?* That unfortunate comment has just taken on a whole new meaning. Archibald's mind is assailed by a tornado of what-ifs and maybes. *What if Mum was right? Maybe this house was an orphanage. Maybe the really sinister sort of orphanage. What if Grandma got rid of all the kids in this fireplace? Maybe that's why it's so big!*

Archibald is staring at the pile of ashes in the hearth with sheer dread. That weird, tingly sensation is back in his legs, the peach fuzz on his prune-sized calves standing on end. It happens when he gets really scared of something—usually in the morning, evening, and sometimes around lunchtime as well. Before his whole body turns to concrete, Archibald takes off and runs up to his room.

Now he can't get that nightmarish scene out of his head. As a result, he winds up spending the next two days hiding under the blankets, faking a cold—the whole time tormented by those scary gargoyles making wicked croaking sounds out on the roof, rain dripping from their mouths in loud, blood-curdling gushes.

Only when Christmastime shows its snowy nose does Archibald get somewhat of a break. The afternoon of December 1st is still a tough one. William Tanner ridicules him once more at the bus stop after stealing drawings out of his backpack—caricatures of macaques, baboons, and orangutans.

"Archibaldo thinks he's Picasso!" shouts Tanner, exhibiting the sketches.

The bully monkeys around until other students point out a rather intriguing detail: one of those funny apes seems to have a lot in common with Tanner himself. Is it the teeth, fanned out like the prongs of a garden rake and leaving daisy patterns on toasts and apples? Maybe it's the leafy ears, quite convenient for picking up free satellite TV but rather hazardous on a windy day. Unless it's simply the eyes, intense as pond goop and in such close proximity to one another they seem about to overlap.

Whether it be one or all of the above, this probably-not-so accidental resemblance earns the artist one more smack behind the head and three extra knots in his school tie.

Archibald will have to wait until nineteen minutes past five o'clock for his life to get better. That's when he gets home. Hands deep in his pockets, looking down, kicking rocks on the driveway, his face lights up at the sight of Bartholomeo dragging a ten-foot tree into the house—a Christmas tree! It's also seven feet wide, which matters greatly since that means it is big enough to conceal most of that evil fireplace from Archibald's view.

The family spends a whole quarter of an hour decorating the massive noble fir with just enough tinsel, baubles, and lights to cover the bottom fifth of its branches.

"I guess we'll need more ornaments," notes Stuart. "This is slightly bigger than the pine tree we had last year!"

"The one barely taller than Archibald, you mean? The one we put on the kitchen table?" says Hailee, chuckling.

"It was not that small!" protests Archibald.

"It was very cute," says Kate, coming in with several gifts in her arms, placing them under the tree.

"Where's mine?" asks Archibald, not seeing his name on any of the tags.

"You'll have to be patient," says Kate. "We thought about a gift for you, but—"

"Does it bark?" interrupts Archibald.

"No, you're not getting a dog," says Kate. "It's far too much responsibility, and you are not ready for that."

"What about a pony?"

"What's next? A flock of sheep?" asks Stuart.

"That's a great idea, Dad! Think about it: no more mowing the lawn! And there sure is a lot of lawn around here!"

"Okay, look," says Kate. "For the last four years, you've turned Christmas into an Easter egg hunt, wreaking havoc on the apartment looking for your present. That cannot happen here. Therefore," she pauses, gearing up to break the news, "we have not bought it yet."

Archibald cannot believe his ears. This is the biggest letdown since that guy on the *Eaten Alive* show was *not* eaten alive.

"What?!" he shouts. "But if you wait, there'll be nothing left!"

"Don't worry; we'll get it before Christmas," says Kate. "You're eleven. You're a big boy now. You can wait a few weeks, right?"

Archibald's answer comes only after some deep thinking. "If I'm a big boy, can I get a cat, then?"

"Oh my!" sighs Stuart.

Feeling crushed, Archibald retreats behind his curtain of long hair, gobbling down his fifth candy bar of the day. His disappointment is not so much about the gift itself as it is about the tradition. Dead set on keeping it alive, and convinced his mum is fibbing, he will wait until after dinner to start his search.

Kate and Stuart have to leave to visit Grandpa Harvey. The timing couldn't be more perfect. This year's hunt won't be easy, though. First, it will require that risk-averse Archibald stray from the "safe zone" he has stuck to for the last two months. Since moving in, rarely has he stepped outside a narrow track leading from the kitchen to his bedroom—except for a few daunting trips at night to the gargling toilet down the hall. Second, this is not the tiny two-bedroom, one-and-a-half-bath apartment the family lived in before. There must be hundreds of closets in this manor. Bartholomeo would say sixty-three, and he would be right. Archibald starts with the ones lining the hallways. As he quickly finds out, they're all empty. Same thing for that cupboard under the stairs, where he finds nothing but an old pair of round glasses.

One door left and Archibald will be done with the hallway on the top floor—a door much shorter than the others, which he always believed to be a broom closet, until he steps inside. Nothing much to step *on*, in fact, since it turns out there's no floor there at all.

For Archibald, it's like missing a step—a very, very high step. Totally caught off guard, he topples over. His heart drops, but *he* doesn't. He has grabbed onto a rope strapped to a pulley above. After a few twists and shouts, he finally stabilizes, stuck in a most precarious position. Turned into a corkscrew, his entire body ends up suspended in the air—his entire body, minus the big toe of his left foot, still hooked onto the edge of the hallway floor. Glancing at the void below, Archibald preserves an uneasy balance between that big toe and both his hands, moving up and down with the rope, as if he were milking a cow. Should he let go of either side of the rope, he would tumble to who-knows-where. The pressure on his limbs and lungs is such that he can't even call for help.

"I'm gonna die," he coughs out.

About to give up, Archibald swings his body back and forth, lunging forward with all his might. Miraculously, he lands back on safe ground, amazed he managed to dig himself out of this hole.

"Holy bejabbles!" he lets out. "Is that a dungeon?"

Getting on all fours, Archibald leans over carefully to check the depth of the pit. He fishes a penny out of his pocket and drops the coin into the hole. One, two, three, four seconds go by and still no sound. Not a clatter. Not a splash. No echo. No sign of a bottom.

"A tunnel to the center of the earth!" gasps Archibald.

He hurries down to the floor below, trying to find a similar opening. There's none. Then he remembers seeing another dwarf door downstairs, between the living room and the library. That one's no broom closet either. It's the bottom of the shaft, and nestled inside is a wooden cart attached to the rope through another wheel. Archibald's penny fell not in China but straight onto a stack of bedsheets in the cart.

"Doorknobs for giants and now this? An elevator for elves!" he exclaims.

"And I thought you were clever!" drops Hailee as she walks by.

"What is it, then?" he asks.

"You don't know, genius?" she says, savoring this moment. "It's for laundry! Bartholomeo said to leave it alone. It's broken. By the way, careful with that small door upstairs; it's dangerous."

"Gee, thanks for the heads-up."

"Come to think of it, do me a favor—use that door," Hailee grins.

For a moment, Archibald imagines climbing into the cart as though boarding a launch pad that will propel him from the earth to the moon. *Nah, that was enough of a scare for tonight.*

After grabbing a flashlight to avoid another whoops moment, Archibald turns his attention to the bedroom closets. He is in for another surprise. Each of them is packed with linen gowns and dresses that were last fashionable when the queen of England was a king.

"What's with the old costumes?" he wonders aloud, exploring every dark corner. He doesn't venture too deep inside, for fear of getting lost or trapped among the layers of fabric that feel like cobwebs. He flinches as a stray sleeve brushes his shoulder. *Was that a hand?* He won't stick around for an answer.

Conveniently skipping Bartholomeo's quarters and the ogre-like snoring echoing from that area, Archibald takes his quest to his parents' bedroom, a relatively safe terrain. He combs through it quickly, in case they come back early.

"Where aaaaaare you?" he sings, calling for his gift to magically reveal itself. "I'll find you!" he says, zeroing in on his mum's dresser. That's where she put that painter's kit last year. No luck this time, though. Just in case, he also checks under the bed, where Stuart admitted to hiding a game console three Christmases ago.

"Looking for monsters again?" asks Hailee as she enters the room, seeing him crawl on the floor.

"The only monsters are those gargoyles on the roof. They make the same noise as the toilet," he says.

"What's a gargoyle?" asks Hailee. "Wait, no—who cares? Look, if you don't get your own room soon, I swear I'll tell everyone at school you're afraid of the dark and monsters."

"I'm not afraid of anything," he says, "except those creepy dolls . . . Wait, that's it!" he shouts, banging his head on the bed slats.

"You are so weird!" hisses Hailee, as Archibald zooms past her shouting, "The library!"

After scanning the room and its roughly five thousand books—the exact count known only to Bartholomeo—he endeavors to pull and tilt every one of them to get a quick glance behind— while also trying to evade the all-seeing eyes of the hairless dolls, which is no minor feat.

"I won't look at you, so don't even try," he tells them in a bid to avoid a staring contest he knows will be unwinnable.

When finished with the books at ground level, he turns to the ladder. Mounted on wheels and attached to a shiny bronze rail near the top, it is built to slide all around the room—a convenient tool to reach higher shelves, although Archibald might have a different purpose in mind for it right now.

"Let's see what you've got," he says, testing the wheels back and forth in a sawing motion. Apparently, it didn't elude Archibald that the room is shaped like a peanut, meaning a figure eight . . . or a racetrack. After taking a few steps back to get a good run-up, he rushes forward. Pushing the ladder as hard as he can, he runs alongside, then climbs onto it. It's like catching a moving train— and probably the closest he'll ever get to that sort of thrill.

"Here I come!" he shouts, riding the ladder like he would a horse, waving the flashlight above his head.

It all goes well until he reaches the main curve in the wall of books—a turn the sliding ladder was not quite designed to take that fast, especially with someone on it.

"Slow down!" begs Archibald, suddenly aware of the hiccup about to happen. But it's too late. No time to jump off this train. The wheels come to a squeaking halt. The next instant, Archibald loses his grip on the ladder and is thrown against the wall of shelves, some of which tilt forward, unloading an avalanche of books on his head as he lands with a thud on the floor.

It takes Archibald a few seconds to stand back up, dazed but unharmed, mainly worried about the mess he's just made.

"Mum's going to kill me."

Scrambling to put the books back together, he catches sight of something on an upper shelf, half-empty now that eleven of the fifteen volumes of Jules Verne's *Voyages Extraordinaires* have been toppled.

"What is that?" he mumbles, not quite sure what he's looking at. Something square for sure, but beyond that, no certainty, just a hunch that his quest might finally yield a result. He moves the ladder over and climbs up. *Victory at last!* Between *The Child of the Cavern* and *Twenty Thousand Leagues under the Sea*, he finds the Holy Grail: a brown box, cocooned in a shell-shaped alcove.

"I told you I'd find you," he says to the box.

Archibald drags it forward. It's heavy—a good sign. This is a substantial present we're talking about. *Mum definitely lied. But, of course, she's forgiven already.*

Archibald descends the ladder with his prize and sits on the floor as he folds open the flaps. And there it is, the sought-after present, the gift that took his parents weeks if not months to find, that special something, that unique reward for a unique son, that . . . dull, used, yellowish "thing" that smells like a mix of sweaty sneakers and hot croissant.

Archibald's expression shifts from excitement to confusion. Pulling the object out of the box, he discovers a twelve-inch terrestrial globe as old as everything else in the house.

"What is *this?*" he lets out, pouting.

Not quite what he expected, that's for sure. Still, it's *his* stinky globe. He decides to bring it back to his room.

"What is that piece of junk?" inquires Hailee as soon as Archibald enters with the globe in his arms.

"My Christmas gift! I found it," he declares, full of pride.

Hailee doesn't care much, anyway, busy looking at herself in the mirror, holding a pink T-shirt up to her chest that clashes heavily with her school uniform (striped tie, white shirt, gray sweater, pleated skirt, and winter tights).

Archibald places the globe on his desk, getting a first close look at his find—an all but ordinary find, undoubtedly.

Mounted on a wooden base consisting of three carved lion paws, the frame is made entirely of bronze, with that unique fool's gold tint. Studded with rivets, two rings wrap around the globe itself to meet again at the top, where a contraption resembling a crank handle seems a bit out of place.

"I hope it lights up," mutters Archibald.

Not seeing any cord or switch, he turns the crank like an old clock, winding it as far as he can, as hard as he can. But nothing happens.

"No light, I guess," he pouts.

As his dad comes in, Archibald tries to act normal, striking an awkward pose in front of the globe to hide it.

"Grandpa Harvey says hello. He can't wait to have you guys over in a couple of weeks."

"Can't wait!" says Archibald, sounding abnormally thrilled.

"Can't wait," echoes Hailee, with a sigh.

Only when he's about to leave does Stuart notice something new on Archibald's desk.

"Where did you find that?" he asks.

"What?" answers Archibald, now leaning on the desk to better block his present from view.

"That!" insists Stuart, pointing at the globe.

Archibald gives up, but not without a fight.

"Nice try, Dad. I must say—the library, behind the dolls, on a high shelf? You guys did pretty well this year. It took me forever to find it, but I did!" brags Archibald, his arms crossed high on his chest full of air.

"Oh, I see. You think this is your Christmas present?"

"Of course it is. Why would you hide it so well if it wasn't?"

"I'm telling you it's not, but you don't have to believe me."

Doubts start creeping into Archibald's mind. He knows his dad would never lie—not to him, at least.

"Maybe it was hidden for a reason, like a treasure," says Stuart.

"A treasure?" mutters Archibald, thinking pirates, black sails, rum breath, wooden legs, and eye patches, even though that cardboard box was no captain's chest.

Stuart examines the globe. "One thing is for sure. It's really old," he says.

"How old?" asks Archibald.

"So old that America is barely on here, that's how old! Look—it's just a smudge of a continent!" exclaims Stuart. "This globe was made four, maybe five centuries ago. I mean, everything on here is in Latin. I know you're smart, but you don't speak Latin, do you?"

"I know pig Latin!" quips Hailee, giggling.

"I'm not sure that's going to help," grins Stuart. "Anyway, I think it's broken."

"Broken?" groans Archibald.

"Well, it doesn't spin," says Stuart, trying in vain to rotate the globe on its axle. "And it's dented," he notes, showing a hole right in the middle of Europe. "Did you stick your finger in here?"

Archibald shakes his head in denial.

"Wait, what is this island right here? This island doesn't even exist," Stuart points out, referring to an unknown piece of land off the coast of Ireland. "Same thing with this one over here by Spain. Another mysterious island! I guess they still had a lot of exploring to do. Fascinating, isn't it?"

"Yes, amazing, Dad," nods Hailee from her bed. "Nerds," she whispers, rolling her eyes.

"And look at all the strange beasts everywhere," adds Stuart, poring over the globe. "What's this? A winged snake with an eagle's head? What did they call that thing?"

"A basilisk?" says Archibald.

"Yes, that's it! Of course you know!"

"Of course he knows," repeats Hailee, irritated.

"What a fantastic creature, able to kill with just one glance," adds Stuart. "I bet if you look closely, you'll find all the monsters that kept people up back then."

"Monsters?" asks Archibald.

"You know, werewolves, dragons, manticores, griffons."

"But those don't exist!" grins Archibald.

"You're right; they are legendary creatures. But in any legend, there's a kernel of truth. Just a slightly distorted truth, that's all."

"What do you mean?" asks Archibald.

"These beasts weren't born out of nowhere, Arch. They reflected people's fears. And believe me, people had a lot to fear back then. Imagine: waiting for the night to come, the darkest of nights, with no lights but torches, being surrounded by the woods, humongous, deep, impenetrable woods. A world where every shadow gave birth to a new monster. And a new tale. And beyond that, the oceans, even more vast, unexplored, full of danger and mystery. Think about sailors; think about what it meant to go to sea at that time. They must have been terrified. So what did they do? They exaggerated their stories. Squids became sea serpents or giant krakens threatening to sink boats. Remember; the unknown is always scarier than what you can see and understand."

Archibald is breathless and speechless, staring at the globe. His chest has deflated, and his mouth has fallen wide open. He is in awe.

"Dragons and griffons . . ." he mumbles.

Glued to a handheld magnifier, Archibald's oversized right eye travels around the globe. Naturally, he is most interested in the strange creatures populating the map. He has just spotted a rather interesting specimen near the city of Herculu by the Strait of Gibraltar, the funnel commanding the entrance to the Mediterranean Sea.

"What are you?" Archibald wonders aloud, addressing what looks vaguely like a pig endowed with two mouths, eight legs, fangs made of branches, and the tail of a lizard.

"A cat!" he exclaims a minute later when he stumbles upon a special breed of his favorite animal on the island of Sicilia, south of Italia. Part octopus, that feral feline fellow has tentacles all around its neck and eyes all over its body, scattered in a cheetah pattern. Unusual for sure but almost tame compared with the unique bear he locates nearby on the coast of Slavonia.

"A bear with a porcupine coat!" whispers Archibald. Bloated like a blowfish, the entire body of that behemoth is indeed studded with horns of different lengths.

"Are these feet?" questions Archibald. "And that face, it's so human," he adds, noticing perhaps the strangest detail yet, lending more mystery to these weird creatures. Each of them seems to possess a humanlike feature, from a head to a toe.

Drawing with quick, self-assured strokes, Archibald sets out to reproduce each monster on paper. A day, a night, and another day go by, and his bedside gradually turns into a mini zoo. Soon, his full-length portraits, claw details, and snout close-ups cover an entire wall and a third of another, creeping toward Hailee's side of the room.

"Can you stop already with that freak show? I'm going to have nightmares!" she yells.

"What about *your* freak show? Don't you think it gives *me* nightmares?" he replies, referring to the posters pinned above her bed featuring various teenaged heartthrobs.

"Look, after Christmas you're out of here," says Hailee. "In the meantime, stay away from me and don't invade my space, okay?"

Archibald just nods. Anyway, they couldn't put any more distance between their beds, crammed in opposite corners of the room.

"And stop wearing my sweatshirt!" begs Hailee.

"It's not even yours. It's Mum's from college, and it's been washed so many times it fits me better now," corrects Archibald, readjusting his hoodie with three Greek letters printed across the front: omega, delta, psi—Kate's old sorority at Harvard.

Archibald is now studying a monster at the foot of the Pyrenees in southern Gallia (France). It appears to be some sort of horse with the head of an owl and a pair of wide bird wings. He is trying to get every detail right when his magnifier wanders to the side by accident. That's when he notices the crack his dad had found, located near a country called Moldavia in Eastern Europe by the Pontus Euxinus (the Black Sea). The edges are too sharp and too straight for that hole to be a crack. It looks machine made. And his dad was wrong on another point: Archibald's finger wouldn't fit in there. He does try, but even his pinky is too small. Instead, he sticks his pencil into it. A faint click occurs right away, followed by a louder intestinal tumult of gear wheels and springs. Slowly, the bottom of the dent rises back up, ending flush with the surface.

"Holy bejabbles!" utters Archibald.

Moving his magnifier as close as he can, he discovers other hidden cutouts on the globe. He can feel them under his jittery, half-gnawed fingernails. Again using his pencil, he presses down on one of them right next to Bohemia, part of the larger country of Germania, near the border with Polonia. This time, the tiny square insert sinks into the globe with another ruckus of moving nuts and bolts. Archibald doesn't quite know what those indents do, but it doesn't matter. "This is the best toy ever!" he exclaims, holding the globe above his head like a trophy.

Hailee makes a mocking comment, but he doesn't pay attention. Looking at the globe from underneath, he notices something he had not seen before: a hole lined up with a pin inside one of the rings connecting the globe to its base—an odd-shaped hole, rimmed with notches revealing its true purpose. "It's a keyhole," mutters Archibald. "But where's the key?" he wonders aloud.

"What key? What are you talking about?" asks Hailee, exasperated.

"Nothing—go back to your phone," he tells her.

Archibald goes through each drawer in the kitchen, living room, and library. He looks into that little cup by the front door where Stuart always leaves the car keys. And, of course, he checks behind the Jules Verne books where he found the globe. No luck. Time for bed. He passes an exhausted Bartholomeo snailing up the staircase. The old man looks more hunched than ever. Just the other day, Archibald overheard his dad say that "Bartholomeo is the main pillar of this house." And according to his mum, "without Bartholomeo, this house would collapse." *No wonder his back is so bent*, thinks Archibald, *with all that weight on his shoulders!*

The poor fellow walks like a gorilla, his arms dragging so low that the keys he carries bang against the stairs. The clanging sound stops Archibald in his tracks. He's just connected the dots.

"He has it," he whispers, staring at the ring of keys.

No doubt his parents gave Bartholomeo the key to the globe, entrusting him with a sacred mission. After all, in every tale and adventure Archibald has ever heard of, there's always a gatekeeper denying the hero his prize. If not a three-headed dog, it's a two-faced giant or a single burner dragon, so why not an ogreish butler?

Sure, Archibald could ask him for the key, but that cranky old man might say no—like the other day when he denied Archibald a ninth serving of ice cream. Besides, it's so much more fun and challenging to try to steal it from him. Let the showdown begin. Archibald shall defeat the creature standing in his way.

He starts following Bartholomeo everywhere, except into that small patch of woods on the south side, deemed "half woods" by Stuart based on the trees' short supply of branches, lack of twigs, missing foliage, and scarcity of life in general.

Besides that, he pretty much shadows Bartholomeo, scrutinizing his every move, waiting for that bony hand to let go of those skeleton keys. But the watchful Bartholomeo never leaves them out of his blurry sight.

When he prepares breakfast, lunch, or dinner, the keys are on the countertop next to a set of long, scary knives. When he retires to his room for one of his five daily naps, he takes the keys with him. Those keys are to Bartholomeo what chips are to fish, yin is to yang, and candies are to stomach cramps—inseparable.

Archibald has a plan. He's going to trick Bartholomeo by diverting his attention. One morning, before school, he bursts into the kitchen, gesticulating wildly, pulling his hair.

"Mum fell into that laundry elevator!" he shouts. Bartholomeo rushes, slowly, to help—but grabs the keys on his way out.

The day after, Archibald tries something else, taking the drama up a notch. This time, it's Hailee who's supposedly in trouble.

"She got lost in the half woods!" Which of course she would never, for she fears them as much as Archibald does. Yet again, Bartholomeo comes to the rescue, limping across the backyard—with the keys.

Archibald doesn't give up. Day after day, he keeps trying, coming up with fresh ploys to catch Bartholomeo off guard.

Friday: "Mum ate one of Grandpa's biscuits; she can't breathe!"

Saturday: "Hailee dropped her phone into the well and jumped in to get it!"—the most credible of his claims by far, if, in fact, there were a well on the property . . .

Sunday: "Dad got stung by a thousand bees! He's got hives on his face bigger than Hailee's pimples!"

Bees out and about in the middle of winter? Really? You would think Bartholomeo would stop paying attention. But the loyal butler doesn't take a chance. He always responds to the call, never forgetting his keys.

Somehow, Archibald's technique pays off in the end. All that "running" has drained the juice out of the already quite dried-up Bartholomeo. By Sunday evening, the old man can't make it to his bed and falls asleep on a chair in the library. Better yet, the ring of keys is hanging from his long fingers as if to say, "You win."

This is a once-in-a-lifetime opportunity. Archibald approaches the snoring giant carefully but flinches when he realizes that one of Bartholomeo's eyes is wide open. This is not a six-eyed Cerberus Archibald is facing—but a Cyclops. Gently, he frees the ring of keys from Bartholomeo's weak grip and rushes up to his bedroom.

Most of the keys look way too big for the globe's keyhole. Only four smaller ones might qualify. "What are these?" asks Archibald out loud, since these are definitely no ordinary keys. Instead of the usual notches, teeth, and ridges resembling a skyline of trees and rooftops, one has the outlines of a bearded old man, another is shaped like a cobweb, and the last two end with a moth and an open hand, respectively. Archibald almost wonders which side to hold them by!

Detaching one randomly from the heavy ring, he starts with the bearded man, who doesn't have a beard so much as five long mustaches tiered beneath his chin. Archibald brings the key near the globe, when his hand starts shaking. If his eyes are not playing tricks on him, the man's mustaches have just twitched a little. A few inches closer and this time he could swear the old man frowned at him for an instant. With a stifled gasp, Archibald springs back and drops the key to the ground, where it turns solid again.

After one gentle kick, three pokes, and two taps (works for cockroaches), Archibald is convinced the creature has been rendered harmless. He picks it up and moves it nearer to the globe. Not only do the mustaches wriggle anew but they also curl up into swirls with a low groan. Almost simultaneously, the old man closes his eyes. In one swift move, Archibald inserts the key—to no effect. It spins endlessly within the hole. The second Archibald pulls it out, the old man shakes his head, then freezes, his five mustaches flat again as if nothing had happened. "Holy bejabbles," blurts Archibald, a phrase as suitable as can ever be.

Startled yet curious tenfold, he sets his sight on the key with the moth. Grabbing it eagerly, he wonders what sort of neat trick it has in store—maybe it will fly away! Nothing happens before it's almost inside the globe. Just then, the moth's wings contract and fold tentlike over its body, wrapping around it until the insect is fully cloaked in a spiky cocoon. This key doesn't fail to astound Archibald, but it does fail to unlock the globe.

He hopes to be more successful with his next pick, the hand-shaped key with all fingers spread out. The first signs of "life" are not promising. Upon approaching the globe, the fingers have spontaneously clapped shut into a fist. *I guess that's a no*, thinks Archibald. He is about to move on to the last key when the index finger flicks out of the fist, pointing toward the lock. Each remaining finger unfolds one by one, either straight or curved, until the hand looks more like a claw. It turns out to be a perfect fit. Following a series of intricate noises like those a bank vault makes as it unlocks, the pin that kept the sphere immobile is released. Archibald can finally rotate his toy, which, to his surprise, is now glowing with a bluish light.

"So it *does* light up!" he says.

"Can you turn that off?" asks Hailee, annoyed.

Something else happens—something really strange. When Archibald spins the globe a bit faster, he can feel it pulling him, like a magnet. At one point, his hair starts floating in the air toward the globe. Some of it even gets snatched off and disappears! Archibald gasps and leans back in his chair. Terrified, he runs downstairs with the ring of keys and places it back in Bartholomeo's hand.

That night, he hides deep into his bed with his flashlight, lifting the blankets just enough to keep a wary eye on the mystery globe. At least it's not raining, so the gargoyles are silent.

Archibald has learned his lesson. *That's what happens when you give in to the temptation of an adventure,* he reminds himself. Now he has a missing lock of hair on the side of his forehead. Burned to the root, it might never grow back. His mother wouldn't mind. At least now she can see one of his eyes at all times. But Archibald fears this will draw even more attention at school, and he surely doesn't need that. It's decided: he will stick to caution and stay away from the globe, no matter how badly he wants to know more about that mysterious light.

He'd like to put the globe away,
but he is scared to even touch it.
When he is ready for bed, he goes
up and tries his best not to look
at it, not even a glance—the
same way he vanquished the
bald dolls.

The strategy works,
until that fateful evening
when Archibald forgets to
close his bedroom
window. Not the kind
of forget that should
have dire consequences,
you may think. And
yet, through the open
window comes a
hissing wind. The
curtains shiver. So
does the globe,
spinning slightly.

Back from the
hallway bathroom,
Archibald realizes
something. "I forgot to
lock it," he cringes.

"Yes, genius, you
forgot to lock the window.
It's freezing in here now,"
complains Hailee, who's just
climbed into bed, ready to write
her last fifty texts of the day.

"No, the globe," he mutters, realizing he'd given the key back to Bartholomeo.

The wind blows once more, opening the window a bit wider, making the globe spin faster. And now it's glowing again.

"Will you please turn that off?" says Hailee, just about to lose it.

Archibald squeezes his eyes almost shut. The outer shell of the globe seems to have completely vanished, morphing into an abyss. There's something going on inside. Archibald gets closer. Only a few inches away, he can now peer through the glow, like a fortune-teller staring into a crystal ball. The spectacle is mind-blowing: lightning strikes exploding against a background of dark, angry clouds. A dormant storm has awoken.

As the glow dims down, Archibald can't help himself; he gives the globe a gentle tap to keep it alive, followed by a stronger push. At the top, the crank handle he tightened so hard has begun to unwind, slowly at first, but quickly gaining momentum. The globe itself accelerates as a result. Suddenly, a blinding flash lights up the entire room, followed by a huge clap of thunder. Hailee lets out a loud and strident scream. Before Archibald can react, he is absorbed into the globe with a brief suction sound.

Stuart and Kate barge in within seconds. All seems normal, except that pretty much everything is gone from Archibald's side of the room. His desk. His chair. His stuff. Everything has disappeared except the top half of his bed—and the globe, tilted on its side.

"What happened? Where's Archie?" asks Kate, panicked.

Hailee can't say a word. Curled up on her bed, she is frozen with fear.

Bartholomeo reaches the room out of breath. His eyelids are so heavy with fatigue that he needs to tilt his head back to see anything. When he does see—the globe on the floor and the coral-shaped burn marks veining the walls—his eyes open so wide they seem about to pop out of his head.

"Oh no," he croaks, a man of few words.

Lifting his hunched torso one vertebra at a time, he freezes, standing straight for the first time in nearly thirty-three years. Seeming to exhale his whole life with one deep sigh, he topples backward onto the floor—dead. The ring of keys is still clenched in his hand.

The wind is getting stronger outside, and snow is drifting in through the window in bursts. Stuart looks out and shouts, "Archibald! Archibald!" But the night gives no answer—only an echo of his broken voice.

$$\mathsf{X}$$

It's the calm after the storm. Or perhaps a lull before the next one. Stuart doesn't quite know. Sitting at the dining table, his head down, he is staring into the darkest, most opaque cup of coffee, his fifth of the day. Still no answers.

Kate brings extra cups for two inspectors who've just arrived from London. These are supposed to be the big guns, Scotland Yard's finest, and it's as though they are trying very hard to fit the part—rough, tough, cold, and almost rude. Quite a contrast to the warm and considerate local officers who had stopped by in the morning. These two even refused to take off their coats, letting water drip all over the parquet floors. No room for smiles on their tight lips. No time for small talk or comforting words either.

"Do you know of any reason why your son would have left like this?" asks one of them.

"He did not leave," says Stuart.

"Well, he's not here now, is he?" says the inspector.

"He didn't leave on his own," corrects Stuart. "You know what I mean," he says. But they obviously don't.

"I see here that you adopted Archibald," says the other officer, reading from his notes. "Any problems since you got him?"

"Like what? Overheating? We didn't *get* him! He's not a vacuum or a car! We welcomed him into our life," corrects Kate, obviously on edge. Stuart takes over.

"Archibald doesn't know he was adopted. We never told him," he explains.

"Even his sister thinks he came from my belly," says Kate quietly, looking around, worried that Hailee might hear.

"Maybe he escaped," says one of the officers.

"Escaped from what? He is happy here," replies Kate hotly.

"Kids at school—they talk, you know," says the other cop.

"What did they say? Do they know something?" asks Stuart.

The officer glances at his colleague. He seems embarrassed. He explains, looking at his notepad, "It's still early. We could talk to only a handful of students, but they said your son had some kind of a bruise on his forehead."

"You know how that happened?" inquires the other inspector.

"We thought he had gotten into a fight," says Kate. "He is constantly bothered at school. It's that bully, William Tanner."

"Are you sure?" insists the inspector.

"Wait—are you implying that *we* did that to him, so he ran away?" says Stuart. "How do you explain the missing furniture? Did he take all that in his backpack?"

Kate puts her hand on her husband's.

"Do you know whether your son was into chemical experiments or anything of that sort?" asks the same inspector.

"What does that have to do with anything?" asks Kate.

"We did buy him a science kit for his birthday, but it was more of a toy, really," notes Stuart. "My wife is right, though; how is that relevant to the matter at hand?"

"Well," says the officer, "there are some substantial burn marks on the walls, consistent with a fire—"

"Brilliant!" quips Kate, cutting him off.

"What my colleague is trying to say, Mrs. Finch, is that perhaps your son set his room on fire to conceal his escape."

"What?" Kate erupts.

"Don't be silly," says Stuart. "We're talking about a boy here. He's only eleven."

"Because thunder stealing your son is a more plausible theory?" says the inspector. "Why not aliens, then?"

"Have you seen the scars on the floor and the walls?" says Kate. "What could cause something like that?"

"You're right; those marks could've been caused by lightning," says the other inspector. "But with all due respect, Madam, we have to look at all *plausible* scenarios and the most *probable* causes first—including child abuse. Your daughter is barely talking; she seems traumatized as well," he notes with suspicion in his voice.

"Of course she is traumatized—her brother is missing!" says Kate, barely containing her anger.

Upstairs, Hailee ducks under the yellow police tape and past an outline of Bartholomeo's body drawn in white chalk. Going straight for the globe still on the floor, she squats down to pick it up but hesitates for a second. Finally, she takes a large breath and grabs it with both hands as if she were holding her brother by the shoulders.

"Where did you go, Arch?" she asks, staring into the globe.

FROM LONDON TO GRISTLEMOTH

Archibald wakes up peacefully, with a yawn so long he can talk through it. "It was just a bad, bad dream," he kind of says.

It's still dark. He pulls the cover up to his chin. His eyes full of sleep, he discovers the blurry twinkle of small red lights above him.

"Christmas!" he rejoices.

Using the energy of an even bigger yawn, he sits up and rubs the back of his head, which feels awfully sore for some reason. To his astonishment, what he thought to be his blanket is actually a leaf as large as an elephant's ear. And he is lying on the ground, outside!

Archibald's first thought, aloud: "Hailee kicked me out!"

His second thought, even louder: "I'm gonna kill her!"

But wait . . . his bed is here, about half of it, at least—the bottom part—bent down by his feet. Also nearby is his desk, a few leaves away, covered with the usual desk mess of books and candy bars. Only the lamp got knocked over, along with a few books now sharing the ground with Archibald's drawings strewn around, some of them burned around the edges.

His head is boiling up with a million questions. Well, to quote the late Bartholomeo, just twenty: *Where am I? Why am I here? How did I get here? Who did this to me? Where is the other half of my bed? Am I going to die? Is my hair okay? Am I dead already?* And about twelve more like these. More importantly, and that's a much more verifiable number, he has zero answers.

After scanning the surroundings, Archibald is sure of one thing and one thing only. This is not *his* backyard, unless he has somehow landed in the dreaded "half woods" behind the house, that uncharted land from which some have never returned (or so

Hailee says). It seems unlikely, as the trees here are much higher and the vegetation much more dense.

"Hailee . . ." he murmurs. "Dad . . . Mum . . ."

Suddenly realizing he is on his own, lost in a totally unknown setting, Archibald panics and ducks under his desk. Dead set on hiding there forever if he has to, he tries to grab his flashlight from under the table, tapping around with his hand. It takes him a minute, but he eventually gets hold of it. He uses the same technique to get his candy bars, slowly gathering quite a healthy stash: three Kit Kat, two Galaxy Ripple, two Twix, and one Yorkie.

"At least I have food," he huffs, although a rigorous recount has him convinced there's a missing Yorkie up there, and, indeed, there is. It's already open, but he took only one bite of it yesterday, so it's definitely worth finding. Archibald is back on the hunt for that stray bar. His hand, with almost a life of its own now, snakes out on the desk again, pushing aside crayons, eraser, magnifier, books, and miniature dog sculptures molded in Play-Doh. His fingers are getting warmer, only a few inches away from the Yorkie, when a tremendous noise interrupts the search.

The desk is shaking and squeaking. Someone, or something, has jumped or landed right above Archibald, who has stopped breathing entirely. Paralyzed by fear, he can't even command his stubborn hand to get back down with the rest of his trembling body. There is some sniffling going on up above, mixed with some growling. Archibald is pretty sure he's even heard a side note of purring! Maybe it's one of those scary boars Bartholomeo showed him last week behind his prized hedge of rhododendrons. Some intimidating beasts, those wild pigs, with heads like ploughs gouging up half the frozen lawn scavenging for food.

Archibald's face is stuck in a painful cringe, his eyes closed, his body twitching in sync with any vibration in the desk. His eyes snap back open suddenly. He can now feel whatever is up there breathing on his hand. He is trying not to scream. One more minute of this and without doubt he will faint. And then, as abruptly as it showed up, that something or someone takes off and disappears with a massive racket, causing the desk to crack and partially fall apart. Archibald gets only a glimpse of a shadow vanishing behind the trees.

Only after a couple of hours does he manage to emerge from under the desk, still on his guard, moving in slow motion, alert for the faintest sound. First assessment: whatever that thing was, it/he/she ate his Yorkie bar, leaving behind eight tablespoons of drool that looks as unsavory as the mint jelly Bartholomeo liked to smear on everything.

"Gross!" he comments when dipping the tip of his finger into that gob, then almost throwing up when smelling the tip of that finger. Why did he do that? He is just one of those many people who like to smell their fingers.

As he tries to dispose of the sticky gunk, he notices a strange white powder coating the fern leaves he is using as wipes.

"That's not snow—just dust," he mutters, realizing the vegetation around is half-dead, smothered under the grayish veil.

Too bad that flashlight is not big enough or Archibald would gladly hide behind it, which is exactly what he's trying to do, holding it with both hands right beneath his nose. Not that he needs it, really. The sky has enough of a glow to light his path through this terra incognita—the regular glow from a moon-full night, plus a reddish undertone.

Maybe Mars replaced the moon, he says to himself. Archibald can't actually see the moon, so it doesn't seem like such a crazy thought. As it turns out, the red glow seems to be coming from the lights he woke up to. Those are some really strange stars! Not only are they red but they're moving. Archibald has heard of falling stars, of course, but these are different. They are not quite falling *per se*. They are spinning and swirling. What a fascinating spectacle! Archibald stops in the middle of a clearing in the woods to enjoy the show blazing overhead.

"These are incredible!" he exclaims, squinting at the UFOs.

One of them even seems to grow right before his eyes. Wait— it has now split into two separate stars getting bigger and bigger, in fact getting closer and closer. Archibald doesn't worry much about it until he realizes those stars seem to be carrying a dark mass along with them. *Is that an asteroid?* He rubs his eyes, for he thinks he might be dreaming still. It has just occurred to him: what he thought to be stars are not stars at all. They are eyes, with some sort of enormous bird attached to them!

Archibald runs for cover, looking for his desk but unable to remember where it is. The tingling in his legs tells him to play possum. Or should he try his chameleon thing? Leaving his dilemma behind, he bolts for his life and won't stop screaming.

The bird has landed. *Is it even a bird? It can't be; it started running like a buffalo!* It's now in pursuit, smashing every tree branch in its way.

Archibald has never run so fast—even faster, perhaps, than that day William Tanner hustled after him at school to feed him soap. And that was a memorable sprint! Thankfully, he has his favorite sneakers on and not those unwieldy slippers his mother usually makes him wear in the evening.

He glances back over his shoulder from time to time but can't really figure out what's chasing him. A bird? A hog? A camel? A mixed breed for sure! There was a circus in town just a couple days ago. Maybe one of their exotic animals escaped! *Or maybe this is the same beast that ate my Yorkie earlier*, thinks Archibald. That gives him an idea. He fishes in his pocket for another candy bar and lobs it in his pursuer's path. It's a dud. The beast zooms past it without paying any attention.

He can't smell it! realizes Archibald. He has to think and act fast. He grabs another bar, only this time tears it open before dropping it. It works! The beast stops to snatch it. Archibald gives a proud "Yes!" but his victorious cry is short-lived. This is the equivalent of him gulping down one reasonable scoop of ice cream. The beast is far from stuffed. And back on the hunt within seconds.

Nearby, Archibald's screams have caught the attention of three young girls carrying bunches of herbs and logs in their arms. They don't just seem to be from another country—like those relatives you've never heard of from Ireland who show up at your door one day. They seem to be from another time period altogether—like those relatives you've never heard of from Ireland who show up at your door one day.

The giveaway? Probably the long-sleeved embroidered blouses, topped with gray linen tunics stamped with a sort of wave pattern on the chest. Tied at the waist, those thick aprons end in a skirt partially covering fluffy black pants. Though usually praised as a fashion must, layering in this case would be more of a faux pas, possibly even worse than wearing socks and sandals together.

And that's not even mentioning the water flask, horn, and sickle attached to their belts, in addition to several pouches hanging like grenades from a shoulder strap. One of them even has a

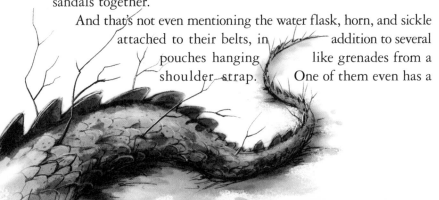

bow and arrow strapped to her chest! Compared with the rest of these outfits, the conical, pointed hats, extending all the way to the width of their shoulders would almost look normal, except for the twigs and leaves scattered on top.

One more high-pitched scream from Archibald and the three girls drop their wood, herbs, and whatever it is they were doing.

They start running in his direction right away and quickly reach the edge of a ridge overlooking the dramatic scene unfolding about twenty feet below. Despite Archibald's good pace, the beast is gaining on him and will soon catch up.

"What do we do?" asks one of the girls, with fear in her voice.

"They're heading to Wigzigor's mouth; we gotta hurry!" says the taller and apparently older one, who's obviously in charge.

Archibald is running out of breath. To make matters worse, he comes face-to-face with a massive rock formation shaped like a crescent and profiled like a wave—Wigzigor's mouth. That cliff must be thirty to forty feet in height at least, ending in a curling top, making it impossible to climb.

Archibald is trapped.

His back against the wall—literally—he seems to have given up.

Seeing the beast moving toward him at full speed, he is surprisingly calm. Or maybe his blood just froze along with every muscle, nerve, and organ in his body.

It's funny, he says to himself. *I always thought that big, foul-mouthed William Tanner would be the one killing me.*

To his left, the three girls have made their way down the hill, but they're still far away. What could they do, anyway? They've apparently picked up a few stones, but their improvised weapons seem rather pathetic in the face of this goliath. Perhaps of less futile assistance, one of them takes aim at the beast with her bow and arrow. Against all odds, cutting through leaves and flying between tree trunks, her projectile hits the beast in the rear. An absolute feat given the great distance and countless obstacles in the way—but an exploit with no effect whatsoever on the monster's formidable velocity. No effect, that is, if you leave out the brief, radiant shockwave, sparked by the arrow, that ripples across the beast's body. But again, it doesn't even so much as flinch.

As if to try to see what will soon devour or obliterate him, Archibald points his flashlight toward his nemesis. He turns it on moments away from his certain demise. Blinded by the light, the creature turns its neck at a quarter-to-noon angle, but without veering much off course. The collision seems inevitable. Archibald has shut his eyes tight. Seven-eighths of a second later, a loud boom echoes throughout the forest.

The three girls arrive at the scene expecting the worst but hoping for the best, following an old Confucius proverb, itself based on a fortune cookie—or vice versa.

They push aside one more fern bush and discover Archibald on the ground in one piece. He sits mute. The beast is lying just six and a half inches away, inert and twisted like a paper clip. It had crashed against the cliff.

The size of a European car, that thing has a coat made not of fur but of dead leaves, making it hard to see where its body ends and the ground begins. In shape it vaguely resembles a rhinoceros, only a rhinoceros that can fly. Indeed, protruding from its back are two pairs of bat wings. As for the tail hanging from the rear end, it belongs to a rat—a giant rat, that is. If it's still alive, the beast will owe its survival to the carapace on its head, a massive horn that arcs all the way to its spine, similar to the front shield of a beetle, connected to two more horns curved around the mouth, like the whiskers of a catfish.

What Archibald finds the most intriguing, though, is the face under those horns, for it is 100 percent human, hairy and scary as hell, but human still—just like two of its six legs, by the way, which seem shockingly dull within this overall display of oddities.

"Blimkey!" blurts out the tallest of the girls. "How did you do that?"

"I just used my flashlight," answers Archibald, stunned by his own prowess—and obvious luck as well.

"Your what?"

"My flashlight," he repeats, turning it on, shining it in her face.

Little does he know that he has just done the unthinkable—the girl cries out frightfully, covering her head as if to protect herself, the two younger ones joining the madness and screeching as well, not too sure why, perhaps simply out of sympathy and solidarity.

Archibald immediately turns it off, and the screaming

slowly subsides.

The victim rubs her face and checks her hands, arms, and hair, asking the others whether she's okay, which of course she is.

As for Archibald, he'd like to feel sorry but doesn't quite know why he should. Baffled, he inspects his flashlight to see whether it might have some special attributes he was not aware of.

"What is your magic?" inquires the girl with the bow.

"My magic? I don't have any magic," he says as he stands up to straighten up his pajama bottoms.

Big collective gasp among his audience, with the smallest one, baby-faced, slapping her hand on her mouth.

"Gollygosh! Is she a boy?" she asks, sizing him up.

"She? What? Of course I'm a boy!" confirms Archibald, offended, uncovering his face fully by pulling his long hair behind his ears and, of course, puffing up his chest.

All three girls are looking at him with equally startled faces. Already intrigued by Archibald's sneakers (quite different from their boots made of cloth and crisscrossed with laces), they seem unsettled by his sweatshirt, the sorority hoodie he borrowed from his sister that she herself borrowed from her mother.

"Are you a wizard?" asks the main girl, now cold and inquisitive, while the other two whisper things to one another.

"I wish," says Archibald. "My sister would be a toad by now."

"Where are you from?"

"London," he responds. "I mean, technically outside of London, because, see, my grandma died, and we—"

"Oh, keep your flummadiddle to yourself!" snaps the girl.

"My what?"

"Your balductum! Your hogwash! You know what I mean!"

"Huh?" interjects Archibald, still in the dark.

"He doesn't even speak English," she says, turning to her

friends, who grin. Then back to Archibald, "Your horse manure, your nonsense!"

"Oh, okay," says Archibald, finally getting it.

"What brings you here?" she now asks.

"Not sure. I was up in my room with my Christmas gift and—"

"Oh, shush at once!" she spits. And he zips it, making his lips disappear into his mouth. The girl taps her index finger, curved into a question mark, on her chin. She is brooding, her eyes fixed on Archibald the entire time.

"Okay, you'll accompany us to the village," she finally says. "But first, hand me your weapon."

"My weapon?" he asks.

She points at his flashlight.

"Oh, this—sure," he says, extending it toward her, making her jump.

She detaches one of the burlap pouches from her belt and motions for him to drop the flashlight into it. After he does, she shuts it tight and hooks it back onto her belt.

"We'll get to the bottom of this in Gristlemoth," she tells him.

"Wait, Grease what? I can't; I have to go back to—"

"To where, huh? London?" she cuts in. "Let's see . . . you're only five, maybe four, weeks away—that's if you walk fast, of course, and can swim for twenty hours straight."

While Archibald tries to comprehend what that bossy girl just said, she gives instructions to her companions.

"You take care of this one," she says, jerking her head toward the beast. Then turning to Archibald, "You, follow me. Close."

"What's with the hat?" he asks.

"Where have you been all this time? Under a rock?" she jokes.

"Under a desk, actually," he says, in the most genuine tone.

"You know, camouflage," she explains. "It's made of the same things you find on the ground. Wood, dirt, leaves. From up there, the Marodors can't see us—we blend in. So, again, you stay close. We're lucky; we've got all sorts of night creepers around here but not many land Marodors. We'll avoid clearings—you never know."

Again, Archibald doesn't have the faintest idea what she is talking about. But, man, is that girl impressive! So he just nods and goes shoulder to shoulder with her, craning his neck to try to match her height. Other than that time he fell asleep against Emily Dorsey on the bus, he can't recall ever being so close to a girl before. It feels strange.

As they walk away, Archibald looks back and sees the two other girls kneeling on the ground, placing around the beast the stones they were holding.

"Is that thing dead?" he asks.

"Of course not," says the girl.

When he checks again seconds later, the beast slowly rises in the air, frozen, as if carved out of stone or freshly stuffed, its tail and wings dragging on the ground. Archibald swallows loudly, now wary of the strange girl next to him as well.

"What's that monster?" he asks her.

"Surely you've heard of Marodors, right? Don't tell me you haven't. Then I'd say you're talking knavery for certain. You don't want to talk knavery to me, do you?"

"Knavery?"

"Knavery, you know—guilery, falsary!"

Archibald shakes his head again.

"Trumpery?"

This definitely speaks more to him, but it's still not all that clear.

"Impostry! A ruse! A lie! You don't want to lie to me, do you?"

"Of course not, I just meant what *kind* of . . . merdar is it? I know what a merdar is," he mumbles. "I know everything."

"That sounds so cockish. Nobody knows everything!"

"It's not something I brag about; that's just the way it is. I don't know why, but I know everything."

"It's funny; you don't strike me as someone who knows everything, but we'll see," she says in a challenging tone.

Archibald has to admit, though, there's a lot he doesn't get about this place, starting with that creature he keeps glancing at.

"By the way, 'merdar,' is that French?" he asks.

"What?"

"No, nothing," he mutters.

"So how many Marodors have you defeated, with that weapon of yours?"

Archibald hesitates and starts counting on his fingers.

"Not sure," he dares to say.

"That many, huh?" she exclaims, truly impressed.

"You know, it's hard to stop yourself. You see one; you've gotta fight it, you know? You can't just let it get away, right?" he brags nervously, all the while staring down, unable to meet her gaze.

"It's weird; if I didn't know any better, I'd say you were trying to run away earlier," she says.

"I know! It looks like it, to people like you, I mean, who are not familiar with my moves and tactics. I get that a lot. Common mistake."

"And the screaming, that's part of your tactics?"

"Part of it? It's half of it—at least. You need lots of screaming."

"Good to know, because it sure sounded like you were calling for help at one point."

"See, I'm so glad you thought that; it's *exactly* what I wanted the beast to think. It's key to my strategy, confusing the enemy."

"Well, you succeeded. It sure was confusing!"

"If you don't mind, I'd rather not say more about it, for now. I could teach you one day."

"I can't wait," she nods, not quite convinced, but after all, he did vanquish that Marodor.

"What is your name?" she asks.

"Archibald," he says in a sorry tone.

"Pleased to meet you. My name is Faerydae."

"Fear of what?"

"Fear of nothing! It's Fae-ry-dae."

"And I thought *I* was the one with the funny name!" he chuckles.

She stops, obviously offended.

"I didn't mean it that way. It's just that people usually mock me because of my name."

"I don't know why; 'Archibald' is so common," she says.

"I know you're saying that to be nice. But thanks. What're *their* names?" he asks, turning to the two girls a couple hundred feet behind walking on each side of the levitating Marodor, holding out the stones—which are now glowing.

"That's Rhiannon and Maven."

No doubt she's pulling his leg, thinks Archibald.

"Any middle names I'd have heard of?" he asks.

"Cinnamon and Hazel; it's short for Hazelnut."

"And what's yours, Nutmeg?" he chuckles.

"I have two, actually, Dawn and Orla."

"You're not from around here, are you, Faerydae Dawn Orla?" jokes Archibald, looking at her from head to toe, hinting at the outdated outfit on top of the weird names.

"Who is, really?" she answers in a deep manner, almost sad.

"By the way, nobody mocks someone just because of their name. They mock someone because he or she did or said something others can laugh at. Usually something stupid."

Archibald doesn't know what to say to that, and it bothers him.

"Anyway, it doesn't matter. When we arrive in Gristlemoth, your name will be Ivy."

"What? No! Why?"

"Yes, when we get there, you'll be a girl. You'll understand."

"No," he repeats with force, making her stop abruptly.

"All right, we'll have to leave you here, then. I'll keep your weapon. Good luck to you, friend!"

"I have to think about this," says Archibald, taking ample time to answer—meaning two seconds. "Okay, fine, I'll be a girl," he says reluctantly.

"That's what I thought!"

Withdrawing a dark moss-green cloak from her bag, she throws it around his shoulders and fastens it at the neck with a string, covering his sweatshirt.

"This will help," she says.

"What will it do? Make me invisible?" he asks.

"No cloak has such powers. But this one will do the trick," she says, as a green-clad Archibald begins to blend in with the foliage.

"I'd love to be invisible and just disappear," he sighs.

"Trust me, I wish you would," sneers Faerydae as they get back on their way.

♫

Between the trees, Archibald catches sight of a light in the sky, standing out against the night. But what it is exactly he cannot discern.

"Is that the moon?"

"Did you fall on your head or something?"

"It's huge!" exclaims Archibald, who can't stop staring at the bright halo.

"There is no moon. That is Gristlemoth," says Faerydae.

As they get closer, Archibald can make out the shape of an almost perfect circle with jittery edges detaching from the surrounding darkness. Inside, it's blue sky and white fluffy clouds—and no Marodor to be seen.

A few more steps and he can see the timber rooftops of a small village located right under the glowing hole in the sky. Rays of sunshine pour a bright glare on dozens of homes—huts more than actual houses.

"How's that possible? How can it be nighttime here and daylight right over there?"

"I thought you knew everything?" mocks Faerydae.

"At home I do," he says with a questioning look. Could it be that his burdensome curse has been lifted at last?

"It's a wonder you survived all these years," says Faerydae, pressing ahead.

They soon reach the edge of the village, surrounded by giant boulders marking the limit of the area soaked by the sun. Strange waves of light are also rising from the large rocks—a green-and-white glow the likes of which Archibald has never seen before, except maybe on a screensaver. The closest comparison would be the aurora borealis. Those hypnotizing lights are usually found by the North Pole, though, not in the London suburbs!

"Holy bejabbles!"

"Remember: your name is Ivy," whispers Faerydae.

"Okay, Ivy it is," replies Archibald, trying to talk like a girl.

"Oh, no need to change your voice."

"What does that mean?" says Archibald, on the verge of a fit.

"I'm just shenaniganning with you. Keep your hair in your face and your mouth shut and it will be fine."

Oddly, the dirt road comes to an end, the huge boulders blocking the way. Faerydae blows her horn, producing an enchanting two-tone sound that carries over a mile.

"What now?" asks Archibald.

"Are you always so impatient?"

He is about to answer when the boulder right in front of them starts shaking—making *him* shake.

The monolith wobbles a bit more before slowly detaching from the ground, as if on hinges. And to the side it swivels, like a fifty-ton door naturally would.

"Voilà!" says Faerydae with a smile. Archibald is stunned.

The small convoy composed of the three girls, half a boy, and the floating Marodor passes the narrow opening manned by four girls with the same kind of stones gleaming in their hands. Archibald looks with apprehension as the revolving rock thuds shut behind them.

"We don't need these anymore," says Faerydae, removing her hat and unleashing a flurry of wavy curls topped with a braided crown. The golden hair brightens up her face, making it all the more soft and angelic. Archibald can't help but stare at her, his mouth wide open. Faerydae is the most beautiful creature he has ever seen. He would call her bedazzling and mesmerizing, if only he had the courage.

"Close your mouth, Ivy," Rhiannon whispers in his ear while escorting the Marodor down a side road, to the cheers and applause of an improvised crowd.

Archibald regains his composure somewhat and takes in the beautiful simplicity of Gristlemoth. This is a small town, as in "no red light around" small, not even a stop sign small. Spread out before him is a summer camp more than a village, dotted with small cabanas and lots of trees sharing a gently sloping landscape. Surrounded on three sides by the woods and anchored to a high cliff on the other, Gristlemoth covers a fairly vast space, shaped like a rugby ball. An eagle flying at an average eagle speed—say, thirty miles per hour—would tell you it takes him about four minutes to cross Gristlemoth from north to south and a minute less from east to west. That's if there was an eagle around, but there's none.

As a matter of fact, the sky and the trees alike are empty. No screeching eagle. No cawing crow. No dooking ferret. Not the slightest trace of non-Marodor creatures.

"Where're all the animals?" asks Archibald.

"Only bugs around here. The rest live on in our memories and up there," she says, gesturing toward carvings on the cabanas' rooftops whose crossbeams end in double-headed hawks, foxes, bears, snakes, beavers, and wolves, among others.

"Even in the half woods there are animals," mumbles Archibald.

He might be able to handle Marodors. But a world without animals? That he can't imagine. Wait, there might be hope after all. He's just spotted something brown, white, and fluffy zooming through a field of flowers.

"A dog!" he exclaims, his joy quickly dashed as arrows start raining on the fur ball.

"What are they doing?" he screams, running to confront the archers who've just reloaded their bows.

"What got into you? It's just a pile of gubbins for target practice!" shouts Faerydae.

"Gubbins?"

"Mullock! Garbage!"

"Garbage that *runs*?!" cries Archibald, certain he sees the outline of an animal in the fleeing prey. What animal exactly, he has no idea. But there is undoubtedly more to it than garbage. Sure enough, among patches of matted fur, twigs, moss, and leaves, Archibald spots the features of something not far off from a dog—starting with legs. More like roots ending in twined feet than anything else, but they are legs nonetheless. And how could that clump of feathers be anything other than a tail? It is wagging, is it not? If further proof of life were needed, Archibald finds it on the creature's opposite end, in what appears to be a face.

Nothing is quite where it should be, though: the eyes are severely askew and at odds with one another—the left one rather large, protruding, and swollen; the other much smaller, smashed in, and half shut. Maybe the archers are to blame for that unfortunate jumble. However, nothing can explain the rest of the creature's mug, especially its fanged mouth, completely off-center, much like its snout, which thrusts in the opposite direction.

Somehow, this motley mound of mullock acts exactly like a dog. The arrows bouncing around it, on the other hand, act nothing like arrows, their tips not sharpened to a deadly point but rather capped with a rounded helmet. The way Archibald sees it, "Those arrows are wearing gloves!"

That's not the least strange thing about this place. Not only can he still not see any (real) animals but there also seem to be only girls around, all very young, none older than fifteen probably.

"Am I the only boy here?"

"No Ivy, you're not," answers Faerydae with a smile.

Everyone seems to be part of a small army—an army of girls: some sawing wood, some washing clothes, others carrying baskets and rocks. Whatever their outfit, trousers and tunics or long aprons, they all have that same double-wave pattern logo sewn on the chest. Archibald wants to ask Faerydae about it, but he's already intrigued by something else—the curious hand gestures she's making toward those in her path.

"What's that you're doing?" he asks, trying to mimic her.

"You don't know sign language either?" sighs Faerydae.

Archibald admits he doesn't—a rather rare occurrence.

"Well, you know how to shake your head; that's a start," jokes Faerydae. "See, when we first moved here, there were people from all over the world with many different languages, making it hard to understand each other. So we developed this common language. It changed everything. We still use it from time to time, especially when we're not right next to each other, so we don't have to yell across the village. It keeps us more peaceful."

Following in his guide's footsteps, Archibald waves at everyone meeting his gaze and gives some a thumbs-up, which Faerydae slaps down right away.

"What did you do that for?" he asks.

"Stop being a mope!"

"A what?"

"A nup, a liripoop, a saddle-goose, a fopdoodle!"

He doesn't know any of those names—who does, really?

"A fool?" she sums up.

"Why am I a fool? I'm just doing what you're doing."

"No, we don't use that kind of sign around here," she explains. "Don't you know where it's from?"

Of course he knows. But he'd rather play dumb. So he shrugs.

"The Roman Empire? Rings a bell? Giant arenas, gladiators, stupid games, thumb up you live, thumb down you die."

"I didn't think of that."

"You mustn't do that again. It's totally barbaric."

As they stride deeper into the sun-drenched village, another odd reality starts to register with Archibald: there are no adults around either.

"Your parents are away or something?"

"You can say that, I guess."

"I'm sorry; I didn't know," he says. "Last week, my dad met one of those orphans my grandma rescued. That's what he kept saying, that his parents were away. It's terrible."

Faerydae just nods, more concerned about some kind of crackling sound in the background.

"Did you hear that?" she asks.

"It sounded like firecrackers."

"Gadzooks, not again!" she thunders, picking up the pace,

her eyes fixed on a cloud of white smoke billowing above the tree line. "It's coming from the river."

By the time they get there, most of the smoke has evaporated, but not the mischievous twinkle in the eyes of four girls squatting on the ground. If it added guilt to their faces, the sight of Faerydae didn't put an end to their misdeed—on the contrary.

"Hurry!" says one of them as she stands up in the middle of their circle, pressing two stones against her chest. Three more are tied up with strings around her ankles. A few words are recited and—WHOOSH!—the stone-laden girl is projected up into the air in a geyser of sputtering sparks. Her accomplices are blown off their feet, balls of light whirling over their heads.

Only after two erratic somersaults and a painful twist does Rocket Girl finally come back down, crashing to the ground on her back.

"Lenora!" screams Faerydae, rushing to the scene.

"Are you tired of life?" she asks, kneeling by the girl still reeling from the fall.

"But . . ." utters Lenora, befogged and disoriented, her sleeves smoking. "I almost made it; did you see?" she says, holding her elbow in pain.

"Will you be all right?" inquires Faerydae.

"I think so."

"Good, then you know where you're headed! No such experiment shall ever happen again," hammers Faerydae. "Is that understood?"

The girls give a reluctant nod and walk away. Lenora cracks a smile as Archibald gives her a thumbs-up.

"What are you doing? Don't encourage her!" fumes Faerydae.

"Sorry, it just seemed fun!"

"It was foolish! She could have gotten herself killed!"

Faerydae collects the mysterious stones strewn around, some

blackened, some still glowing.

"What are these?" asks Archibald. "They look like those stones Raymond and Maverick used on that beast earlier."

"It's Rhiannon and Maven," snaps Faerydae, "and I'll tell you what these are *not* intended for—fun. Whatever *fun* even means," she says, bashing two stones against one another, knocking the light out of them.

"Fine, don't tell me. They're just stones, anyway," he says.

"Just stones?" repeats Faerydae angrily. "Follow me."

Just what Archibald had hoped would happen. He conceals a smile.

Right around the block, merely a stone's throw away, they enter an immense garden and weave their way between rows and rows of cabbage, potatoes, celery, and all sorts of weird-shaped vegetables, some with hair growing on them, some with warts, some with eyes even! That awful sight quickly makes Archibald sick to his stomach. When a "yuck" turns into "burp" and that belch turns into gagging, he looks for a quick escape from this scary maze, but Faerydae has just found someone she knows.

"Aye up, Naida! This is Arch—Ivy," she says, biting her tongue.

"Hello, Ivy. Where are you from?" says Naida, with a warm voice spiced up with an exotic accent.

Not sure what to say, Archibald responds with a weird cough mixed with a hiccup, followed by the oddest nod and shrug. Faerydae elbows him, urging him to act normal.

"By the way, what was that noise earlier?" asks Naida.

"You know, Lenora and her experiments," sighs Faerydae.

"You can't blame her for trying."

"Oh yes, I can," says Faerydae, rolling her eyes. "So what are you doing?"

"I was just about to plant some carrots!"

"Yuk!" blurts Archibald, swallowing back two still undigested candy bars that had moved back up to fill his mouth. Faerydae elbows him again. Then turning back to Naida, "Go ahead,
show us."

They all kneel down on the ground. Naida proceeds. Brushing aside the long black curls that blend with her skin, she pours a few seeds in the ground, to which she adds a bit of water. Other than that, there is nothing too out of the ordinary in her routine, until she opens a bag full of those strange-looking stones. She surrounds the planted area with three of them, two black and shiny, one brown and translucent. Archibald is close enough to notice the markings on the stones, basic signs made of lines, rectangles, and circles, similar to the hieroglyphs used in ancient Egypt—like nothing he has ever seen outside of a book, though. He is also close enough to hear the strange words Naida is muttering but can't understand any of them. One thing he can see clearly is the result of her mumbling. The stones start glowing, causing a tiny stem to emerge from the ground almost immediately, turning into a fuzzy green bouquet in the blink of an eye.

"You think they're done?" Faerydae asks Naida excitedly.

"Only one way to find out," says Naida, who wraps her hands around the crown and pulls up swiftly, unearthing the fastest-grown carrots ever.

Even though Archibald hates carrots, he is amazed. Still, he does hate carrots, so when Naida shakes them in front of his nose, he takes a step back with a profound look of disgust on his face.

"What's wrong? You don't like carrots?" asks Faerydae.

"No!" he says, as if the question itself is offensive.

"What do you eat, then?" asks Naida.

"Real food," he says proudly, taking a Kit Kat out of his pocket.

"What is this?" asks Faerydae, pulling him aside by his cloak. "It'd better not be another one of your magic tricks. What kind of potion is this?"

"Just food. You're kidding me, right? You think my flashlight and my candy bars are magic? *You* have the magic!" he says, pointing at Naida's carrots.

"Don't be silly. We're no magicians, only witches."

Shocked and awed, Archibald gulps—in fact, swallows the whole piece of Kit Kat he has just put in his mouth.

"Are you all right?" she asks as he slowly gets a grip on his fear.

"I'm sorry—what did you say you are?"

"Witches!" she repeats, with that "no big deal" look on her face. "I mean, unfortunately, that's what people called us, you know, that and other bad names like sorceress, she-devil, or eye-biter."

"Eye-biter," repeats Archibald, shielding his eyes with his hands and rapidly turning as green as those veggies he hates— not "ate," or he would then be turning purple.

"We actually call ourselves witches; we don't mind. We wear that name as a badge of honor. We are so much more than the caricature, though. Personally, I see myself as an enchantress. It sounds better, too, don't you think?"

"Enchantress," Archibald mutters slowly, his lips trembling.

He squints at Faerydae. *Is there something I missed about that girl?* he wonders. She doesn't quite fit the stereotype of the witch. For one, her nose is rather small and cute, not swollen and crooked like a banana. Neither is her chin. And there's no giant, coarse, multilayered wart growing on that nose—or the chin, for that matter. Sure, she was wearing a peaked hat earlier, but it definitely looked more weird than scary. Besides, she seems to have all of her teeth, not just two or three moldy ones sticking out of her mouth. Faerydae can't be a witch! Unless this is the disguise of an old hag, as beautiful as it is deceitful.

"I have to go home," says Archibald.

Faerydae seems surprised and disappointed by his reaction.

"If you put it that way," she says, coldly. "But let me show you one more thing before you go," she adds with a much nicer tone.

"I'm not sure I have time."

"I would feel insulted. We wouldn't want that to happen, right?"

Archibald shakes his head, stiff and fearful.

"That's what I thought," smiles Faerydae, motioning for him to follow her. Naida can tell something fishy is going on.

Using an arched bridge, they cross the narrow river running through Gristlemoth. There's nothing much on the other side except for three tiny cabanas in a rather remote area of the village. Faerydae leads Archibald to one of them right next to a small graveyard—which does not reassure him about the young witch's intentions.

"I really have to go," he repeats.

"It will just take a minute. After you," she says, politely inviting him to go in.

As soon as he does, she bangs the door shut and locks it with a wood plank swiveling from vertical to horizontal.

"What are you doing?"

"I don't trust you."

"But I did everything you asked! I just want to go home."

"Sorry, but you shall not. I have to figure out what's in you. Until then, I will see to it that you don't go anywhere," she says, walking off.

"What if I want to go to the bathroom?"

"That *is* the bathroom!"

"Are you joking?" he chirps, sighing in the same breath when he sees a bed in the corner of the room.

Archibald is trapped. He can't see much between the wooden slats of the door—just enough to realize Faerydae is indeed striding off. He doesn't seem too mad, though. He even breaks into a smile.

"She thinks she's so smart," he mumbles.

From the sweatshirt under his cloak, he pulls out three stones he obviously stole from Naida in the vegetable garden.

"I'm going home!" he says, in a highly confident tone.

Imitating Naida, he lines up the stones at the foot of the door. Then he takes a step back and, extending his arms and waving his fingers toward the door, he orders, "Shazam!"

He walks to the door, which, to his surprise, is still locked. He takes another step back. This time, no doubt—he's got it.

"Abracadabra!" he yells, pushing on the door, which apparently didn't quite get the message.

"What is it she said already?" he mutters.

Scratching his head, he tries something else. "Balamoo Ragadoo Malabarus Malvoye!"

Close. But the door still doesn't budge. Shocker! Somehow, it just doesn't speak Archibald.

Realizing he won't hocus-pocus his way out of here, he sits on the bed, the only thing in this windowless room. The floor is dirt. The walls are dirt. If not a bathroom, this certainly looks like a jail.

"Are you done in there?" asks a voice coming from outside.

"Who's that?"

"I'm in the hut next door," says the voice, which sounds familiar.

"Lenora?"

"That would be me," confirms the stunt girl.

"They put you in jail too?"

"It was well deserved. Besides, this is not really a jail."

"That girl Faerydae, she's so tough!" he whines.

"I know, right? I wish I could be just like her."

"What? Are you serious?"

"Of course, she's like a big sister, a role model for all of us."

"A role model? But she's barely older than you."

"It doesn't matter. Just in the last hundred years she has been in more battles and captured more Marodors than all of us combined. To be honest, I thought you were her secret boyfriend."

"What? No. I can't be! My name is Ivy."

"I'm not stupid, you know."

"I don't know what you're talking about," tries Archibald.

"Anyway, she seemed pretty mad at you. What did you do to get locked up?"

"Nothing. I just want to go home."

"Don't we all?" says Lenora.

"I thought you were from here."

"None of us is, really."

"What?" mumbles Archibald, not too sure what to make of these foggy comments.

"Sorry, my whole body hurts; I'll try to rest now," she says.

"By the way, what were you trying to do back there?"

"What we all want to do—fly! To fight Marodors on equal ground."

"Or escape them?"

"That too."

"But you're a witch, aren't you? Don't you have a broom for that?"

Lenora cracks up. "That's a good one. All right, good night . . . Ivy."

"G'night, then," he says, lying down.

Through the top part of the roof, where tree branches meet in a cone shape, Archibald experiences his first sunset in Gristlemoth. The night comes like an eclipse, slowly filling the hole in the sky, from an orangey blue to a creamy yellow, to finally blend in with the darkness around.

With no flashlight to keep him company, Archibald finds some comfort in those strange lights rising above the village, undulating like sheer curtains in the wind and rippling against the night.

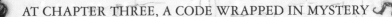

HERE BE DRAGONS

Hailee has spent the last two days wandering around the house. She gathered the scary drawings Archibald left behind, scribbled on napkins and toilet paper. She folded some of his sweaters, T-shirts, and socks. The rest of the time, she just went through countless pictures of that dear, beloved, and missed brother she wished gone just a few days ago.

Now she is on her way back to school, sharing the 8:00 a.m. train with gaggles of other teenagers. Most of them are texting and goofing around. She is not. The tears streaking her cheeks mirror the raindrops slaloming against the window. Her lost gaze detaches from the blurred horizon to drift to the seat next to her, where her coat partially covers a cardboard box.

An hour later, in history class, that box is sitting at her feet. Obviously unfazed by Archibald's disappearance, notorious bully William Tanner is trying to get Hailee's attention by throwing air-kisses her way and paper balls on her desk. Her friend Emily picks one of them up and opens it. It's Tanner's theorem, a blend of subtlety and finesse, reading: William Tanner + Hailee Finch = two stick figures he's drawn exchanging what vaguely resembles a kiss.

"Gross!" says Emily, showing it to Hailee, who has no apparent reaction. Inside, though, she's boiling up.

Closing her eyes, she pictures herself jumping from one desk to another, going to that jerk and shoving the stupid paper ball in his mouth. *Why not?* she says to herself. *What a great way to channel all that stress and blow off steam!* Not that her teacher would care.

As usual, Mr. Hickinbottom doesn't see any of William Tanner's shenanigans. A five-thousand-pound Marodor could walk through the classroom in a Santa suit asking for directions, and Mr. Hickinbottom would still be completely oblivious to what's going on. Once more, he is too busy discoursing on his favorite subject: what happened to the passengers and crew of the *Mary Celeste*, the ghost ship found empty at sea in 1872. Totally outside of this year's curriculum—any year, in fact.

For the first time, Hailee is listening to the story with a totally different outlook, but no one else is paying attention. Besides, Mr. Hickinbottom is always hard to understand, as if he had wet vermicelli stubbornly stuck between his tongue and his palate. Bored students spend the hour challenging each other to count the hairs left in his comb-over. Some say twenty-three. Some bet on twenty-five. Others, more audacious, speak of thirty—but that's probably far-fetched.

When the school bell rings out, Mr. Hickinbottom dives into his notes, wagging his index finger in the air.

"Please read the first chapter of *The Making of the Modern World*. We'll discuss it on Thursday," he reminds all.

When he lifts his head back up, all have scurried off except Hailee.

"Do you have a question, Miss Finch?" he asks.

She approaches his desk with the box in her arms.

"I was hoping you could help me with something."

"Of course, young lady. But first let me say, if I may, that it is very courageous of you to come to class today, considering what happened to your brother. I commend you for that. What a shame—a great student, that Archibald."

"I know," sighs Hailee, still a bit tired of hearing that.

"Now, what can I do for you?"

Hailee pulls the globe out of the box.

"Well, well, well, what a fine piece of history you have here!" says Mr. Hickinbottom, tilting his head back and adjusting some old-fashioned spectacles to see more clearly. "A family heirloom, I presume?"

Hailee goes straight to the point. "Have you ever seen a globe like this?"

"Not exactly, no; this looks quite old and rare," he answers. "It's too bad, though; it seems broken."

Again, the globe doesn't spin. It must have locked itself automatically after Archibald used it, but, of course, neither Hailee nor Mr. Hickinbottom is aware of that.

"What can you tell me about it?" she asks.

"What do you want to know?"

"Anything, really," she sighs.

"Well, the first thing you'd want to find out is how old it is and where it was made. That's usually a good start. Wait, does it say 'Made in China' right here?"

"Where?"

"I'm sorry; I'm just pulling your leg," giggles Mr. Hickinbottom. "Now, let's see what we've got here," he says more seriously.

Hailee bends down to explore the globe with him, not too sure what to look for.

"Well, you don't see this too often!" says Mr. Hickinbottom.

"What's that?"

"Right here—*hic sunt dracones*," he says, reading from an inscription at the top of the globe.

"Is that some kind of code?"

"In a way, yes. It's Latin. It means 'Here be dragons.' You'd find that on ancient maps. A code, indeed, to identify territories still unexplored. Dangerous lands, obviously, though it doesn't mean there would be actual dragons there. Besides, the creatures on this globe don't quite look like dragons—wouldn't you agree?"

Hailee nods in approval.

"Now, did you see any other markings that would be of any help in this matter?"

"I don't think so. Just a few letters on this arm, right here." Hailee shows him the engraving on one of those ribs circling the sphere:

LDVMDXV

"See, Miss Finch, this is not an arm. It's called a meridian. And these are not quite letters. They are Roman numerals," he corrects.

"What's that?"

"That," emphasizes Mr. Hickinbottom, "is what we spent an hour discussing in class just last month, Miss Finch."

"I'm sorry."

"It's all right. Given the circumstances, I won't increase your burdens," he says, tapping her gently on the shoulder before heading to the chalkboard.

"It's fairly easy, really," he says. "Do you know what this is?" he asks, writing a capital I.

"That stick?"

"Not quite a stick but rather a number one in Roman numerals, Miss Finch," says Mr. Hickinbottom, rolling his eyes in dismay. "But don't worry—I have heard that before, unfortunately. In fact, I think I've heard it all."

"I knew that was a one," says Hailee, semi-honestly.

"But of course you did! So from here, to make a two, you'll need two sticks, and for a three, you'll need three of those . . . sticks," he says, turning around with a teasing smile.

"That's pretty easy," comments Hailee.

"Well, it gets a bit more complicated. Five is this capital V. The reason I skipped four is because you need to know five before you can make a four. Since four is five minus one, we'll just place that capital I before our capital V, which you'll just reverse to get a six. Are you following?"

"Yes."

"Good. Same for ten, with capital X as ten. Then based on the same logic, you'll have fifteen made of a ten followed by a five, and then twenty, thirty, etcetera, until you reach fifty."

"Is that five Xs?"

"No. You see, to make things more convenient, they came up with specific signs for some numbers. Remember when I told you ten was X and five was V?"

Hailee nods.

"So fifty is capital L. Then C equals a hundred, D five hundred, and M a thousand. Are you still following?"

"Yes."

"Perfect. Now let's apply this to your globe. So what do we have?"

Hailee starts reading the numerals on the meridian, starting with L.

"That's 50," notes Mr. Hickinbottom, writing it down on the board.

"D," continues Hailee.

"That's 500."

"V."

"That's 5."

"M."

"That's a thousand," he says, pausing suddenly. "Wait, no, you must have read this wrong. Can you please start over?"

"Okay: L-D-V-M-D."

He interrupts her. "I'm sorry—that can't be right. We have 50,

500, 5, and then a thousand. There is no logic to this. It's simply impossible to make a date out of it."

Mr. Hickinbottom checks the globe for himself. "I'm sorry to tell you this, but I think this is a copy, a forgery, which could explain why they made a mistake when engraving the numerals. That's the only thing I can think of."

"I see," sighs Hailee.

"I'm sorry I couldn't be of more assistance. Now, if you'll excuse me, I have a teachers' meeting to attend, and I'm quite late already."

"Of course, I understand," she says, putting the globe back in the box.

As Hailee is about to exit, Mr. Hickinbottom has one more piece of advice for her: "Miss Finch, I'm thinking you might want to bring your globe to an antique store; perhaps they could help you further."

"I didn't think about that. Thanks, Mr. Hickinbottom," she says before leaving.

Back home, sitting on her bed, Hailee is looking at those puzzling Roman numerals, flipping the globe upside down, when her dad knocks lightly at the half-open door.

"Hailee?" he calls.

"Come in."

Stuart sits next to her on the bed. "You know, your mother and I were wondering . . . maybe you should move into another room, you know, just for now."

They both take a quick look around. Archibald's side is still strangely empty. The room has been cleaned up, but the burn marks on the walls are still visible under a fresh coat of paint. As for the floor, it seems scarred forever.

"No, I'm fine, Dad. I'll stay here until Arch comes back."

"Okay, we'll leave it up to you."

An awkward silence ensues. Hailee can tell her dad obviously has something else on his mind.

"What's wrong, Dad?"

"Nothing, why?"

She tilts her head and stares at him, meaning, "I know better."

Stuart hesitates a second. Then he begins, "I don't want to upset you. I just wanted to know if . . . perhaps you could tell me more about what happened that night."

"I told you already. There was a big, bright light, the sound of thunder, and then nothing. Arch was gone. That's it."

"I'm sorry," says Stuart, putting a comforting hand on her leg. "Anything else, though? Any other detail you could think of?"

Hailee looks down at the globe sitting on her lap.

"Arch certainly loved his globe," Stuart notes with a smile before standing up and heading out.

"Dad . . ." says Hailee, calling him back in.

She looks conflicted. She wants to tell him the bright light emanated from the globe, but what would he think? That she's crazy. Or that she made it all up like so many other things she lied about these last few years.

"No, nothing," she finally says.

"I'm here for you, okay? Anytime, sweetheart."

Hailee nods, smiling weakly as Stuart exits the room.

Hailee is carrying her box under a mix of cats and dogs, unless it's just rain and snow. She's roaming the narrow streets of Covent Garden in the center of London, scanning the storefronts.

Enchanting as usual, the holiday decorations are totally invisible to her eyes, bloodshot after another restless night. Hailee passes by clothing stores she would normally be glued to, now without even a glance. Obviously, it's something else that brought her here.

"There's one!" she says suddenly.

Her pick is Edmund's Antiques, with a façade becoming an antique in its own right, thanks to custom cracks and a paint color nearly impossible to replicate—greenish moldy gray.

"Ching-a-ling." Attached to the door in clusters, jingle bells awaken an old man napping in the back. He looks very much like an Edmund, his pants and four-button waistcoat blending in perfectly with the striped fabric of a moth-eaten sofa. He is up in a jiffy and with a wince.

"Hello, hello!" he says, greeting Hailee in the warmest tone. "How can I help you? Looking for a gift?"

"No, not real—"

"Don't tell me!" he shouts, cutting her off. "I know—it's for your mother. You want to surprise her, and instead of buying one of those cheap knickknacks online, you said to yourself, 'I'll go to Edmund's and make my mum happy.' Well, you were right. As they say, come to Edmund and he'll give you the moon!"

Spinning around while a few cuckoo clocks go off, he's like one of those toys that just got wound up and won't stop until the stored energy is all used up.

"I have just what you need," says the salesman, and before Hailee can utter a word, "I know what you're going to say. You've seen these somewhere else, but, no, they don't make them like this anymore. Just between you and me, the Duchess of Cambridge herself wore these for her first ball. Who could say no to these, huh?" asks Edmund, pulling out the most hideous pair of shoes ever made: yellow, with purple stripes, orange polka dots, and a missing heel—a flaw of which Edmund has apparently just become aware.

"That's a quick fix. I'll glue a heel from another shoe. Free of charge. The color might not match exactly, but your mum deserves something unique, right? And 5 percent off! What do you say?"

"No, sorry, I'm not here for shoes."

"A necklace, then?"

"No!"

"Pearl earrings?"

"No!"

"I know—a purse. I have one just for your mum."

"Please, no. I'm not here for my mum," says Hailee.

"Don't tell me. It's for your best friend, isn't it?"

"No."

"Your sister?"

"No!"

"Your brother?" he says, cringing at the shoes he's still holding.

Hailee shakes her head. "I'm not looking for anything! I just need some help with this globe," she says, opening the box.

Edmund barely looks inside. "Of course, young lady. Why don't you take a seat and we'll look at it together?" is the reaction Hailee expected. Edmund's is a tad different:

"Sorry, miss. I have enough globes to create my own solar system," he tells her, pointing at shelves after shelves of globes covered with dust.

"You don't understand. I'm not trying to sell it; I just need some information about it."

"Information? What do you think this is? Booble? Or one of those Yahoos? You're at Edmund's here; you're not on the Internets. I happen to work for a living, miss. I sell things. Can't you see I'm a busy man?" he says, as he stands there in the middle of mountains of unsold bibelots, with a spider already starting to build a web from the corner of his hat to a chandelier above.

Back on the street, Hailee starts looking around again. No less than five times within an hour does she get a variation of the same answer from different shop owners, whether they be old or young, male or female, awake or not. Hailee wants to call it a day. A bad day. She heads back to the Tube entrance. She has almost reached the Leicester Square station when she sees one more antique store across the street—the Realm of Antiques. She gives it a shot.

This time, Hailee makes it a point to be crystal clear as soon as she enters. "Hello, sorry to bother you. I'm not here to buy or sell anything; I just want to know more about this globe." That's when she realizes there might be no one in the store, until a voice responds, coming from behind a desk—a rather young voice.

"I'll be with you in a minute," it says. About a minute later, a head pops up from behind the desk—a rather charming head, which is not lost on Hailee.

"Sorry, I was cleaning up," says a boy around her age with a rough look to him and no trendy clothes—very different from the boys at school. She is taken aback and still a bit wary.

"As I said, I'd just like to know more about this globe," she explains, glancing at her box on the counter.

"A terrestrial globe?" asks the young man.

"Yes."

"I love those. Let's put it over there by the light," he suggests, motioning toward a table by the entrance.

"Great!" says Hailee, startled by such a rare display of basic kindness. She pulls the globe out for him to look at.

"Nice!" he says right away, before getting closer.

As he starts inspecting the globe, Hailee starts inspecting him. "This is not your store, is it?" she asks, making him chuckle.

"No, I'm only fourteen. It's my dad's."

Hailee nods.

"This is very interesting," he says.

"Very," she concurs, not sure what she is referring to exactly, him or the globe.

"The monsters, the map, all of this was painted by hand. Can you believe that? It's great."

She nods. "Anything *different* about this globe?"

"Ancient globes like this all have their own little quirks. Some maps showed California as an island for a while. Others even had a totally fictitious mountain pop up in Africa—the Mountain of Kong, they called it. I'm not kidding. That mistake lasted for almost a hundred years. But in general, most globes and maps have a lot in common, just because they're based on science, you know, triangulation—that's just basic geometry."

"You talk like my brother," says Hailee, but she wants to remain focused on the questions that brought her here. "By different, I meant something out of the ordinary, something strange—you know what I mean?"

"You want something out of the ordinary? This is, right here," he says, pointing at the carvings on the meridian.

"Yes, I know, but it doesn't make any sense," she comments.

"LDV," he spells out.

"Those aren't letters, actually. Mr. Hickinbottom, my history teacher, told me those were Roman numerals. No offense, by the way. I made the same mistake."

"Well, Mr. Hickinbottom is only partially right. See the four letters that follow LDV? Those *are* Roman numerals, and they read fifteen hundred and fifteen. I'm not certain, but most likely that's when this globe was made. These three letters before that are actual letters. And they tell you something out of the ordinary for sure."

"What's that?"

"They tell you who built this globe."

"Who's LDV?"

"Leonardo da Vinci. Ever heard of him?"

Hailee is amazed, her thoughts instantly awash with images of well-known drawings and paintings from the Italian master. She has seen them in class, online, or in museums.

"So I guess you *have* heard of him!" says the boy, noting Hailee's awe.

"I saw some of his stuff in Paris a couple years ago. But I didn't know he built globes. I thought he was just a painter."

"Believe it or not, there's only about fifteen paintings by him out there. But thousands of drawings! Wait a second," says the boy, heading to the antique books section of the store.

"Here," he says, pulling a weighty tome from the bottom shelf and opening it on the table next to the globe. Of course, it's a book about Leonardo da Vinci.

"Let me show you. That guy was a genius," he says, leafing through. "Look, not only was he a great artist but he also invented tons of things. The first tank, that's him. Same thing for the parachute, his idea. And look at his sketches for a flying machine. Remind you of something?"

"It looks like a weird helicopter."

"That's exactly what it is. He was such an incredible designer."

"I didn't know that," says Hailee, amazed by the level of detail in the sketches.

"Most people know da Vinci for the *Mona Lisa* and that's it—kind of sad," adds the boy, going back to the cover.

"That would be me, most people—kind of sad," says Hailee, joking but almost ashamed at the same time.

"I didn't mean it that way; I'm sorry. By the way, it's never too late to learn. Look, now you know," he says, bringing a smile back to her face.

"Another Archibald!"

"What do you mean?"

"My brother, he knows everything. It's annoying sometimes."

"Well, *I* don't know everything; nobody does."

Just then, the front door swings open. Someone barges in—a frail little man, gangly frame, skinny arms, and slumping knobby shoulders, all bones and nerves crammed into overly tight clothes. He brings a whiff of cheap wine along with the outdoor breeze.

"Didn't I tell you to call me when we've got a client?" yells the man, sounding drunk. And to Hailee, with a slightly nicer voice and a forced smile, "Hello, young lady, good day. What can I do for you?"

"Sorry, Dad, I didn't want to bother you at the pub," says the boy, apologetic and submissive suddenly.

"Oliver, that's the point of me having a drin—a coffee right across the street, so I can be here in a twinkle," says the man, nearly losing his balance.

Pushing his kid aside, he turns back to Hailee. "What were we saying?"

Hailee doesn't know how to respond. Oliver comes to her rescue.

"Dad, she brought a globe she'd like you to look at."

"I don't need no globe," answers the father.

"Dad, I really think you should look at it," says Oliver, grabbing the globe from the table.

"I told you, boy; I don't need no goddam—"

One glimpse from afar is enough for him to stop talking at once. He approaches the globe with obvious interest. He takes it from his son and inspects it from top to bottom, passing his hand gently over the surface.

"Could this be?" he mumbles.

"I told you, Dad," says Oliver.

"How much?" the shop owner asks Hailee.

"No, I'm not here to sell it; I just—"

"Everything has a price, young lady—name yours," he says, staring at her, his eyes hesitating between creepy and drunk.

"I'm sorry, sir; as I said, I'm not interested."

"Miss!" he yells.

Oliver puts his hand on his dad's shoulder to stop him. "Dad! She's not interested."

His father looks at the hand on his shoulder and manages to calm himself down. "Okay, okay, no problem, young lady," he says in a much more conciliatory—and clearly fake—tone. "What is your name, sweetheart?"

"Hailee," she answers, fearful.

"And Hailee, where is it that you live?"

Now she is really freaked out. "I'd like to go now; it's late," she says in a trembling voice. Indeed, it's getting dark outside. "Can I have my globe back, please?"

"Of course you can!" says Oliver, prying the globe from his father's hands and putting it back into the box.

Hailee leaves without turning back.

Oliver's dad watches her through the window as she enters the nearest Undergound station. He then turns to his son, grabs him by the collar, and pushes him against the wall.

"Do you know what you've done?"

"I didn't do anything."

"You've just ruined our lives. Mine. And yours."

"I was just trying to help her."

"Your job is to help *us*! Have I taught you nothing?"

"I'm sorry."

"What did you tell her? And what did she tell you? I want to know every detail," says the creep, pressing up on his son's throat.

"Nothing, I just told her that history teacher was wrong," says Oliver, now struggling to breathe.

"A history teacher, huh?" says his dad, loosening his hold.

A few minutes later, Hailee is sitting semi-safely in her train, clutching her box to her chest the way she hugged her stuffed rabbit until just a few years ago.

Meanwhile, Oliver's dad is dialing a number on his old rotary phone, holding a business card.

A deep, cavernous voice answers, "Who is this?"

"Mr. Heinrich?"

"Yes. Who is this?"

"Mr. Heinrich, this is Mr. Doyle, James Doyle. I'm the owner of the Realm of Antiques, in London. We met a few years ago—you came to my shop. You bought that old book from me, the *Malleus* something. Pardon me, I'm getting old."

"Go on."

"Well, maybe you don't remember, but back then you told me you were looking for something dear to you, a very particular globe, a terrestrial globe. You called it the missing link or something like that."

"Continue," says Mr. Heinrich with the same monotonic, almost robotic voice.

"I don't know if you're still interested, but if you are, I think I can make you happy, Mr. Heinrich. We would just have to find an agreement of some sort, of course," says Mr. Doyle.

An eerie silence shrouds the other end of the line.

"Mr. Heinrich, are you still there?"

"I'm in New York. I'll be at your shop in the morning," says Mr. Heinrich, before he hangs up.

"No more debt," mumbles Mr. Doyle. He is smiling. Oliver is not. Hiding behind an armoire, he listened to the entire conversation. He looks really worried.

GOLEMS
VERSUS
MARODORS

The day has just dawned on Gristlemoth. Archibald wakes up with another long yawn, talking through it with essentially the same thought. "What a bad dream," he says sleepily.

Of course, giant boulders don't just float in the air. Nor would carrots ever grow that fast—thank goodness! No way did he feed a Marodor his candy bar. Merdar or Marodor, there's no such thing, anyway. Besides, even if he were running for his life, he would never waste a Kit Kat like that. And what did that girl call him? A liripoop? A fool? How could he imagine such a fallacy? No one talks to Archibald Finch that way.

"And you're a puggard!" yells a voice, startling him out of his fantasy. It's Faerydae. She has just discovered Naida's stones scattered on the ground behind the door.

"Nothing but a petty puggard," she repeats, fuming.

From the bewilderment on his face, she quickly understands he doesn't understand. "You're a goodfellow!"

"That doesn't sound too bad."

"Maybe you didn't hear me well! What about gonof, snatcher, thief?" she yells.

"No, I just borrowed these."

"Again, your flummadiddle!"

Archibald pouts, finding nothing to say in his own defense.

"If I am to trust you, we have to set some clear rules," she yells.

"Like what?"

"Like you won't lie or steal anymore. Can you do that?"

"I think so," he says, not that convincing.

"Can. You. Do. That?" repeats Faerydae.

"On one condition," requests Archibald, sheepish.

"I'm not sure you're in a position to bargain, but what would that be?"

"That you don't turn me into a rat or anything like that."

Faerydae cracks up. "And why would I do that?"

"Because you're an eye-biter, an enchantress."

Faerydae bursts out laughing again. But she also sees an opportunity to use his fear to her advantage. "You're right. I *am* a witch; I *could* do that, and you will do well to remember it. But you have my word—if you stop lying and stealing, I won't turn you into anything."

Archibald looks relieved. "Okay, then I'll stop," he promises. "One more thing, though."

"What now?"

"The stones—will you show me how they work?"

"Well, if you really want to know, you'll have to go to school."

Archibald doesn't like the sound of that. "Please, no. I'm on vacation. I hate school," he laments.

"How can you hate school? It's whimsifulous!"

"Whimsifulous? If that means anything close to great, it can't apply to school, or we're not talking about the same thing."

Faerydae has walked out, leaving the door open, but Archibald seems in no hurry to follow her.

"I don't want to go to school," he whines.

"Don't forget your cloak," she shouts.

Borrowing Bartholomeo's unique style as a marathon runner, he drags his feet out of the cabana just as that doglike moving target comes zooming by, panting, tongue out, and with the most frightened look on his scrambled face. Five seconds later, a horde of archers follows, led by Rhiannon.

"What a freaky place!" blurts Archibald.

He slowly catches up with Faerydae, making no secret of his lack of enthusiasm for a last-minute trip to school, however whimsifulous she thinks it might be. He pouts, he sighs, he huffs, he puffs, he looks down, he helps his shoulders sag, he kicks some rocks. He uses every trick in the book. And why not? It worked more than once before with his mother. Each time, they ended up spending the day watching TV at home instead.

"Why don't we go fishing or something?" he suggests.

"Stop it! I'm telling you: you're going to love it," she assures.

This is real torture for Archibald. In fact, looking at his face, you would believe he is being dragged to his death. Or at least that he has just caught an instant case of the plague. Nothing could make him feel better, not even the gigantest scoop of ice cream. Nothing except, perhaps, what was hiding past that green curtain of tall elm trees . . .

"Welcome to the Hive!" announces Faerydae, as a large structure comes into view.

"Holy bejabbles, that's not a hive; it's a castle! Just like in my history books," says Archibald, stunned.

This is Gristlemoth's Rome. All roads lead to it, at the very center of the village. Unlike all the mud and wood dwellings around it, the Hive is made out of stone—massive blocks of stone. From the crenelated fortifications to the arrow slits, deep moat all around, and turrets on each of six corners, it has all the attributes of a medieval fortress.

"That's your school?" he exclaims.

"The Hive has been many things to us. A school today but mostly a shelter to begin with, the heart of our colony. It's not just shaped like a honeycomb. We *were* like bees in there when we arrived, hiding in the dark, building our defenses, resisting the siege from Marodors, and coming out to sting them," recalls Faerydae.

Archibald cannot quite picture Faerydae and her friends fighting off armies of monsters from behind these ramparts.

"Not quite the fairy-tale castle I expected," he comments.

"Don't tell me you believe in fairy tales," says Faerydae, amused. "'Cause this is no fairy tale. It's the real thing."

He would have imagined something a little different, more "girly" for sure—maybe some larger windows, a few towers of all sizes here and there, with funny, pointy roofs and probably some pink little flags fluttering in the wind. The only flag up there is more on the gloomy side, emblazoned with that obscure double-wave symbol—cream on a brownish-red background.

Past the moat, over a wobbly drawbridge, they enter a wide courtyard effervescent with laughter, discussions, and prayerlike recitations. While some girls are studying or reading on benches, many others are seated or lying directly on the ground. All faces, though, are turned toward three large chalkboards around which most of the action seems to revolve. The drawings on the boards include some trees, plants, and flowers, but the focus is definitely on Marodors, featured in parts or whole. Arrows point at the beasts' weak points, sides to avoid, and danger zones. Also specified are more basic yet potentially lifesaving details, such as head and tail, which for some Marodors are rather hard to figure out—like that round millipede with about ten separate heads, puzzling to many inspecting it.

"Where's the teacher?" asks Archibald.

"We are all teachers," explains Faerydae. "We all have things to learn from one another. The key to learning lies in observing, listening, and sharing. And that's not just true for Marodors."

Archibald is fascinated, though his main takeaway from her speech is rather predictable. "No teacher? That's so cool!"

"I told you you'd love it."

Past the chalkboards, Faerydae leads Archibald inside the

castle itself, through a gloomy corridor carved under a huge double staircase, the walls lined with luminous jars that seem to be humming. The first room they access spans both sides of the hallway. On the right are mounds of herbs and flowers covering three workbenches almost entirely, with more waiting in baskets on the floor.

"Our apothecary," Faerydae says proudly, her broad arm gesture guiding his gaze toward hundreds of bottles, flasks, and vials crowding the cabinets and shelves around the room. "With six different kinds of herbs: healers, damagers, protectors, numb-makers, paralyzers, and brain-crackers."

"I think I'll pass on the tea, thanks," jokes Archibald.

Faerydae shakes her head. This is serious business. "Many of our plants are unique. To locate them, we've traveled weeks, crossed valleys and peaks, often to the far edges of the world," she explains. "Itch weed from Worgonia, mugwort from the Sargung River, voodoo lilies from Arachnagar, Dracula orchids from Lobulia, octopus stinkhorns from Gurguria. Some you see here you cannot find anymore."

"I hope so," he mutters under his breath, guessing the potency of these herbs solely based on the frowning faces of those cutting and bunching them together.

Across from this collection of stinky rarities, Archibald discovers a grand library, very much like his grandma's but with a twist. Running from floor to ceiling, the shelves continue on the ceiling itself, where books are somehow hanging upside down without falling. It's all the more impressive that the books are enormous, some of them taller than Archibald, looking as heavy and overwhelming as the knowledge they surely carry. The students working here don't seem too inconvenienced or deterred by this sort of detail. With the help of a few glowing stones, they have made those oversized books lighter than feathers, passing them to each other across the room—an unusual ballet that has all but hypnotized Archibald.

Faerydae pulls him along. Maybe he will get some answers down the hallway, where unfolds the holy of holies, the main workshop for manufacturing those mysterious stones. The well-oiled production line is organized around a single, extremely long table. At one end are unloaded buckets of rough rock fragments. By the time they reach the opposite end, the rocks have become a more finished product shaped like a big bar of soap, thanks to the work of many hands polishing in concert. The stones are now ready for their markings. Armed with hammers and chisels, Maven is among those taking care of the engraving.

"Are these the magic rocks?" Archibald asks them.

"Golems, these are golems," corrects Maven.

"Golems? What are those signs you're carving on the stones—I mean, on the golems?"

"It's what makes a golem a golem—the runes alphabet," says Faerydae, as if it were self-evident.

Archibald examines the stones scattered on the table, fascinated and confused at the same time. Some of the carvings look like regular letters, but not really. There's one that could almost pass for an N, if not for the arrow running through it— ᚾ . The ᚱ is rather unbalanced for an R and seems just about to fall on its back. One of them might have been an E at one point, before it was most certainly struck by lightning— ᛇ. As for the ᛒ, that's one angry B, giving the others a "Don't mess with me" attitude.

Most runes, though, are as close to regular letters as margarine is to butter. From a tree of arrows ᚧ, to a swirl ᛰ, to another cryptic symbol vaguely resembling a snake's head ᚦ, this is a different language altogether.

"That's one complicated alphabet!" says Archibald.

"A bit trickier than *a*, *b*, *c*, *d*, etcetera, if that's what you mean," says Maven. "These might look childish, but don't be mistaken. They're based on ancient signs handed down from our ancestors."

"How many letters?" he asks.

"It depends," says Maven.

"It depends? How can it depend? Try to remove the *T* from the alphabet, and let's see how we . . . alk," chuckles Archibald.

"It's not set in stone, if I can say that," Maven chuckles back.

"We constantly have to adapt to new breeds of Marodors," explains Faerydae. "As a result, runes change over time. Some disappear; others are born. It's just the regular cycle of life. That's why their number varies. Right now, we're using around thirty."

"Once a rune is etched on a stone, they become one, sharing powers and a name," explains Maven. "This is my favorite—Moonascendum," she says, grabbing a golem with a pyramid marking on it **Δ**.

"So what does . . . Moonascendum do?"

"Oh, nothing much—it just links the earth and the sky," she smirks, "with the ability to defy the burden from the heavens, you know, the weight that keeps your feet on the ground."

"As in gravity, you mean?" notes Archibald.

"What's that?"

"What you're describing—I'm pretty sure it's gravity."

"Uh-huh, the burden from the heavens," repeats Maven.

Archibald just nods, yielding to the poetry of that synonym and eager to learn more. "So this rune can make you fly?" he asks, looking excited.

The girls grin from ear to ear.

"Not quite, but it can move mountains," says Maven, giving an indication as to how she made that Marodor hover aboveground and how those books can remain glued to the ceiling next door.

"You know, your friend Lenora, I think she'd rather fly than move mountains," he says.

"Lenora doesn't need to fly; she already has her head in the clouds!" sneers Faerydae.

"She might have better luck with this one," says Maven, switching to another stone on the table engraved with three stacked-up horizontal lines ☰.

"What is it?" asks Archibald.

"Eolare, focused on wind power," says the teacher. "And one of our base runes—the key runes, if you will," Maven explains.

"Hey, it's that sign you guys wear on your clothes," he exclaims, grabbing a golem with a wave engraving ≋.

"Another base rune, Aequae, linked to water," says Maven.

"The source of life," adds Faerydae. "We chose it as the emblem of our colony," she says, placing her hand on the patch embossed on her tunic, as if pledging allegiance to a flag.

"What about fire?"

"Yes, that's the third base rune," confirms Maven. "And since most Marodors spit fire, that's a crucial one."

"Spit fire? Like dragons?"

"Not *like* dragons; most Marodors *are* dragons, but you know that, right?" questions Faerydae.

Archibald nods nervously, a slight tremor of tingling itch going through his spine. "Dragons and griffons," he whispers, echoing his reaction to Stuart's stories the night he found the globe.

"If we're talking fire, it rhymes with 'Ignifera,'" says Maven, picking up a stone with another pyramid, this one made of dots: ∴. "And there you have your three base runes, the most important."

"Which doesn't make the others negligible," notes Faerydae. "Yes, base runes trigger or multiply the powers of sister runes, but they all have a crucial role to play."

"Abbreviae, for example," says Maven, pointing at the stone Archibald just picked up, with a rune shaped like a target ⊕. "It can compress, squeeze, or shrink pretty much anything."

"Marodors' heads, mostly," jokes Faerydae.

"There's a crack in it," notes Archibald, sticking his finger through a small hole in the stone.

"It's not a crack," laughs Faerydae. "It's a slit we drill into some golems so they can be mounted on arrows and reach their target more easily."

"Arrows with gloves," remembers Archibald, amazed at the basic ingenuity of this weapon.

"Rhiannon tried that against the beast chasing you, but it was already too late. There was no stopping that thing, not with one golem, at least," she says.

"Artificio did a good job. You never know what kind of awesome effect you'll get with it, and that ripple of light was quite bewilderful," comments Maven as she holds up a stone carved with a rough square ◇. "It's true, though; a golem can't do much on its own," she says, going through the stack. "Don't get me wrong. Take Tremora here ⟋. Like Artificio, it sure knows how to put on a good show—a good shake, actually. Same with Fraxinus ✗; it will break something when you need it to. A log or a bone, it will break it. But it takes more than that to defeat Marodors."

"It takes teamwork," continues Faerydae. "Golems are made in our image. Alone, they won't achieve much. But combine them and you've got real magic on your hands," she says, adding a stone to the ones Archibald is holding already.

"The best part is there's an infinite number of combinations," says Maven, walking up to another blackboard against the back wall of the workshop. No Marodor on this one. Instead, a web of those arcane symbols scrawled into different sets of equations in which variables are runes.

In fact, the sum of each formula is not a number either. In Gristlemoth, ᛒ + ∞ + Δ or ✗ + ≋ + ᛕ does not equal anything but a headache, a real headache, among other medical conditions and ailments listed on the board—some relatively mild, such as dizziness, loss of balance, blurred vision, or nausea; others a tad more severe, like total paralysis, hallucinations, legs crumbling, instant weight loss, or ribs crushing.

"This has nothing to do with growing carrots, does it?" comments Archibald. "These are magic spells!"

"You can call them that," says Faerydae. "What you see here is more of a battle plan. That's the number one purpose of runes and golems, to fight Marodors."

"To hit the beast from within, you have to add Vixeneme," Maven advises a girl stuck on one of those equations.

"I get the legs crumbling or the ribs crushing, but what's a looping tail?" he asks, reading from the board.

"That's a good one," chuckles Maven. "It's when we make a Marodor tie up its legs with its own tail."

"I have to say, this is much more fun than math class," notes Archibald.

"And I had to drag you here," smiles Faerydae.

"Have you shown Ivy the fish?" asks Maven.

"Not yet."

"What fish?" asks Archibald, excited again.

"This workshop is only the tip of the iceberg," explains Maven.

∴

Making their way south, Archibald and Faerydae soon find themselves near the cliff Gristlemoth is leaning against. Riddled with holes of all sizes, from huge at the base to small toward the top, the steep rock façade has been terraced over time to progressively turn into a gigantic staircase—surely a way for giants to reach for the skies, at least in Archibald's mind. Each step is connected to the next with ladders. Two dozen girls are digging and scraping at the mountainside with shovels and picks, while buckets are floating up and down, like the books in the library.

"This is where the golems come from," says Faerydae as she picks up rock fragments from the ground. "We also use amber from trees, but this is much better."

"What is it?"

"Magnetite—it's charged with natural energy," explains one of the girls using golems to keep the gliding buckets in line.

Archibald recognizes her despite the mask of dust on her face. "Lenora?"

"Aye up, Ivy!" she says, confirming she is indeed the acrobat who shot up in the air and nearly killed herself yesterday.

"They let you out already?"

"The door was never locked. I went in there on my own."

"What? That stunt must have damaged your head! Who would choose to go to jail on their own?" he chuckles.

"I told you; it's not like that."

"It's about acknowledging our mistakes," explains Faerydae, "and taking time to reflect on those mistakes so we don't repeat them."

"Sounds real good," he says, skeptical. "So, Lenora, you've learned your lesson? In one night? You'll never do that rocket thing again?" he asks, drawing loops in the air with his finger.

Even under Faerydae's stare, Lenora struggles to offer a

straight face. "I shall not," she finally swears to Faerydae in an overly theatrical tone, punctuating her oath with a wink to Archibald. By a rather fitting twist of fate, she drops one of her golems in the process, causing all the buckets to tumble to the ground.

"That's what I thought," laughs Archibald.

"Those buckets don't feel pain, but *you* sure will the next time you fall," warns Faerydae.

"By the way, why is *my* door locked, then?" asks Archibald.

"Let's just say that some people need more reflection than others," smiles Faerydae.

"I'm fine. Nothing to improve, thanks."

"We all have it in us to be better; we just need a little push. Take this magnetite. It's born with great powers—but even greater potential. So we add a little something to it," she says, moving toward two canoes sitting by the river nearby.

Lenora runs ahead, picks up bread from a basket, and throws some into one of the boats. Archibald takes a look inside.

"Fish!" he cries out.

"We rarely use these boats, so we converted them to raise our Raad," explains Faerydae.

"Raad? What kind of fish are these?"

They are indeed unique, with their long, thin tails, bug eyes, and flat, wide bodies that look like they've been squashed between a rock and a hard place—or inside a huge waffle maker.

"They have so much energy they can multiply the power of these rocks by a hundred," shouts Lenora.

"How?"

"Just like this," says Faerydae, dropping a piece of magnetite in the boat. As soon as the rock hits the water, several fish wrap and spin around it. Their dance makes the water seem to boil instantly.

Lenora swaps her loaf of bread for a pair of large tongs. She carefully extracts the stone from the tight embrace of the Raad.

"Hot, hot, hot!" she says, fishing it out.

"It will cool down and go back to its original state, but now it's fully charged," explains Faerydae. "Magnetite has unique qualities. It can attract and repel, energize and weaken. We use the runes to reactivate and harness those powers when needed. But none of this would work without the herbs and plants I showed you earlier."

"What are those for? Seasoning?" jokes Archibald.

"Well, we do boil them with the magnetite. They definitely spice things up," smiles Faerydae. "Only then can the rocks be sent to the workshop."

Archibald is feeling dizzy.

"Energy stones, thunder fish, poison plants, tricky symbols, crazy names, freaky spells—those golems are one hell of a magic weapon," he says.

"And don't forget the bread."

Archibald laughs. "What do you call that bread, by the way?"

"Just bread. What do you want to call it?"

"I don't know; it's just that you have all those funky names for everything, so I thought . . ."

"What?" she asks, obviously not seeing his point.

"Never mind," he says, biting into one of his candy bars.

Smarter than he may sound, Archibald starts connecting the dots.

"Those big stones around the village, are those golems too?"

"Good thinking," confirms Faerydae. "They took years to install. We used them as a shield at first, then at one point they liberated enough energy to carve a hole in the sky. *That* was magical and key to creating more colonies. We even have one in Umbraea now."

"Where's Ombreya?"

"Umbraea," she corrects, stunned he wouldn't know.

"Remember Naida? My friend with the carrots?"

Archibald nods, twitching his nose.

"That's where she's from," she says. "Where's Umbraea . . ." she adds under her breath, shaking her ahead in both amusement and disbelief.

"What's wrong?" he asks.

"You said you'd stop lying. So I'm going to ask you a question, and you'd better not lie," she says, waving for Lenora to go away. "Who are you?" she asks, her expression darkening.

"I'm just . . . Archibald," he answers, a bit frightened.

"When we showed you the runes earlier, you acted like you didn't know anything about them."

"Because I didn't."

"So what is this, then?" she asks, ripping off his cloak and uncovering his hoodie with the $\Omega \, \Delta \, \Psi$ letters sewn across.

"That's just my sweatshirt," says Archibald, on the defensive.

"Just a sweatshirt? You have three of our most powerful runes drawn on your clothes, and you're saying it's just a coincidence?"

Archibald is really scared now. Maybe Faerydae will turn him into a skunk or a turkey after all.

"It's my sister's; I took it from her," he says, as honest as it gets.

"Stole it, you mean?"

"Yes," he admits.

"Where's your sister?"

"In London."

"Will you stop saying London?" snaps Faerydae. "There's only one colony in Gulli Terra—Whifflecliff."

"I'm sorry; I thought it was Cuffley. I'm not too familiar with the names. We just moved there a few months ago, but I trust you," says Archibald.

Faerydae calms down a little. "All right, it's your sister's. It makes sense, I guess. Sorry about your cloak," she says, trying to put it back together around his neck.

Archibald is off the hook. Or maybe not. Faerydae grabs him by the shoulders suddenly, scaring him again. But her face is softening.

"Look, I'm trying to put myself in your shoes, whatever shoes these are," she says, glancing down at his sneakers. "I know it must be hard for you just to be here, as a boy. I mean, you're only a mislimp after all."

"I'm what?"

"A mislimp, you know, an accident. I can only imagine how it feels," she confides. "I'm sorry if I was a little rough with you."

Archibald smiles really big. He is amazed and relieved that she seems to know everything.

"Rough with me? No, I'm used to much worse—trust me." Images of William Tanner and his sister come to his mind instantly. "I find you pretty chill, actually!"

"Chill? Are you saying I'm cold?"

"Not at all—what I meant by chill is you're cool, you know?"

"Wait, so I'm not cold, but I'm cool. Isn't that essentially the same thing?"

"Trust me—where I come from, it's a compliment. Don't ask me why; I don't even know. I just really like you!" he exclaims.

Faerydae is taken aback. She blushes a little, looks away, runs her hands through her hair, unable to avoid looking awkward.

"Oh, um, okay . . ." she mumbles. "Well, I'm sorry, but I'll still have to put you in that cabana and lock the door, for your own safety. You don't quite know your way around. Living here can be challenging, you know. I'm not sure you're ready yet—that's all."

"I've heard that before," groans Archibald.

Another morning, another instance of talking through yawning for Archibald, who still dreams of getting out of this nightmare.

"This was just a bad, bad—nope, still here," he mutters as he opens his eyes once more to the blue sky of Gristlemoth and the comfort of his charming cabana/prison.

He digs into the right pocket of his hoodie, surprised to find nothing. He tries the left pocket. Nothing there either. The wrapping papers scattered on the ground confirm his worst fear: he has run out of candy bars.

Faerydae is knocking at the door. "Can I come in?"

"Sure," he answers weakly.

"Everything okay?" she asks, noting the worry in his pout. "I have something to cheer you up, something I've been working on for quite a while now," she adds, handing him a thick book.

"Wow, it's heavy!"

"That's centuries of research—what do you expect?"

The title reads:

THE GRAND
(PURPOSELY INCOMPLETE)
BESTIARY OF MARODORS
CAUGHT & WITNESSED
(OR DEPICTED BASED ON
FAIRLY RELIABLE DESCRIPTIONS)

In order to read all the fine print (where the devil usually hides), Archibald has to brush aside clumps of feathers, leaves, fur, and pine needles sewn on or glued to the wood cover.

"What's all this, a bunch of charms?" he asks.

"Nope, just some of the many things Marodors are made of."

"Kinda looks like Paws," he says.

"Who's Paws?"

"Him," says Archibald, pointing under his bed, where Faerydae finds the pile of gubbins used around the village for target practice—cowering and trembling like a scared puppy.

"I can't believe you gave that thing a name!" she chuckles, struggling to make heads or tails of it. "Well, you're not that far off. This *is* what that—what your *Paws* is made of," she says, stroking the bestiary's thickly adorned cover.

"What?"

"Scraps! Leftovers from Marodors. One day, we were cleaning their cages, and one of the girls threw a bunch of fur and junk away along with some old golems. Next thing we know, that ball of jinx—Paws here—comes flying out of the bin!"

"Paws is . . . garbage?"

"Pretty much! Or whatever these weirderies are shedding," she says, opening the bestiary.

Page after page, Archibald discovers the most outlandish, ragtag menagerie. Winged or scaled, horned or clawed, furry or bald, all Marodors look like the product of some botched experiment. The sum of their many parts, whether they be from animals, birds, or insects, hints at something gone terribly wrong. And that's not even mentioning the human parts, chief among them that ghostly face many seem to have in common.

Each Marodor, fully drawn or roughly sketched, is scarier than the last, with names alone capable of inspiring the worst fears. Humciferae Sulfuratus, Choleoptus Mortifare 1, 2, and 3 (depending on the head count), Megaptera Plaguare, Enominum Obscurus—just whispering some of them makes Archibald tremble.

"So they weren't scary enough; you had to give them crazy names too," he comments.

"These are just their official names—their smart names, if

you will. All plants and animals have those, you know," explains Faerydae. "But, of course, every Marodor also has a more common name. See right here," she says, pointing to the "also known as" section in the Marodor's description chart (on the opposite page).

"Socks . . . Clafoutis . . . Dingo . . . Stripes . . . these sound more like pet names."

"It's just a way to show we're not afraid of them, even though we are, of course," she jokes. "The point is: we have nothing to fear but fear itself."

"Sounds good!" concurs Archibald, who might have heard that somewhere before.

Not all of those nicknames have a friendly tone, though. Some, like Booger, Meathead, Doomdumb, or Big Bertha, are clearly intended to ridicule the monsters. Some seem more rooted in history—the darkest side of history.

"Genghis Khan!" exclaims Archibald. "That's one bad boy right here."

"Considering he's responsible for the death of millions, yes, I think you can say that. They really look similar, though. I swear, sometimes I think the actual Genghis Khan got reincarnated into this thing."

Messy blend of cat and moth, plus bits and pieces of cockroach, the Ulanbatore Golgothae indeed owes its nickname to an obvious resemblance to the bloody Mongol conqueror, from the long goatee to the thin, scary eyes—and possibly the rough childhood.

"That's not even the worst! Check out page 125."

Archibald finds it quickly. "Maculatus Ferocipare, also known as . . . Arthur. That doesn't sound too bad."

"It is; trust me. I named it after an ex-boyfriend. They both had really bad breath."

Archibald cracks up, while also turning his head discreetly, blowing into the palm of his hand—just to make sure.

"As long as you didn't name him Archibald."

"No, Archibald is page 173."

He has stopped laughing suddenly, not eager to reach that page. When he does, he is definitely not too pleased with the DNA of that particular beast: naked mole rat, locust, and snake, among other weird bits.

"Looks terrible! What's wrong with this one?" he asks, exploring the chart that details his average size, weight, speed, capture location, strengths, and weaknesses.

"If I remember correctly, this Marodor has multiple tongues. Naida picked the name. Another ex-boyfriend, I think. Terrible kisser, I heard."

"Really?"

"I'm just bourding with you," she laughs. "This is a pretty average Marodor, nothing too special about it. Sneaky creature, though; you never quite know what its next move's going to be, so you've got to keep an eye on that thing."

"It's weird; it says nothing about that in here."

"Trust me: I know *all* about the Archibald," says Faerydae, in a not-too-subtle nod to her experience with this boy from Cuffley—or wherever he claims to be from.

"And it's a crawler—that's just great," sighs Archibald, reading more details about the weird beast that bears his name.

"Yes, some of them crawl, some of them fly, some run, some swim. And some, well, they do all of the above."

"What a freak show!"

"Hey, look! This is the Marodor who chased you," she says, showing him the Apiumare Mellifera, aka Ram, on page 29.

"Who drew all these?" he asks.

"This is kind of my pet project, but I'm not very good at it, so others contribute. One of my best friends, Parnel, she drew a few," says Faerydae, looking sad suddenly.

"I don't think I've met Parnel yet."

"Not yet," she sighs.

Flipping through more pages, Archibald pauses at one beast, the Tetradonte Bacillus (page 111), that looks strangely familiar.

"Hey, I've seen this one before!" he exclaims.

"I doubt it," says Faerydae, "but, again, you fought so many."

"I did? Oh—yes, yes, I did, so many!" he corrects, reminding himself of his own lie.

"I'm impressed. This Marodor is rather rare. No one I know has ever seen one. In fact, I've never seen one."

It's some kind of bear—not black, not white, not brown either, or maybe it is. But it's not the color one would remember. What makes this bear so different is the pair of huge horns in the front and a hundred smaller ones shielding his body. It suddenly comes back to him—that's one of the monsters he was drawing at home.

"I know where I saw it. On my glo—"

He is interrupted by a loud rumbling noise from down under.

"What was that?" asks Faerydae.

He knows. He just doesn't wish to tell her. But the roiling noise is back, even louder and more of a gurgling sound this time.

"Was that your stomach?"

Archibald nods, reluctantly.

"What happened to your *real food?*" she inquires, using air quotes.

"I finished it all."

"Well, let's go to the kitchen and see what we can find for you," she says, pulling Archibald outside.

"Where's the kitchen?" he asks.

Archibald has been in Gristlemoth for only two days, but he already noticed a curious pattern. Every evening around the same time—hard to tell when, exactly, since there's no clock around—all the cabanas, and the village as a whole, empty out at once.

Where's everyone going? he wondered each time, peeking through the door of his cabana. Now he knows—to the Hive, across the courtyard, up the grand double staircase, all the way to the second floor, into the majestic hall where he has just followed Faerydae.

Archibald can't believe his eyes.

No, his astonishment has nothing to do with the size of the cauldron sitting in the middle of the kitchen, even though that giant pot could easily cook two hundred pounds of rice in one batch.

It's not the size of the dining hall, designed to feed an army, with dozens of tables organized in circles around the cooking area.

It's not even the chandeliers, as whimsical and unique as they can be, made out of dead oak trees rising from all four corners of the room, with constellations of glowing jars in their arms extending left, right, and center, sometimes overlapping one another.

No, Archibald is in awe because there's a man in that kitchen! A real man, with hair on his hands, on his knuckles, on his arms, on his cheeks, and plenty more in his nose and ears, some even growing *on* his ears—but none where you'd expect it the most, on the top of his head, smooth as a polished golem.

"That's a man!" he shouts, a big smile on his face.

"It sure is." confirms Faerydae, as if she needed to. "That's Wymer, the best cook in the world and the best handyman in the world. Wymer, this is Ivy, and she's hungry."

"Ivy, huh?" says the round-bellied, barrel-chested man, with a fatherly voice. He doesn't seem too convinced. "Okay, Ivy, I am indeed Gristlemoth's cook, and Faery's right, the best one in town. Probably 'cause I'm also the only one in town," he chuckles. "And, yes, I'm the handyman around here as well, so I'll try not to put too many nails in your mint sauce!" he adds, chuckling some more.

"Mint sauce is bad enough," jokes Archibald.

"What are you preparing?" asks Faerydae.

"Not carrots, I hope," Archibald mumbles.

Wymer heard that, but he's not the one answering.

"No carrots today," says a metallic voice.

"What was that?" asks Archibald, trying to figure out where it came from.

"Oh, that's just Karl," answers Faerydae, giving the cauldron a friendly tap.

"Karl?" asks Archibald, now distinguishing a face on the cauldron that sits on its own three hands. "You turned him into a crockpot!" he says, fascinated and afraid.

"The opposite. Wymer was a little lonely cooking in here by himself, so we gave life to his cauldron," she explains.

"Hello, Ivy!" says the cauldron.

"Hey, you," calls out Archibald, waving, full of amazement.

"Since Karl felt lonely as well, we gave him some company. That would be Karla, over there," explains Faerydae, motioning toward a smaller cauldron lost among pots and pans.

"Pardon her; she's sleeping. She cooked a heavy meal last night," says Karl.

"It's like Paws," says Archibald. "Only a bit more . . . human."

"To be honest, Karl was more of an accident, too," explains Faerydae. "We were boiling golems in the cauldron, and we got this unexpected . . . side effect."

"A side effect?" says Karl, his feelings hurt.

"Yes, but a very welcome side effect, with the most fantastic taste buds," says Wymer, patting his cast-iron sous-chef.

"So what's for dinner?" asks Faerydae.

Archibald is glad to hear carrots are not on the menu, but a quick look at the ingredients lined up on the table does not reassure the picky guest.

"Let me see," says Wymer. "What do we have here? Stale bread, fish, black treacle, cinnamon . . . what could I be making?"

"Flummadiddle!" shouts Karl as Faerydae high-fives Wymer.

Archibald has heard that word before. "I thought flummadiddle was some kind of nonsense?"

"What do you think this is, if not nonsense?" Wymer chuckles again.

"That's where flummadiddle comes from. We just mix a lot of things that shouldn't really be mixed together—it's *total* nonsense!" sums up Faerydae. "The bug patties make it pretty tasty."

"Did you say *bug* patties?"

"You know, caterpillars, termites, cockroaches. Worms and larvae are the most nutritious, though," she assures him.

Archibald is looking pale again.

"The only bugs we don't eat are these," says Faerydae, pointing up at the glowing mason jars.

"That's why those lights are humming?" asks Archibald, squinting at the swarm of tiny bulbs, remembering the sound he heard yesterday in the workshops downstairs.

"Our dear fireflies. All those years we were lost in darkness, they were our only hope. You can't imagine how much they mean to us."

"I can, actually," he sighs.

"Way too precious to end up in a crockpot," she adds.

"Lucky them," mumbles Archibald, as he watches insect heads, tails, and wings getting smooshed under Wymer's rolling pin.

"You're supposed to use pork fat in flummadiddle, but the only pig we have is a Marodor with a pig body," explains the chef. "We're not gonna eat that!" he laughs.

"What do you mean you have a Marodor with a pig body?" asks Archibald. "You keep those things around here?"

"Wanna see that book of monsters come alive?" asks Faerydae.

ß

Ten minutes later, she has led her curious guest to the very edge of Gristlemoth, opposite from the cliff. They're strolling alongside the giant golems and the dancing lights surrounding the village when Archibald recoils in horror. Two Marodors come careening down on the other side but pull out of their dive suddenly. They flap their wings furiously and swerve away, as though an invisible brick wall was standing in their way.

"Don't worry; we're fine here," says Faerydae. "You can enjoy your pudding!"

"Is that what this is, pudding?" he says, gnawing off a chunk of a thick slice of dark-brown cardboard he has a hard time chewing—not to mention swallowing. "And I thought Grandpa's pudding was gross!"

Faerydae laughs.

"By the way, what was going on in the kitchen? I saw you guys doing those weird things with your hands. Were you making fun of me?"

"Not at all. It's just part of our sign language—remember, I told you about it?"

"I guess," he says, unconvinced.

"We actually borrowed a lot of those signs from monks. You know, in monasteries. They don't really have the right to talk, so they came up with a whole system of signs. It's pretty ingenious."

"What does this mean, then?" he asks, forming a circle with his hands by joining his thumbs and index fingers.

"Bread! I was just asking Wymer to make more for dinner."

"That's pretty neat."

"I know, right? For fish, you do it like this," she explains, waving her hand, mimicking the tail of a fish in water. "For the Raad fish, it's like this," she notes, making her hand shake frantically as if electrocuted.

Now it's Archibald's turn to laugh. "So when you fight Marodors, do you use signs like these?"

"Yes, just simple ones. They've got to be. When you're in the middle of a fight, you don't have time for anything complicated. For example, when we're ready to approach a Marodor, we do this," she says, turning her hand into a bird's head shape, her fingers all curled up together. "To retreat, it's the same sign, just the opposite direction," she explains, now pointing toward her chest. "There's also this one, to create a diversion," she says, placing her left-hand fingers into the palm of her right hand.

"You're like a commando, or a ninja."

"I'm not sure what that is, but thanks, I guess."

"Okay, give me one more."

"Well, there's this thing you can do when you really care about someone," she says, crossing her arms on her chest.

"Like this?" he says, doing the same. Faerydae nods, gazing gently at him. The moment is about half a second from getting awkward when a dreadful scream soars from the area ahead, quickly followed by another.

"What was that?" asks Archibald, dropping his arms.

"That would be the Marodors."

"It sounds like they're crying."

"I wouldn't say crying, but are they happy we caught them? Probably not."

They soon enter a woodsy area that gets darker and darker as the trees get bigger and taller. Regardless of the time of day you choose to come here, you will most likely be surrounded by shadows, for only the top third of the canopy manages to capture the sun's life.

Flaming torches light their way. The moaning is growing louder. They are close.

Some cages come into view, dark and dreary, covered with a thick layer of branches blocking the few rays of sun that manage to pierce through the trees above.

The Marodors are barely visible, pacing in the shadows, popping out for brief moments, one scary glimpse at a time—here a growling muzzle, there some salivating saber teeth, next door a semihuman hand with nails long as knives scratching the ground.

"Eeuww!" yells Archibald, breathing in a stench of near death that makes his flummadiddle smell like cotton candy.

Patrolled by a few girls armed solely with golems, the sinuous path divides into secondary arteries, each lined with cages on both sides. There must be a hundred of them scattered across a rather large swath of land, making it a village within the village.

"Wow! This would make a great ride at the fair," mutters Archibald, advancing between two walls of frightening mugs.

"Just make sure you stay in the middle of the road. Don't go too near the cages."

Naturally, there are no markings on this dirt road, but

Archibald definitely sticks to the center, curled up into a turtle posture, chin tucked deep between his shoulders, arms glued alongside his body.

"You said the book would come alive, but these creatures look dead almost," he comments, noticing that most Marodors, if not wounded, are in really bad shape.

"That's the thing. Marodors won't die, so we have to park them here," notes Faerydae. "Look: here's the one that attacked you," she says, pointing at one of the cages.

Its neck still painfully bent, the Marodor also seems to have lost one of its eyes, since only one glows red.

"We'll call this one Cyclops," jokes Faerydae.

Archibald is amazed, scared, and sad all at once. Even though these are obviously horrible monsters, they remind him of the animals from that shelter he visited last month with a friend.

"We keep them in the dark, their natural element. We don't want them to go too crackbrained in the sun."

Another word Archibald obviously doesn't get.

"Too crazy," she translates. "Anyway, just being here makes them extremely weak. Not only do the golems around the village keep the Marodors out, they also sort of hypnotize the ones inside. Be careful, though; they are still dangerous," she warns.

"What happens if they catch you?"

"You don't know?"

"I have an idea," he sighs. "I saw the graveyard by my cabana."

"That's different; those sisters died in battle. Marodors don't usually try to kill you. At least they don't mean to."

"That's reassuring," jokes Archibald.

"If they do kill you, it will be by accident, most likely, or because you made them really mad."

"I don't understand. What do they do to you, then?"

"Something worse than death."

"What can be worse than death?" argues Archibald, not really eager to find out.

"Just a few weeks back, a friend of mine got too close to a cage. Within seconds, it was too late."

"I'm sorry. What was her name?"

"Parnel."

"Wait, that's the one you told me about earlier, right? She drew some of the Marodors in that book!"

"Yes. She was so talented, so beautiful, and so full of life."

"What happened to her?"

"When one of us gets caught on the battlefield, we are never to be seen again. We are usually lost forever, probably for the better. This was definitely not easy to witness."

About a hundred yards later, Faerydae stops in front of a cage isolated from the others.

"This is Parnel."

At first, Archibald can see only an undefined shape curled up in a corner, until a pair of eyes light up, bright red. Coming out of the shadows, a pale face emerges, that of a young girl. Faerydae was right; she is beautiful. Parnel would look almost normal, if not for the huge roots creeping up her neck.

The rest of her body slowly unfolds. Her arms look intact, but her legs have partially disappeared, replaced by claws and a double hook at the end of a curved tail. It's as if she was being devoured by a giant pincher bug.

"It's horrible," cries Archibald.

"She is slowly turning into one of them," explains Faerydae, fighting off tears. "This is what Marodors do to you. It's one way for them to multiply."

"What causes that?"

"We call it the final embrace, or the hug of death."

"How does it work? They suck your brains out or something?"

"No, they don't take anything from you. They inject something into you, some sort of virus or poison. We still don't know exactly how it works, but it happens quickly. You can get infected within seconds."

Parnel is crawling on the ground, moaning, trying to get closer to them, but she is having a hard time.

"She seems in pain," says Archibald.

"When she got caught, we tried to rescue her. The problem

is, by using our golems on the beast, we hurt Parnel in the process. I think her arms are broken. We don't know, though. She has not said a word since."

Parnel suddenly shrinks back to her corner when two girls come hurtling, screaming Faerydae's name.

"Willow, what's happening?" Faerydae asks one of them.

"It's Naida," says the girl, out of breath.

"Is she okay?"

"She saw something," says Willow. "You've got to come with us."

Archibald and Faerydae find Naida on the way to the Hive surrounded by many. It looks as though half of the village has thronged to hear what she has to say. Slumped on the ground, she is obviously shaken.

"What happened?" asks Faerydae, kneeling next to her.

"I was out looking for new herbs. That Marodor appeared right behind me. It's enormous. I've never seen anything like that before," explains Naida, fear imprinted in her eyes.

"Can you describe it?"

"It was so dark. I didn't see much—a shadow, mostly. I just ran, sorry."

"Don't be sorry; you did the right thing. Any detail you remember? Anything at all?"

Naida leans over and starts drawing something on the ground with her finger. The beast takes shape little by little: first the legs, arched and wide, then the serpentine necks, twice as long, four in total.

"That's impossible," whispers Faerydae.

Maven has brought the *Bestiary of Marodors*. Faerydae knows it by heart. She jumps to page 155.

"Is this it?" she asks, almost scared of the answer.

"I think so," nods Naida. "Only . . ."

"Only what?"

"With more necks."

Unfinished, the drawing itself doesn't offer many more details than Naida's sketch in the dirt.

Archibald peeks over Faerydae's shoulder, discovering the one they call Krakatorum Gargantus, a meaty and mighty beast with two faceless necks mounted on an eight-legged furry body.

"Two nightmares in one: 50 percent spider, 50 percent basilisk," says Faerydae.

"And 100 percent spine chilling," notes Maven.

"A basilisk? Is that the one with the death gaze that can petrify you?" asks Archibald, remembering his dad's story.

"Not quite," smiles Faerydae. "Don't get me wrong, though. Could you be petrified by just looking at the basilisk? Certainly, but petrified with fear you will be. That's probably where the legend comes from. I'm sure the Krakatorum is a sight to behold, but only for those lucky enough to actually remember. The thing is, most who laid eyes on this beast probably never survived to tell of their encounter."

"Is that why the drawing isn't more detailed?" asks Archibald.

"When you witness something like this, you do the same as Naida. You run—you need not stick around for details," says Maven.

"What's a Krakatorum doing here, anyway?" wonders Faerydae out loud. "I thought they lived deep in the forests of Basquery." Then turning to Naida, "Where were you when you saw that thing? How far?"

"Near the Neander Pass," says Naida, triggering a loud gasp

throughout the crowd.

"That's less than ten miles from here," realizes Faerydae, even more worried now.

"The Krakatorum is said to be a slow crawler," notes Maven.

"Still, it would take it only a day or two to reach us," fears Faerydae.

"We're fine here, right?" asks Archibald.

"Maybe, maybe not," answers Faerydae.

"But you said the golems around the village would protect us?"

"They should. Those golems can resist regular Marodors, but the Krakatorum is much larger and much more powerful. Most likely, our arrows will have no effect on a monster like that. Gristlemoth could fall," she predicts.

"It happened to Tungolwald a few years ago, in Myrmecia. I was there," recalls Naida. Her eyes say it all.

"Why don't we just stay here and wait? Maybe it will just go away," suggests Archibald.

"No, we can't take that risk," says Faerydae. "We'll have to fight it outside."

She turns to the crowd to address everyone.

"There is danger at our walls, but I have some great news for us all," she adds, calming the clamor a bit. "We have a secret weapon that was sent to us at this very uncertain and perilous time."

Archibald looks relieved. He can't wait to hear more about that secret weapon.

"Here it is," she says, yanking Archibald's cloak and unveiling his hoodie with the three Greek letters—which to the girls in the assembly read as runes, of course.

"His name is Archibald. He is a great wizard!" shouts Faerydae.

Archibald is stunned and overwhelmed as weak applause turns into cheering to greet the coming of the savior.

"I think it's time I give you back your magic weapon," says Faerydae, handing him the pouch containing his flashlight.

THE DARK PRIEST

Until Hailee's visit, James R. Doyle thought of his life achievements as lying behind him, meager and questionable. No truth serum needed. Though only forty-five, to all he looks sixty, anger often adding another ten years to his grim, wine-soaked mug. If a turn of fortune is in the cards, it will happen today. Of that, he is certain. Oliver's father arrived at his antique shop at 7:00 a.m., two hours earlier than usual, in case his esteemed client showed up first thing. He has sobered up. He is wearing his nicest suit, two sizes too small, washed out, and adorned with a mustard stain from a 2001 wedding, but his nicest suit nonetheless. His only suit, to be clear. And a wrinkle-free shirt of the yellowest white, matching the false teeth he made sure to soak all night in mint water with five cleaning tabs. Now he keeps looking at his watch, getting impatient. After all, Mr. Heinrich said he'd be here in the morning but didn't give any specific time. Mr. Doyle peeks out the window once more, biting his fingers, nearly losing his dentures in the process.

A long black Mercedes pulls to a stop curbside. The driver comes out first, then two more men from the back seat, each panning left, right, and back, like owls. Only after that routine does a tall, shadowy figure finally emerge, his face obscured by a fedora. The man is escorted to the door hastily. Mr. Heinrich comes in, followed by one of his bodyguards, a muscleman with a chest so wide and arms so short that clapping is not even an option. Because henchmen usually come in pairs, like pliers, sneezes, and bad news, his twin brother blocks the entrance, squeezing his square peg of a body into the oval frame of the doorway.

"Welcome!" shouts Mr. Doyle warmly.

He offers a handshake that only meets the hat his guest has just removed, revealing a monk's haircut that screams 1455. Archibald got the same two years ago—by accident. His mother was in a hurry. She placed a pasta bowl on his head and, following the edge, trimmed everything sticking out. He got teased at school for three weeks. Mr. Heinrich's mistake possesses one unique twist, though. Cut short on his forehead, the scattered line of hair ends abruptly in a dent right above his left ear: a dark, slanted dent that runs all the way to the back of his head,

as if a chunk of his skull and brains had been chopped off by a sword.

Despite the high collar of his black leather coat covering part of his chin, Mr. Heinrich's face looks unusually long and emaciated. Due to a receding tide of skin never to rise again, the arched bones protrude around cavernous eyes besieged by deep shadows. All features have collapsed to form two deep parentheses framing a tight mouth, itself sagging at both ends. To sum it up, an ideal face for a radio career.

"Where is the globe?" he asks right away, quite nicely.

"Why don't we sit down?" suggests Mr. Doyle. "Please make yourself comfortable. I have tea in the back if you wish. I think there are just a few details we need to discuss first, to make sure we are on the same page."

Mr. Heinrich remains silent, simply slapping the palm of his left hand with one tight leather glove he has just stripped off.

"Of course, I'm prepared to be reasonable. By the way, just out of curiosity, what did you have in mind?" asks Mr. Doyle, rubbing his hands together, swallowing his saliva, as if getting ready for cake.

"I'm not happy," murmurs Mr. Heinrich.

"I beg your pardon?"

"You said you would make me happy. I'm not happy," says Mr. Heinrich.

Before Mr. Doyle can even think of something to say, Mr. Heinrich repeats, "Where is the globe?" and lets out a cough mixed with a scary growling sound.

"Look, I don't need to tell you how this works. We are both businesspeople here—am I right?" tries Mr. Doyle.

Mr. Heinrich slaps his hand with his glove again, only harder this time, yet showing no pain. "Boris," he utters, motioning for his bodyguard to make a move. And a swift move it is. With one heavy blow to Mr. Doyle's chest, the colossus tackles him to the floor, pressing a size-sixteen boot right against his neck.

Mr. Heinrich clears his throat and comes close, towering over poor Mr. Doyle.

"Don't you dare insult me with your cheap bargaining tactics," he yells. "Money is not an issue. This is so much bigger than you and me. This is about history. This is about fulfilling a promise made half a thousand years ago."

"Did you hear what Master Heinrich told you?" asks Boris, blessed with the singular talent of talking from the back of his throat while barely moving his razor-thin lips.

Mr. Doyle can't talk, so he offers a whimpering nod.

"Good," says Mr. Heinrich. "So I'm going to ask you one last time, Mr. Doyle. Where is the globe?"

Boris lets go of Mr. Doyle, who painfully gets on his knees—the perfect position to beg for his life if need be.

"It's complicated," he says. "I might be able to locate it; give me a few days."

Boris grabs onto his suit again, ripping off the sleeves and using them to tie Mr. Doyle's hands behind his back.

Mr. Heinrich approaches. He takes off his second glove, uncovering a wooden hand with metal wires running across the palm and connected to each finger.

"Do you know what this is?" he asks, making every articulation of the prosthesis move like tentacles.

Mr. Doyle shakes his head, nervous.

"This is an automaton," says Mr. Heinrich. "One of the first robotic hands. A pure marvel of technology, nearly four hundred years old. Unfortunately, it was built with a flaw," he explains, clutching the frame of a chair. "See, instead of just grabbing onto things, this hand compresses them, crushes them, breaks them," he says, as the piece of wood in his grasp starts cracking and splintering.

Mr. Doyle looks terrified. Mr. Heinrich lets go of the chair.

"A shame, really. The first owner of this automaton killed his wife and child because of it. A tragic accident, really. Needless to say, he was not thrilled with it. I, however, happen to find the flaw very useful," he continues, approaching Mr. Doyle, whose chattering teeth have now detached from their gums.

"I wanted it to be fully mine, to be a part of me. So I had this machine connected to my nervous system, which can cause it to act a bit erratically. Don't worry; you have nothing to fear—as long as you don't get on my nerves, of course," he warns, moving that fidgety claw close to Mr. Doyle's face.

"That girl, she was here yesterday. She has the globe, but she refused to sell it to me," he explains.

"What girl?" asks Mr. Heinrich.

"I don't know who she is," he says.

Mr. Heinrich seems about to grab onto Mr. Doyle's neck.

"I swear I don't know, but my son—my son knows."

"So where is he?" yaps Boris, frowning so much he's managed to merge his eyebrows with an exceptionally low hairline.

"I have no idea," assures Mr. Doyle. "But he gave me some information about the girl. I can help you find her . . ."

Mr. Hickinbottom is alone in his classroom, getting ready for his next batch of students. The subject will be "The Superpowers' Race to the Moon," as he wrote on the chalkboard. Now he is trying to sketch the moon, biting his tongue. He can't quite draw a perfect circle, and that makes him awfully mad. To make matters worse, he's just heard someone open the door behind him. He sure doesn't need to be disturbed.

"What now? Please, I'm busy," he shouts with annoyance, erasing his drawing one more time.

"Professor Hickinbottom?" a deep voice asks.

"Just Mr. Hickinbottom would do, but thank you, anyway."

Turning around, he discovers Mr. Heinrich and the loyal Boris standing by the door. He is a bit taken aback. Not only has he never seen these two men before but they are also not the kind of people who usually step into his classroom. Mr. Hickinbottom's visitors are more like three-piece suit or tweed waistcoat kind of fellows than leather coats and combat boots. Although he did have that angry parent who showed up in yoga pants a few years back, threatening him with a curling iron after he gave her son an F for spelling Churchill "Churchle."

Hopefully, this is not that kind of scenario, he prays.

"Gentlemen, how may I help you?" he asks.

"Professor, I'm terribly sorry to disturb you," replies Mr. Heinrich. "I'm trying to get in contact with one of your students."

"And who would that be?" inquires Mr. Hickinbottom.

"A young lady, about five feet tall, brown hair, light-brown eyes."

"That sounds like a police report!" comments Mr. Hickinbottom.

"Well, we'll get to that later, perhaps," says Mr. Heinrich in a cryptic tone.

"Is she in trouble?"

"Possibly."

"What's her name?"

"Hailee," says Mr. Heinrich.

"Surely an unusual young lady, that Miss Finch."

"Hailee Finch," whispers Mr. Heinrich.

"Is this a police matter?" asks the professor.

"Not exactly. Not yet. I just need to locate Miss Finch, and I would be thankful if you were to help me in my quest," says Mr. Heinrich.

"Well, I can't just share my students' information with anyone. I don't know what this is regarding, but if you contact the administration, I'm sure they will help you," he says, returning behind his desk a bit shaken.

Mr. Heinrich approaches the desk and opens his coat slightly, just enough to reveal a clerical collar. Mr. Hickinbottom looks immediately at ease. He breathes a deep sigh of relief.

"Hailee Finch brought you a globe recently," inquires Mr. Heinrich.

"Yes, indeed."

"We have reasons to believe that globe belongs to our church. It was stolen just a few weeks ago."

"I asked her whether that was a family heirloom, but she wouldn't say," notes Mr. Hickinbottom.

"I'm truly sorry," says Mr. Heinrich.

"I really thought that globe belonged to her, with her family moving into that manor and all," adds Mr. Hickinbottom.

"A manor?"

"Her grandmother's house in Cuffley. The Finches just moved there. I was so naive. I feel like she took advantage of her brother's disappearance."

"I'm afraid I'm not following?"

"Yes, her brother vanished, into thin air, really, just a few days before she brought the globe to me."

Mr. Heinrich seems troubled by that story.

"We should call the police," suggests Mr. Hickinbottom.

"No," says Mr. Heinrich immediately. "We're trying to keep the police out of this. That's why I preferred to come and see you directly."

"Now I wonder whether that other kid is an accomplice of Miss Finch's," Mr. Hickinbottom mentions.

"What other kid?"

"A young man . . . Oliver Doyle his name was, I believe."

"Doyle?" exclaims Mr. Heinrich.

"Yes, he said he had some textbooks to give back to Miss Finch.

He needed her address. Very strange request, really; I'm not even sure he's a student here. He came in just a few minutes before you."

Without saying another word, Mr. Heinrich and his bodyguard leave Mr. Hickinbottom's classroom. Down the hall, Oliver Doyle is still there, talking to a group of students. He is the only person without a uniform in the hallway. Mr. Heinrich spots him immediately.

"Doyle!" he shouts in the boy's direction.

Oliver looks at him and puts two and two together in an instant. He starts running the opposite way. Mr. Heinrich's bodyguard charges toward him but bumps into clusters of students getting out of class. Oliver disappears down the stairs.

"You can run, boy . . ." whispers Mr. Heinrich.

Hailee is in her parents' garage, rummaging through drawers, shelves, and boxes. It's dark out and fairly dark in this garage as well, green with faint fluorescent light. The lonely bulb hanging from the ceiling certainly won't help Hailee find what she is looking for. She strides out into the hallway and shouts, "Dad! Dad, I can't find those candles; they're not here!"

No answer.

"Of course he can't hear me," she mutters. "How convenient!"

Hailee goes back into the garage and starts looking again. Her task is not easy. It's like trying to find a hair on Mr. Hickinbottom's head. The garage is so big. It was designed for a large fleet of cars—six to eight, easily—which means about fifteen the size of the family Fiat. Right now, it's the only one parked in here, along with the mess from their last place. Oddly enough, every piece of furniture from their old living room is laid out pretty much the way it was in the London apartment.

For Hailee, it's like stepping into a time capsule. She sits on the spongy foam couch, as uncomfortable as it is cozy, because it's full of memories. She rubs a stain embedded in the middle cushion. That's from three Wimbledon tournaments ago. It was on her birthday. Archibald dropped his piece of cake on her lap—officially, by accident—while she was opening her gifts. She was so mad that night. Now she smiles thinking about it. Hazy with tears, her gaze has paused on the dining table. That's where that tiny Christmas tree was sitting a year ago. At dinnertime, Archibald was adding his own ornaments to it—the beans and pasta he refused to eat, making everyone laugh except Hailee, of course. Now, grasping the value of the normality that's been lost, she would give up everything, even her phone, to go back to that moment.

Some noise behind the car interrupts her daydreaming, bringing her back to reality. She jumps.

"Great house! Full of rats!" she mumbles.

She doesn't see any. Instead, she finally spots the candles on the very edge of a shelf. As she extends her arm to grab the box, she notices a weird shadow in the corner behind the shelf. Following the curves of that shadow, she gradually makes out the contours of a chin, a nose, and some hair. Someone is standing there. Hailee has stopped breathing.

Did that shadow just move?

Hailee gasps at the sight of . . . Oliver Doyle, who lunges at her. He claps his hand over her mouth. Hailee is terrified. She is gagged, but her eyes are screaming.

"I'm here to help you, okay—to warn you, actually," he says. "Please don't scream. I'm going to remove my hand from your mouth. Can I trust you?"

She nods. He lets her go.

"What are you doing here? Are you crazy?" she shrieks.

"I know how it looks, but I had to come over before they do."

"What are you talking about? Who's *they*? It's your dad, isn't it? He sent you to get the globe from me."

"No . . . yes . . ."

"Yes?" repeats Hailee, getting ready to scream again.

"I mean, no—it's not my dad. But, yes, they want the globe."

"Who are you talking about, then?"

"That man, he came to my dad's shop. He's looking for that globe you have. For some reason, he wants it really badly. I think it's the same guy who was at your school this morning."

"What? My school? He was at my school? Wait, how would you know?"

Oliver hesitates to tell her, for obvious reasons.

"Because I was there too," he finally says.

"You were at my school? That's it! I'm calling my dad," warns Hailee.

"I had to. You told me about your history teacher. That's how I figured out the name of your school. I mean, there's not that many teachers called Hickinbottom in London!"

"But why would you go there?"

"Because I knew that guy would do the same. It took me, what, five phone calls to locate your teacher. Then ten minutes for some students to tell me you moved here."

"This is crazy," mutters Hailee, her eyes fluttering.

"That guy has a lot of money; I'm sure he has a lot of power too. There's something wrong with him—I can tell," says Oliver.

"What do you mean?"

"I don't know. I think he's a priest, but it doesn't make sense."

"A priest?"

"I saw his collar—you know, that white collar priests wear," says Oliver, pointing at his throat.

"Why would a priest be interested in that globe?"

"I'm not sure, but maybe I should look at it more closely. If I get a better look, maybe I can find out why that priest wants it so bad."

"Oh, I see now. This is what it's all about, isn't it? You made up this whole story just so you could convince me to sell my globe to your dad! I might not know much about Leonardo da Vinci. But I'm not *that* dumb, you know."

"What? No. I swear! I'm just here to help."

Hailee walks toward the hallway again and presses a button on the wall, opening one of the four garage doors.

"If you don't leave right now, I'm going to scream, and my dad will be down here in seconds," she threatens, though she knows he probably won't hear anything. "Then I'll call the police," she assures.

"No, don't call the police; that guy hasn't done anything yet."

"Yet?" asks Hailee. "Oh, so what is he going to do next?"

"I don't know, but I have a bad feeling about it."

"I'm going to give you five seconds before I scream," she warns him.

"Let me just have a quick look," he suggests.

"Four," Hailee replies, starting the countdown.

"I'm begging you; it won't take long."

"Three."

"Just a few minutes, I promise."

"Two."

"I'm doing this for you. Don't you get it?"

"One."

"Fine! Good luck to you, then," says Oliver before he drifts away, disappearing into the night.

Another troubled night for Hailee. More tossing. More turning. More grunting. Barely any sleep. She just can't stop thinking about everything Oliver told her.

Between Archibald, the globe, that weird priest, and Mr. Doyle, this is becoming too much for her to handle. She misses the time when her life was simple, made of texting, shopping, interneting, and, oh, yes, going to school sometimes. It has actually just occurred to her that she has an early class today.

She leaps from her bed, puts on her uniform quickly, grabs her small backpack, and leaves without having breakfast, just giving a quick kiss to her mum.

With Bartholomeo now gone, Kate has been trying to take care of this gigantic house on her own. It takes her two hours just to clean up the living room and library floors.

She has just started scrubbing the kitchen stove when she sees someone wandering around in the backyard. Because of the fogged-up windows, she can't really tell who it is. With his long coat, he looks like one of those inspectors who came over after Archibald's disappearance.

Kate opens the back door.

"Can I help you?" she shouts.

The man approaches slowly, his head down to avoid the rain, pressing on his hat to prevent it from flying away. He lifts his head back up only when he reaches the house. It's Mr. Heinrich.

"I'm truly sorry; I didn't want to scare you. I knocked at the front door, but nobody answered," he says, forcing his face into a smile, which seems particularly painful.

"I know, I'm sorry; we need to install a doorbell. I can usually hear those big knockers, though," says Kate, clearly on the defensive.

"I'm really sorry; I didn't mean to scare you," he says, shaking his coat, letting it fall open to reveal his white collar.

On Halloween night last year, Archibald managed to collect treats from the same neighbor's house three times, simply by switching disguises. (They had the best candy in the neighborhood.) Mr. Heinrich would probably pull off the same feat with only one disguise. His trick worked with Mr. Hickinbottom. It does once more with Kate.

"You don't have to be sorry," she says suddenly, in her nicest voice. "Please come in; you wouldn't want to stay outside in this weather."

"Just a drizzle, really, but thank you," says Mr. Heinrich as he walks in, drenched.

"So how can I help you?" asks Kate, now completely at ease.

"Oh, quite the opposite, Mrs. Finch—hopefully, *I* can help you." Kate is intrigued.

"I'm with the local church," he explains. "We heard from the police about your son. It is in our tradition to try to help as much as we can, to bring comfort to families."

"How kind of you. Thank you so much; but to be honest, my husband and I have not been involved with any church, so—"

"There's no need to feel bad, Mrs. Finch," he says, cutting her off. "We help people regardless of faith or religion; we are all neighbors before all."

"Sounds good; I agree," says Kate.

"See," continues Mr. Heinrich, "we have a large network of followers, all with the good pair of eyes the Lord gave them, and good ears as well. That can be of great help in your son's case."

"Well, I really appreciate it. Would it help if I gave you a picture of Archibald, perhaps?"

"It certainly would."

"Why don't we go to the living room—we'll be more comfortable. I'll make a fire, and tea, perhaps?"

"That would be lovely."

Kate leads Mr. Heinrich to the living room. On the way, he comments on the beautiful library.

"What an impressive collection!"

"We are actually thinking about donating some of these books. Maybe your church would be interested?"

"Maybe, maybe . . ." says Mr. Heinrich, suddenly back to his old weird self. Something else has caught his attention, it seems: a picture, sitting in a frame on one of the shelves, between two rows of books.

"That's Archibald's grandmother, my husband's mother," Kate explains.

Mr. Heinrich moves closer to it. He looks stunned.

"What's her name?" he asks, without taking his eyes off the picture and now looking even more strange.

"Celestine, Celestine Finch," she says.

"Is that so?" he comments, producing that scary cough and growling sound again.

"I'm sorry?" asks Kate, a bit troubled.

"Is your mother-in-law around, by chance?" he asks, going back to a nicer voice and demeanor.

"I'm afraid not; this is the picture we used at her funeral. Celestine passed away recently."

Mr. Heinrich finally detaches from the picture, takes a large breath, and closes his eyes for a few seconds, a slight smirk on his face.

"Her death was very sudden," says Kate. "She left us this big house, and to be honest, we don't know what to do with all of this."

"Well, this house is beautiful, Mrs. Finch; you'll make good use of it, I'm sure."

"Would you like a tour?"

"I didn't want to ask," he says with another smirk.

"There's something I'd like to show you upstairs," says Kate.

Hailee is seated at her deskin Mr. Hickinbottom's classroom. On the chalkboard, the same title as yesterday, "The Superpowers' Race to the Moon." Right underneath, that same drawing of the moon, still unfinished.

Hailee is thinking about the crazy story Oliver told her. She seems worried and lost at the same time. A third paper ball from William Tanner has just landed on her lap. She turns to him with such a furious look that he swallows the whitish tongue he had unleashed from his dirty mouth.

It's 10:05 on the wall clock, and Mr. Hickinbottom is not here yet. Five minutes late: a very unusual occurrence for a man who puts punctuality at the top of a long list of manners and principles to respect—a list three feet long and pinned up at the entrance. Everyone is waiting for him. Instead, it's the headmaster who shows up, looking even more somber than usual—a fairly bad omen. She goes down the aisle and steps up on the podium. She clears her throat. She seems distraught. The students have never seen her like this.

"I'm sorry," she says in a chocked voice. "There has been a terrible tragedy. Mr. Hickinbottom's car swerved off the road this morning, quite inexplicably. As a result of that accident . . ." adds the headmaster, taking a deep breath, "Mr. Hickinbottom is, as we speak, fighting for his life."

Her announcement draws loud gasps from the room. William Tanner digs deep to find an appropriate reaction.

"Coooooool," he lets out, cracking a smile.

"William Tanner!" shouts the headmaster in outrage.

For Hailee, aghast at the news, it echoes as a scary reminder of Oliver's warnings.

"Given these rather tragic circumstances, class is dismissed," says the headmaster. "You are invited to go back home for the day and not return tomorrow. Since your Christmas vacation starts the day after that, we will see you in two weeks."

"Sooo cool!" tops William Tanner.

By the time the headmaster is done, Hailee has already left the room.

Hailee gets off the bus at the Culpeper Lane stop and hikes up the hill to the gigantic manor she still isn't used to. She starts down the interminable driveway. The rain is getting heavier, but she doesn't care. Her light makeup is already smeared on her cheeks. She's been crying.

As she nears the house, she notices a car coming toward her—a long black Mercedes. She has never seen it before.

It's not Grandpa Harvey's car—she would have seen the heavy clouds of smoke coming out of the diesel tailpipe.

Maybe her mother hired a new housekeeper to replace Bartholomeo? No, this car seems way too flashy to be a housekeeper's.

Maybe the police inspectors came back with some good news about Archibald? No, at this point Hailee knows it will take more than the police to get her brother back.

Soon the car drives past her. She can clearly see the driver and his creepy bulldog face, but she gets only a furtive glimpse of the person in the back seat, just enough to see a white priest collar under his chin. Or at least she thinks so. Did she see that collar for sure, or did she imagine it? Hard to tell with the rain and that dark tint on the car window.

A sinking feeling sweeps over her. She drops her backpack and starts running toward the house, a million scenarios twirling in her head about what might have happened to her parents—well, mainly one, actually, closely related to Mr. Hickinbottom's fate.

"Mum! Dad!" she screams as soon as she pushes open the front door.

The five agonizing seconds that follow seem like an eternity. Then, suddenly, coming from the kitchen: "Hailee? What's going on?" asks Kate.

She enters the foyer, and she seems fine. But Hailee asks anyway, "Everything okay?"

"Are *you* okay?" asks Kate, seeing Hailee out of breath, completely soaked, her makeup a mess.

"Where's Dad?" asks Hailee.

"He's at one of Grandma's orphanages. There was a problem. Why aren't you at school, by the way?"

"What problem? What happened?"

"We're not sure. Nothing too bad."

"Who was that in the car?" asks Hailee.

"Oh, you saw Mr. Heinrich leave? Very nice man."

"Mr. Heinrich?"

"Yes, but I guess I should say Father Heinrich; he's a priest."

Hailee's heart stops beating.

"Oh my God!" whispers Hailee, in shock and scared.

"What's wrong? You're so weird today. You want a hot chocolate?"

"What did he want?"

"He is with the local church. He just wanted to know whether he could be of any assistance. He heard about Archibald from the police and volunteered to help. Such a pleasant man! He loved the house. I gave him a tour."

"What? Are you crazy?"

"Hailee! I was just being polite!"

"Did he go into my room?"

"Yes, as a matter of fact he did. I just wanted him to see where Archie was when he disappeared."

"Oh my God, the globe!" mutters Hailee as she sprints up the stairs as fast as she can.

She reaches her bedroom door. It's closed. She takes a large breath and goes in swiftly, her eyes riveted on her nightstand. The globe is gone. It was there when she left this morning, and now it's gone.

Kate comes in, beyond worried. "Hailee, you have to tell me what's going on. You're scaring me now."

"The globe is gone," Hailee mumbles.

"The globe? Archie's globe? I just put it in the living room."

Hailee takes off again, this time dashing back downstairs. She heads straight to the living room. The globe is there, on a table right by the Christmas tree. Hailee squats down on the floor to enjoy this moment of relief.

"I'm losing my mind," she whispers.

Kate follows in a few seconds later. "Okay, please talk to me."

"It's nothing, really," assures Hailee.

"I'm sorry. I shouldn't have moved it without asking you. I had no idea this globe meant so much to you. I just thought it would be better here, so that everyone can enjoy it. Mr. Heinrich liked it very much as well; that's what gave me the idea, actually."

Hailee stands back up swiftly, her fears awoken anew.

"What did he say about it?"

"I'm sorry?"

"What did he say about the globe?"

"Nothing much. He just told me he had one exactly like it when he was young. That's why he'd like to have it."

"Did he offer to buy it?"

"Yes, he did, actually," says Kate, "but I told him it's become Archie's favorite thing, so there was no way we would part with it. He looked disappointed. But he didn't make a big deal about it."

After staring at the globe for a few seconds, Hailee goes by the fireplace to grab an empty gift box. She places the globe inside and adds sheet after sheet of wrapping paper around it.

"I hope you're not planning on giving it away!"

"No, don't worry, Mum. I have somewhere I need to go," she says, heading to the door.

"Can you tell me what's going on, at least?"

No answer from Hailee.

"Please, dear, make sure you don't get back too late," adds Kate, watching as Hailee disappears down the driveway.

Though ice on the railway added twenty minutes to her ride, it is still not quite enough time to convince Hailee that her next move is the wisest one. But it sure feels like the only one.

She is back in the heart of London, breathing clouds into the freezing air. It is snowing now. People are milling around with bags full of Christmas presents. Hailee is holding on to her box as if it were everything she has in the world. Her eyes seem full of doubts, focused on the store across the street, the Realm of Antiques.

After several minutes, she finally convinces herself to go in. She pushes the door open quietly and closes it behind her. She can't see anyone around, but the piles of antiques could easily conceal someone.

"Oliver," she calls, her voice shy.

Getting no answer, she walks deeper into the store. Each corner she passes is a source of fear and anguish. What if Mr. Doyle is standing right behind that mountain of books? Or behind that tall pedestal clock?

Hailee has found a trick. She uses the mirrors of all sizes scattered around to navigate the room and tell her more about those hidden corners she dreads.

One more turn and she will have reached the end of the store.

Hailee braces for the worst—seeing Mr. Doyle's face pop up out of nowhere, for instance—when a voice catches her by surprise.

"Can I help you?" it says, coming from behind her.

Hailee jumps in surprise and wheels around to discover Oliver, who also jumps as a result.

"You scared the hell out of me! You're good at that!" she says, startled.

"Sorry, but what are you doing here?" he asks, a bit cold.

"You were right. I should have listened to you," says Hailee, apologetic.

"What do you mean?"

"That priest, he came to my house and talked to my mother. He asked about the globe. And my history teacher, Mr. Hickinbottom, he is . . ."

"What about him?"

Hailee has a hard time just saying it. "He's at the hospital. Between life and death."

"What?!" exclaims Oliver, in shock.

"They're saying it was an accident, a car accident, but this can't just be a coincidence."

"This is crazy."

"Is your dad here?" asks Hailee, obviously fearful.

"No."

"Is he at the pub?" she asks, looking across the street through the window.

"No, actually, I haven't seen him in two days. I'm starting to worry, especially now that I've heard about your teacher," says Oliver. "He might be back soon, though—come with me," he adds, leading her just a few steps away, to one of the bigger mirrors attached to the wall.

Oliver applies a slight pressure on the ornate frame. A springlike noise rings out, and the mirror swings open like a door, leading to a secret room. It's pitch black in there. Oliver turns the lights on, unveiling a small chamber so clean, so well put together, and so organized it doesn't seem to belong here.

"It's like a museum in here!" says Hailee. "A war museum."

Covered with tufted red velvet, the walls are lined with all sorts of ancient weapons—swords, muskets, halberds, pistols, spears, bows, crossbows, axes, and full body armors.

"We'll be okay here," says Oliver, closing the door. "This room is only for special clients."

"Freaks, you mean?" says Hailee, exploring this caveman's cave further.

"Huge freaks! When it comes to killing, men's imaginations know no limits. People love this stuff."

"What's that?" she asks, gesturing toward a wooden target on the wall, pierced by multiple arrows near the center.

"Let's just say I get bored sometimes."

"Can't you just play darts like everyone else?"

"Sorry, I don't really want to be like everyone else."

"I know you're different. That's why I'm here. I feel like I can trust you."

"Oh, *now* you trust me?" questions Oliver, noticing the rounded bulk of the globe sticking out of Hailee's box.

"I want you to have it," she says.

"Why?"

"Just for now. For some reason, I feel it will be safer with you," she says, handing him the box.

"Are you sure?" he asks, reaching out to take it.

She nods. "There's something else I need to tell you. Something I haven't told anyone."

"Okay," answers Oliver, curious.

"My brother, Archibald, he disappeared a few days ago."

"Really? How?"

"I'm not sure. The only thing I know is that this globe has something to do with it."

"I'm sorry—what? You think that priest took your brother or something?"

"No, that's not what I'm saying."

"I don't understand, then."

"The night Archibald disappeared, I was with him at home. He was playing with this globe. I kept telling him to turn it off."

"To turn what off?"

"The light. The globe was glowing. Then, suddenly, it became even brighter, like lightning. There was a loud thunder sound too. I got so scared—you have no idea. The next thing I know, I opened my eyes, and Archibald was gone."

"What do you mean he was gone?"

"Gone. It's like he had . . . evaporated," says Hailee, about to cry again.

"This is insane."

"I know, but you have to believe me. I have to go. Please don't tell anyone about any of this."

"I won't. I promise."

"This is my number," she says, handing him a piece of paper. "You seem to know so much about everything; I was thinking maybe you can find something about this globe and help me get my brother back."

"I'll definitely look into it."

"Thank you. And by the way, sorry I didn't believe you the other day," says Hailee, heading out.

DAUGHTERS OF NIGHTFALL

Archibald is back in his cabana, only this time, the door is unlocked. He could leave, but to go where? He doesn't even know where he is! So, like any other eleven-year-old boy after dinner, Archibald is studying. Cross-legged on his bed, the *Bestiary of Marodors* spread open on his lap, he is getting ready not for an exam but for a looming battle. That's what it means to do your homework in Gristlemoth.

At his feet, partially hidden under a blanket, Paws, the junk dog—used and abused as a moving archery target—has found a resting place and some temporary relief. He is shivering, though, his eyes bouncing from side to side and up, watching out for the next incoming arrow.

"Don't worry, little guy; you're safe here," says Archibald, giving his makeshift pet a gentle stroke.

He takes the book outside, where a couple of girls are running through high grass waving nets, trying to catch fireflies. Sitting on the cabana steps, he can't take his eyes off the beast he is to face tomorrow—the Krakatorum Gargantus. The lack of detail in the drawing almost makes it more frightening.

Dad was right, thinks Archibald. *The unknown is always scarier than what you can see.*

The stats alone on that monster don't bode well for the fight ahead. With an average height of twenty feet and a weight (estimated) of nine to twelve tons, the Krakatorum is a Titanosaur in the world of Marodors. Under the influence of the night fires burning around the village, the terrifying beast almost seems alive, undulating between shadows and sudden flashes of light. Besides the lack of nickname, two facts on the monster's chart worry Archibald more than others: the date of capture and the list of weaknesses, both left blank.

Not so long ago, Archibald learned in school about rites of passage in certain tribes from Asia to Africa. In his eyes, fighting that monster represents a leap into manhood that is second to none: more unpredictable than the Masai initiation leading wannabe tribal warriors to stalk and kill a lion, armed only with a spear; more daring than the naghol from Vanuatu, in which daredevil boys throw themselves from huge bamboo towers with tree vines wrapped around their ankles, aiming for a well-calculated brush with the ground—and death.

Archibald is looking at his flashlight, turning it on and off over and over until the shaft encircles some of the graves next to his cabana. He has never dared get too close to them. But on a night that feels like his last, he finally does, his eyes lingering on one particular aspect of each grave: the dates of birth and death.

"That can't be right," he mumbles.

If he believes the markings, one girl, Forestyne Emma Payne, was born in 1501 and died in 1733! Another one, Abellana Wren Brickenden, lived from 1487 until 1789. And what about Alvina Millicent Ashdown, who passed in 1869 at age 351?

"This doesn't make any sense," Archibald ponders.

Two people holding torches are heading his way. Even from afar, he can tell one of those silhouettes is Wymer—a fairly easy assumption since the big guy is the only person in the village over six feet tall. He is coming over with Faerydae.

"What have you been up to?" she asks.

"Nothing, really, just getting ready to die," he answers, glancing somberly at the graves.

"I made a little something for you," shouts Wymer, holding that little something in his hand. "Stand up; let's see if it fits."

"What is it?"

"Well, any knight deserving of the title needs proper armor, don't you think?"

"A knight? Me?" asks Archibald, his face lighting up.

"But of course," confirms Wymer. "We had a castle already; now we have a knight!"

The armor is very rudimentary, made entirely of rough slices of bark. Wymer places one piece on Archibald's chest and another on his back, connecting them with ropes over his shoulders and two more tied up at the waist.

"It's a bit tight on the chest," says Wymer. "I'll have to adjust the bark a little. You're stronger than I thought," he says, winking at Faerydae.

"You must be kidding! My armor is made of bark? The only thing protecting me from that Gigantus is made of *bark*?"

"Oh, not just any bark," corrects Wymer. "A mighty strong bark, from Dalbergia Melanoxylon."

"That'd better be some magic bark," hopes Archibald.

"It's blackwood, from Umbraea. The same wood I used to build the tank."

"Okay, but—wait, what? You said tank? You have a tank?" asks Archibald, eyes and mouth wide open.

Wymer just nods and smiles really big, his eyebrows arched high on his forehead.

Wymer is showing the way, but he can barely walk, with Archibald stepping in front of him every five seconds, assailing him with questions. His gesticulating makes Faerydae chuckle.

"How big is the cannon?" asks Archibald.

"Big," assures Wymer.

"Wow! How big is the tank?"

"Big."

"Wow! How fast does it go?"

"As fast as you want it to go."

"Wow! Can it shoot from any direction?"

"From *any* direction, that's for sure."

"Wow!"

Wymer comes to a stop suddenly.

"I'm sorry. I'm in your way?" asks Archibald.

"No, we have arrived!" Wymer says, motioning to a house on the side of the road. Unlike the other homes up and down the street, this one has a huge garage door almost covering up the entire façade.

"That's my house," says Wymer. "Well, this is actually my workshop; *that* is my house," he says, pointing at a tiny hut about five times smaller than the workshop it's attached to. As a result of that rather peculiar floor plan, the building as a whole is profiled like a snail. The head of the mollusk—aka the living hut—is so little that both Archibald and Faerydae wonder how Wymer can even fit in there. It seems hardly bigger than his body!

"I go in there only to sleep. And I never sleep!" he says, grimacing as he cranks up the garage door. He goes in first, using his torch to light up four more anchored to the walls around the room. Little by little, Archibald discovers the silhouette of Wymer's work of art.

"My baby, the Hérisson," the handyman says with pride.

Not quite what Archibald had in mind, which in many ways makes this combat vehicle even more impressive.

Wymer didn't lie. The tank shell is made entirely out of wood. Circular at the base, with a cone-shaped body ending with a pointy observation turret at the top, it can be best described as a cross between a turtle and a teapot.

"I have to say, when we got the plans for it, I didn't really know what I was building at first. I had never seen anything like this before," says Wymer, gesturing to a series of drawings pinned to the wall—intricate hand sketches of such engineering precision and artistic virtuosity they could only be the work of a master draftsman.

"It reminds me of your hat," Archibald tells Faerydae.

And it's not just the conical shape. The wood panels are also covered with the same cloak of camouflage material.

"It does, doesn't it?" says Wymer. "I never thought about that."

Archibald has already shifted his attention to the detail that matters most to him: the cannons sticking out from small openings all around the tank, which to a giant, bearded kid like Wymer might look like the spines of a Hérisson—as some call a hedgehog in other lands.

"These are so cool!" he says, trying to count how many there are—eight total.

"Just like I told you, there's no blind side. You can fire from any angle, 360 degrees," explains Wymer.

Archibald notices something by the turret. "What are those lines up there? Looks like that wave rune from your flag. Nice touch!"

"No, that's no rune," corrects Wymer. "Those are scratch marks from a Marodor's claws, from last year."

"The Tormentare Arnicolare—that was a toughie," recalls Faerydae.

"It sure was," notes Wymer. "But, hey, at least my Hérisson came back in one piece."

Archibald sits on the ground, overcome by doubt again. "This will never work. I mean, no offense, Wymer—this . . .

Hérisson of yours is awesome and all, but that beast seems so big. It's just crackbrained, you know, crazy!"

"You gotta believe in this baby. It can withstand a great deal of firepower," assures Wymer, petting his tank. "We've lost only twelve on the battlefield."

"Only! That's encouraging!" says Archibald, sarcastic, of course.

"Don't forget: we also have your special weapon," Faerydae reminds him.

"That's what's *really* crazy! This is not a special weapon," explodes Archibald, pulling the flashlight out of his pocket. "Don't you get it? This is just a flashlight!" he adds, turning it on and off.

"Don't you point that thing at me again!" says Faerydae, hiding behind the tank.

Even Big Wymer seems afraid. Right now, he would gladly hide in a deep hole if he could, and he does, going down a ladder into a pit dug underneath the tank—a regular pithole like you'd find in any other repair shop.

"I just remembered I have to fix one of the pulleys," he says.

"It's only a flashlight; it will never work," repeats Archibald.

"Well, it worked the last time you used it," says Faerydae.

"That was just luck."

"Luck? Archibald, nobody has ever defeated a Marodor that quickly before!"

"Really?"

"Trust me; you've got something special there—special powers."

"Special powers?" repeats Archibald, inspecting his flashlight closely again.

Is he actually starting to believe that flummadiddle?

ᚱ

The sun has barely risen over Gristlemoth. Wymer's Hérisson is rolling through the village, to the applause of many girls lining the streets. Archibald is enjoying the glory. The top turret is flipped open. He is standing up there, hitting his chest armor with his fist and brandishing his flashlight high in the air. Yesterday a sword, it is now an Olympic torch!

"Here I come!" he shouts, the battle cry he rehearsed in his grandma's library.

Each time he points his flashlight down, many in the crowd, scared and panicked, duck as if trying to dodge a bullet.

Down below, in a cabin lit solely by fireflies twirling around in jars, Faerydae is driving, looking at the road through a slit cut into the slanted face of the tank. Seated on a tree-stump stool, she has her hands solidly wrapped around the control stick, her right foot drumming on the brake pedal. Both are connected to a complex system of pulleys and cranks, themselves linked by ropes to four wagon wheels, also made of wood.

Right behind Faerydae, Maven and Rhiannon are using golems to activate and feed that ingenious engine.

Conveying the not-so-discreet grinding sound of a steamboat engine, the wobbly chariot is actually throbbing down the road at a remarkable speed, threatening to topple Archibald from the rickety ladder he is standing on.

Soon, they cross the limits of Gristlemoth, entering the darkness and Marodor territory.

They follow a sinuous path carved into the woods without a glitch, only a few bumps in the road. Still posted at the turret, Archibald has abandoned his earlier chest thumping. Holding the hatch slightly open above his head, he is trying to hide 99.9 percent of his body inside the tank, worried of what might pop out from the woods around.

"Why is there dust everywhere?" he asks, referring to the

thin powder coat he noticed the day he arrived.

"Ashes, not dust," says Maven.

"Ashes? From what? Is there a volcano around here?"

"Not nearby. But your bet is as good as ours," says Rhiannon. "Most likely just Marodors' breath—we're not too sure."

"You're joking, right?" he says.

"Nope," they respond in one voice.

"Naida says the nutrients in ashes are great for fertilizing plants," adds Rhiannon. "If that's true, this land should expect spring to one day prevail over any other season."

"Well, in the meantime, it's stuck in winter," says Faerydae.

After a six-hour drive, the Hérisson is having a harder time advancing. Behind them are the flat plains and gentle slopes of Gristlemoth. The terrain around here is much more difficult. For the last mile, Faerydae has had to maneuver around rocks and huge tree stumps—a challenge that pales in comparison to what lies ahead. Slapping the murky surroundings with his flashlight, Archibald is first to spot the problem. The dirt trail will soon shrink to nothing.

"Trouble at twelve o'clock. There's no more road!" he says.

"No, there is—just not quite a road, though," says Faerydae.

Archibald's eyes go from squinting to wide open as he discovers a crumbling cut in the middle of a sheer cliff face.

"That's the Neander Pass," says Rhiannon—more of a mule route, in fact, barely wide enough for a car, let alone a tank.

"We can't go through that!" whines Archibald.

"We have no choice," says Faerydae, slowing down to a crawl.

"Have you done this before?"

"Not with a tank."

It's a tight squeeze. Faerydae is biting her lip, trying to stay within the limits of the narrow path carved right off the cliff's edge. Archibald looks down with a fearful gaze, peeking into the blackness of a seemingly bottomless ravine.

What if that Gargantus showed up now? Archibald thinks to himself, right when a loud, walloping noise rattles the cockpit.

"Landslide," whispers Maven, as more rocks come tumbling down from the peaks above.

For everyone on board, the entire stretch of the pass is a heart-stopping experience—three hundred mountain-hugging yards of high stress and sweat.

"We made it!" celebrates Rhiannon when at long last they reach the end.

"Naida spotted the Krakatorum a mile north of here, only a few minutes away. We could see it at any time now," says Maven.

"As soon as the Marodor shows up, you hit it with your magic light, okay?" Faerydae tells Archibald.

"Okay," he says, glancing forward. "But maybe you should get the cannons ready, just in case," he adds.

Just then, the glow from his flashlight gets dimmer.

"Oh no. No, no, no, please, no," he whispers.

Despite his incantations, the glow gets even dimmer, and dimmer, and dimmer, until it dies entirely.

"You wouldn't have any batteries, by chance?" he asks the girls, getting a concert of "What?" and "Huh?" in return.

"Two C batteries," he says after unscrewing the bottom of his flashlight.

"C what, sorry?" asks Rhiannon.

Archibald is getting dizzy.

His body is boiling up inside and out.

He is sweating profusely.

He wants to vomit, but he's afraid his guts would come out all at once in a single chunk—big as a pea.

And that paralyzing tingling is back in his legs.

"We have to go back to the village!" he says.

"Have you gone mad?" asks Maven.

"We have to turn around!" he shouts.

Archibald has turned into a pressure cooker with no safety valve. Seeing that the girls have no intention of changing course, he pulls himself up and slides down the tank and onto the ground.

"What is he doing?" screams Faerydae.

Maven removes from their socket two of the golems that were feeding energy to the pulleys. A quick, loud snap later, the engine has stalled. The Hérisson comes to a grinding halt. The girls leap out through a side hatch. Archibald is sitting on the ground, his flashlight next to him. He looks knocked out.

"Are you okay?" inquires Faerydae.

"No, I'm not okay," he whispers to himself.

"What's wrong?"

"What's wrong? My flashlight's dead. That's what's wrong!"

"It can't die! It's a magic weapon!"

"This is bonkers. How could I be stupid enough to believe you with that whole magic thing? This was never a magic weapon—you didn't want to listen, and now it ran out of batteries!"

"You're saying the magic died?" asks Maven.

"I can't believe this. Why don't you guys use your own magic, huh? What kind of witches are you, anyway? Don't you have a magic wand, like all witches?"

Faerydae looks furious. "Maven, hand me that, please," she says, referring to a crooked twig lying at her feet.

Maven picks it up. "This?" she questions, wondering what Faerydae could possibly do with it. Sure, she knows her friend has more than one trick up her sleeve—"This twig here?" Maven repeats, unsure what's about to happen. Archibald wonders the exact same thing, except he's worried about it.

Faerydae grabs the twig, bends it to straighten it up a bit, and brushes her fingers on the tip before pointing it at Archibald in a threatening manner.

"I told you not to lie anymore or I'd turn you into the little weasel that you are deep inside," she says with a furrowed brow.

Archibald is crawling on the ground, trying to escape, but Faerydae won't let him. She gets closer, now aiming the twig directly at his face.

"Here is what a magic wand can do," she thunders.

Archibald cringes and closes his eye nearest to the twisted twig.

Faerydae seems about to strike. Instead, she breaks the piece of wood in half and throws it on his lap.

"Nothing, that's what a magic wand can do. And, no, we don't have any flying brooms either!"

Rhiannon lets out the most mischievous, spooky, almost devilish cackle.

"Some of us do have a wicked laugh, though," admits Maven.

Archibald picks himself back up, still shaking.

"Now get your weapon to work again," says Faerydae.

"It's not a weapon; don't you get it? And the letters on my sweatshirt, they're just from my mum's sorority."

"Oh, so you like to wear girls' clothes? Maybe your name *is* Ivy?" jokes Rhiannon.

"Don't listen to him; that's just his flummadiddle again," laments Faerydae.

"You're so disguisy," Maven tells him, coming closer, looking mad.

"So *what* now?" he asks.

"Befuddling, always mealy mouthed," says Rhiannon, moving nearer as well.

"Bamboozling, confusing, full of tricks, that's what you are," thunders Faerydae.

"No, I'm not making this up," says Archibald, now surrounded on three sides by menacing figures. "I have no clue where I am or what I'm supposed to do. I just arrived here a few days ago. I had never seen a Marodor before that. I have no magic; the flashlight just followed me here when I got sucked up into that globe—"

All three girls freeze at the same time. It takes a few seconds for Faerydae to digest what she's just heard.

"What did you say?"

"About my flashlight?"

"No, you said something about being sucked up into a globe."

"Yes, I was in my bedroom."

"There is no globe. They were destroyed a long time ago," says Faerydae.

"Wait, you know about the globe too? Is that the way all of you came here?"

Faerydae is stunned. Maybe he's not a hugger-mugger after all.

"Tell us about the globe you speak of."

"I found it at my parents' home. I mean my grandma's."

"What did it look like?"

Archibald doesn't know where to start. "It was round, like a globe, brown, old looking, and with a weird smell."

"What else?" inquires Faerydae, visibly impatient.

"There were monsters all over it. I drew several of them. Some looked like the beasts in your book. What else? Oh, yes, there was a crack in the globe. But it was not really a crack, more like a button you could press up and down. I got the key that unlocked the globe, and—boom, a big flash of light—I was here."

Faerydae is staring at Archibald. He doesn't know how she's

going to react.

"You are speaking the truth!" she says, with astonishment in her voice.

The next second, Maven and Rhiannon start jumping up and down and screaming at the top of their lungs.

"What's happening? We are stuck in this nightmare! What's there to celebrate?" asks Archibald.

"You don't understand. We thought all globes had been destroyed," says Faerydae.

It took some time, but the girls have now calmed down. Everybody is back in the tank, sitting in a circle. Silence has taken over, so deep and heavy it gives a buzzing life to the fireflies' usually muted symphony, increasing the drama of the moment—the moment of truth for all.

"So when did you get here?" asks Maven.

"Just a few days ago. The day I met you."

"When you left, what year was it?" asks Rhiannon.

"2021," he says. "What about you? When did you get here?"

The girls hold each other's hands for a few seconds.

"We couldn't be sure. But based on what you just said, about five hundred years ago," answers Faerydae.

"Yeah, right!" chuckles Archibald. He quickly stops, though, realizing this is no joke just by reading their startled faces.

"But . . . you don't . . . look five hundred years old."

"In Lemurea, you don't get old. Only your mind grows. You learn; you expand your way of thinking. Your physical body doesn't change," she explains.

"What's Lemurea?"

"It's here—in the earth's underbelly, if you prefer."

"No, I don't prefer. I don't prefer at all, actually! What kind of country is that?" asks Archibald, with fear and concern in his voice as this new reality sinks in.

"A country far, far away," says Faerydae for short.

"How far? Like Ireland?"

"Are you sure you're ready for the answer?" asks Faerydae.

"Yes," he says, shaking his head at the same time.

"It all started a long time ago, but the tragedy took a turn for the worse in the fifteenth century. Thousands of women across Europe were hunted down just because they were different, just because they didn't think like everyone else. They were tortured and put to death in the worst imaginable way—hanged, drowned, or just burned alive."

Faerydae's story reminds Archibald of that shocking scene carved on his grandma's fireplace. The same question comes to his mind once again.

"Those women, what did they do to be treated like that?"

"They were accused of everything short of making the sun go down. If you believe their enemies, they were monsters. They killed babies, devoured them, even. Let's see, what else? Oh yeah, they could trigger hailstorms and turn into animals. And, of course, they cast spells causing people to lose body parts and things like that."

"Is that true?" asks Archibald, terrified.

"Not really—greatly exaggerated. Their only crime was to be too caring and way too smart."

"You can never be too smart," objects Archibald.

"Oh yes, you can," she says. "Especially women. They offered alternatives to medicine, to religion, to teaching in general. They became a danger. They were the enemy; they were . . . witches."

"That's why they were called witches?"

"Yes. I know it sounds crazy, but it didn't take much to be

called a witch back then. In reality, they were just nature lovers, believing in the power of plants and herbs. They were healers, they were life worshippers, they were our mothers."

"Your mothers?" exclaims Archibald, not quite following.

Maven and Rhiannon just nod to confirm.

"Imagine what those women had to go through, every single day," says Faerydae. "Imagine what it means to live in constant fear and terror, forced to flee your town to survive, moving from one place to another, hiding. Based on what was happening to them, it was easy to assume that their daughters would meet the same fate. *We* would grow up to suffer the same persecution. Our mothers knew they had to do something to protect us. We were birthed as the daughters of nightfall."

"Is that why they sent you here? To save you?"

"That was the idea, yes," says Rhiannon.

"But it's a bit more complicated," adds Faerydae. "Something else was happening in the world. Always more wars, more massacres, more blood being spilled. What our mothers were trying to heal, or protect, men were busy destroying. The earth couldn't take it anymore. All that blood seeping through the ground gave birth to demons—the Marodors."

"Wait, Marodors are demons?"

"That's why they can't be killed. In a way, they *are* death," says Faerydae.

Archibald's world is thrown off balance suddenly. "I don't understand. Those demons live inside the earth? We are inside the earth?" he asks, panicked.

"Not exactly, no. Lemurea is more like a parallel dimension, some sort of underworld. At first, the Marodors were confined here, with no access to the earth. Nobody could see them. That was until the winter of 1132, when sailors from Ireland got caught in a storm of rare might. Through the power of lightning, that storm created a temporary passage that brought them to the shores of this underworld. They were the first ones to witness the demons. The same storm carried them back to Ireland, where they told their story. They thought they had landed on an island nobody had discovered yet. So people started drawing that island on maps."

"And they drew the Marodors too!" notes Archibald.

"They thought they were just sea monsters," smiles Faerydae. "Our mothers knew better. They knew about Lemurea. They knew those monsters were demons. More boats followed. More storms. More stories. More mysterious islands started to pop up on maps everywhere. And more Marodors. A handful of them even managed to escape Lemurea through those storms. One sank boats off the coast of Ragusa. Another terrorized a village in Carinthia. And the wars didn't stop. With more blood seeping into the ground, there were more and more Marodors. Their power was growing by the day. Our mothers knew it was only a question of time before they'd enter the earth in droves and take their revenge against men."

"Why not let them, if men were trying to kill your mothers?"

"You would think, right? I often wonder why they didn't."

"Instead, they turned you into guardian angels—guardian angels fighting demons."

"I never thought about it that way, but that's the thing: our mothers also believed in the best in men. They believed the human race was worth saving. More importantly, they believed people
could change."

"So what happened?"

"They had two goals in mind. First, put us out of reach of the witch-hunters. At the same time, they knew someone had to fight the demons, not on Earth but here, in the underworld. So they passed down their knowledge and powers to us. Then they sent us here."

"That's what the globe was for?"

"The idea was to re-create the conditions of those storms that allowed sailors into Lemurea. To do that, witches from all over Europe combined their powers, but it was not enough. They had a dear friend in Italy, a great inventor. He found a way to build a machine powerful enough to help us travel here. Putting that device inside a globe was meant to hide it and protect it, and also made it easy to use, with just a spin."

"That man was brilliant. This tank is also an invention of his own devising," says Maven.

"He built a total of five globes," points out Faerydae. "They were taken to all corners of Europe, to save as many young witches as possible."

"What happened to those globes?" asks Archibald.

"Two of them were found by witch-hunters and smashed to pieces. Two were lost in wars. We used the last one, which was destroyed as well. At least that's what we thought, until today."

"What does it change, anyway?" asks Archibald. "I'm here, and the globe didn't come with me."

"It never does. The storm it generates will take anything and anyone within a ten-foot radius. But the globe always stays behind. That's just the way it works, to allow someone else to bring you back, supposedly."

"That's possible? How?"

"I'm not sure. Clearly, no one ever used that trick on us."

"Maybe you can come back with me, then!" says Archibald, with a half smile, thinking maybe this nightmare could end soon.

"I'd rather not get my hopes up."

"You know, where I come from, people don't burn witches

anymore."

"Maybe they don't, but I'm sure they still find a way to keep them silent," notes Faerydae. "What about wars? There are no more wars either?"

"Not too many."

"So why are there more and more demons down here, then?" questions Faerydae.

Archibald doesn't quite know what to say to that. Another question he doesn't have an answer to: why would his grandma have that globe in her house if she hated witches so much, as proven by that horrible fireplace in her living room?

Archibald spent the next fifteen minutes trying to convince Faerydae he was ready for battle. He argued passionately that he had not only the necessary experience but also the required skills to take on the Krakatorum Gargantus. It sounded very much like a job interview.

He bragged about catching a ginormous lizard with his bare hands—so big his arms couldn't stretch wide enough to describe the size of that creature. (In fact, a sixteen-inch gecko that had escaped its container at the pet store and that he had held by the tail for two seconds before screaming for help. But why bother the girls with such insignificant details—cluttering up the story, really.)

He also mentioned his extensive training in aikido, once a week for five months two years ago. "The key," explained the white-belt champion, "is to use your opponent's strength against him. The bigger the opponent, the easier it will be to defeat him." How that technique would translate to fighting a beast like the Krakatorum he did not elaborate. "Just trust the ancient Japanese," he simply said, "and Mr. Edwards," his aikido teacher.

As though to close the deal, Archibald threw in one more accomplishment, admittedly minor but still with the potential to tip the balance in his favor: holding his breath underwater for a full minute—more a survival necessity than a shot at a medal, really, since William Tanner was pressing on his head the whole time, trying to drown him.

When it became clear he had exhausted his collection of highly remarkable exploits, Archibald left it for the girls to judge.

"What do you say?" he asked.

Ω

In the end, Wymer's tank is back on the march, but only after making a U-turn some hours back. Archibald is not at the turret anymore. He is sitting in the cockpit alongside Rhiannon and Maven, with Faerydae still at the command post.

"Why do we have to go back to Gristlemoth?" he complains.

"I told you already," says Faerydae. "Since that magic weapon of yours happens to not be so magic after all, we have to put you in a safe place. We're going back to Gristlemoth, then we'll go fight that Marodor without you."

"That's just whimsifulous," Archibald says grumpily.

"Look, you have to face reality," says Maven. "You don't know anything about golems. In the middle of a fight you'd be a total nuisance for us. Not only would you be of no help whatsoever but you could get hurt."

"You should consider yourself lucky," says Rhiannon. "Back in Gristlemoth, you can have fun with the girls."

"And do what? Laundry?" he jokes.

"What's wrong with doing laundry?" she snaps.

"Look, no offense. I'm not sure if you guys are trying to make me feel better, but, just so you know, it's not working."

"We're just telling you the truth," says Maven bluntly.

"I think I've had enough truth for today, thanks. Enough to last my whole life, actually, and now it might last a thousand years—who knows?"

"Maybe not," comments Faerydae, back to grave and serious.

"What's happening?" asks Rhiannon, getting up right away.

"Marodor, right ahead," shouts Faerydae. "It's the Krakatorum!"

"It's attacking Gristlemoth!" yells Rhiannon.

This is the worst-case scenario Faerydae warned about. In a wheeling movement worthy of Napoleon's most brilliant tactic—or just because it likes to venture off the beaten trail—the Krakatorum Gargantus must have crawled in a semicircle through the woods from the Neander Pass. That's how the beast avoided their tank.

Peering through the slits in the planks, Maven and Archibald discover the extraordinary creature.

"Blimkey!" she blurts out.

"Holy. Giant. Bejabbles," echoes Archibald.

Tall as a palm tree, the Krakatorum is as scary as the drawing could suggest—and then some. The monster is pushing against the wall of golems using its spider legs, some with sharp pikes and some with human hands. Sticking out from that dark mound of fur and leaves are not three but four wormlike necks, confirming Naida's description. Lined with a mohawk of branches, each of the necks ends with a most ghoulish face lost in patches of swampy hair, each human(ish), with eyes glinting like hot coals.

What makes the Krakatorum so awesomely creepy is the look on those faces: utterly blank, lifeless, until the mouth gapes so wide it eats up everything around it—eyes, nose, and chin. One of the mouths has just burst open, spraying fire between fences of crisscrossing teeth. The flames go over the rampart of golems but luckily ricochet off the wall of light.

"We've got a dragon on
our hands!" says Faerydae.
Even though the necks are also covered
with lizard scales, for Archibald, something
doesn't add up. "That thing is no dragon,"
he says, sounding disappointed almost.

"What do you think it is, then?" asks Rhiannon.

"I have no idea, but not a dragon."

"Because you know so much about dragons!" snaps Maven.

"That thing can't even fly," he argues.

"We don't have time for this!" yells Faerydae. "It's trying to break through the wall. If it does, more Marodors will come in, and we all know what that means," she adds, looking at the girls with her most severe face yet.

All four of the monster's heads seem to be acting independently from one another, some focused on the village, others on the incoming tank. It's like fighting an enemy equipped with a second pair of eyes behind his head—three extra pairs in this case!

"Let's fire! Where are the cannonballs?" asks Archibald, lifting blankets but finding only crates of golems underneath.

"Cannonballs would do no harm; Marodors have thick skin! And they don't bleed, anyway," says Rhiannon.

"Then what do we do?"

"We fire these golems, but *you* don't do anything. You just stay put," she says.

"No!" shouts Faerydae. "We'll need all the help we can get! Let him shoot too." Then, sharing a deep stare with Archibald.

"You can help us, right?"

He nods, thankful, smiling with his eyes.

"You know how to aim?" asks Maven.

"Do I know how to aim? I scored eighteen three-pointers and twelve free throws on a video game once!"

"I have no idea what you just said, but fine," says Maven. "Look, the goal is not just to hit the Marodor; that would be too easy. Remember the chalkboard. The golems work together. So we have to fire three of them back-to-back."

"How do I know which golems to fire?" he asks, lost just looking at all the different runes in front of him.

"Don't worry about that. I'll pick them for you. Just make sure you aim right, okay?"

"Okay," says Archibald, taking position behind two cannons.

"Hurry!" shouts Faerydae. "We are almost within range."

Maven is holding her head between her hands, scanning the golems, trying to figure out which ones will work best.

"Vixeneme, Eolare, Abbreviae," she finally says, handing one golem to Rhiannon and one to Archibald, keeping one for herself.

Rhiannon and Maven place their stone in a chamber located at the back of their cannons. Archibald does the same.

"How do you fire?" he asks, seeing no trigger.

"Each cannon is mounted on powder golems—the same that heat up Karl and Karla, only much more powerful," says Maven.

"When you're ready, just push your golem into the slot and say 'Propellia Momentum.' The cannon will fire," explains Faerydae.

"Propel what? Couldn't you guys just say 'Fire'?" he whines.

The Krakatorum is finally within striking distance, about two hundred feet ahead.

Rhiannon taps her golem to load it fully and pronounces the triggering words. Her cannon goes off in an ear-splitting roar. It's a hit!

The golem doesn't quite penetrate the Marodor's body, but it gets stuck right under its skin—its scales, to be exact, layered like the flower buds of an artichoke.

"Your turn, Archibald! Quick!" says Maven.

One sharp poke and his golem is in. He points his cannon at the beast.

"Propellia Momentum!" he shouts.

Another loud bang resonates through the cockpit. It's a hit too! The golem disappears among the multitude of eyes studding the spider's face.

"So much better than video games!" says the sharpshooter.

They have to switch positions since the Hérisson is now facing the wrong way.

"To the other side," says Rhiannon.

That's the point of having cannons all around the tank. Maven fires the last golem of the spell, Abbreviae, hitting the Krakatorum in the belly. All three golems glow at once.

Seconds later, the beast starts coughing and choking.

One after another, the Marodor's heads are rendered all but useless, collapsing and dangling on the side of its body like dirty old socks—two out of four.

"Hurray!" shouts Rhiannon, high-fiving Archibald.

"What was that? Internal boiling?" he asks.

"Close. More like a crushing of the lungs," says Maven.

"What about that other spell—the looping tail?" he suggests.

"This dragon doesn't have a tail," Rhiannon points out.

"So? Maybe we use the necks to tie up the legs?"

"Too complicated, too many limbs to worry about," gauges Maven, and she obviously has the last say.

"Well, we need something and quick!" says Faerydae. "Two of the heads are still working! That's more than enough to destroy Gristlemoth."

In fact, the Krakatorum has managed to partially push aside one of the huge wall golems. The breach allows the dragon to spew lava breath deep inside the village, spreading panic. It is now trying to squeeze in.

On the other side, Naida and others are pushing back, armed mostly with bows. As feared, their arrows are too weak to pierce the beast's carapace.

"The wall won't last much longer," says Rhiannon.

They can't get too close, though. Balls of fire have begun raining their way, ripping through the forest and lighting up the night. Faerydae slaloms between trees to avoid them. Not fast enough. A blazing wave reaches the combat vehicle with hurricane strength. The machine quakes and shivers, like a spaceship reentering Earth's atmosphere. Incredibly, it remains essentially intact. It's no miracle. The torrent of flames has simply rolled up the sloped planks of the tank, licking the turret but frying only the top camouflage. Everyone is relieved, especially Archibald.

"Now I get the whole mushroom shape of this thing!" he sighs.

Another gush of fire is aimed at Gristlemoth, setting ablaze a guard tower where several girls had taken position and were trying to set up an extra cannon. As the tower collapses on the outer boulders, one of the girls is snatched by the spider half of the Krakatorum.

"That's Willow!" screams Faerydae, recognizing the girl who alerted her a few days ago in the Marodor's pen.

Maven is trying to pick a new set of golems, but panic has taken over. She hesitates.

"Please hurry!" says Faerydae.

Prisoner of the monster's arms and claws, Willow has no wiggle room to put up a fight. Only when the spider brings her close does she try to kick that ugly face, but the danger comes from above. One of the Marodor's necks plunges down on the young girl and anchors itself to her back.

In frightened awe, Archibald witnesses that hug of death Faerydae described. The embrace is horribly peaceful. Willow seems to suffocate, as if every ounce of life is being drained out of her. A spark slowly spreads, turning her pupils bright red, the flame soon engulfing her eyes almost entirely.

"Maven! What's taking so long?" yells Faerydae.

The rune expert seems at a loss. Then, "Maybe this: Achillae, Moonascendum, Inflecto."

"What's that?" asks Rhiannon.

Maven just nods, meaning, "Trust me." She fires her golem first, again hitting the Krakatorum in the chest.

It's Rhiannon's turn. She misses. The golem gets lost in the trees.

"Sorry," she sighs. "I was afraid to hit Willow."

"Hurry, or soon she won't be Willow anymore," says Maven, handing her another golem.

This time, Rhiannon adjusts her aim and hits the Marodor in one of its front legs. Her perfect shot causes the beast to let go of Willow and throw her aside, against the wall of golems.

"What have I done?" gasps Rhiannon.

Unable to say another word, she is all but paralyzed. Maven tries to shake her out of her torpor, but nothing will. Everything depends on Archibald now. With all that firing, smoke has engulfed the cockpit. He squints, trying to tune out all the craziness around him. Finally, he gives one more yell: "Propellia Momentum!"

It's also a hit—a close call, though. The golem lodges itself in one of the Marodor's limp sock faces.

"Does it count?" asks Archibald.

"It will do," says Maven, and sure enough, the three golems light up. Their combined energy seems to act as a giant hammer. The Krakatorum is hit with such force to the head(s) that the monster loses its balance. It is staggering, growling, and about to collapse.

That's just the first effect of the spell.

Next comes the impact from Inflecto: several of the spider legs get entangled, and more importantly, the two dragon necks still alive roll around one another to end up tied in a knot.

"We got it!" shouts Maven, confident they have the beast at their mercy.

Suddenly, one of the golems detaches from the Marodor's body, making the other two fade and quickly go dead. Nearly unconscious, two of the beast's faces reopen their glaring eyes. The fire-breathing demon regains its full strength in an instant, using one of its necks to hit the tank ferociously.

The shock is tremendous.

Da Vinci's war machine is sent flying through the air. Countless flips later, it comes crashing against a tree.

Wymer witnesses the drama from another guard tower inside Gristlemoth. His widening eyes soon match the diameter of the funky binoculars rising two feet above his head—some sort of periscope made of concave mirrors and optical glasses linked together through strings and putty.

The Krakatorum approaches the crippled Hérisson, now upside down like a spinning top. Rhiannon is the only one still inside, pinned underneath the planks, her left leg crushed by a cannon. She's trying to grab her bow, but her preferred weapon is out of reach.

Lying nearby, the other crewmembers have been ejected on impact like rag dolls, along with the rest of the cannons and ammunition. They are barely moving. Archibald's vision is blurred, but he sees the Krakatorum getting closer. Faerydae is lying right in the monster's path.

"Careful—it's coming!" Archibald warns her.

Faerydae stands back up painfully. She's not in good shape either. Noticing the golems scattered on the ground, she picks up two of them, punches the stones deep in the earth, and utters,

"Foraterebra," before running out of the way.

When the Krakatorum charges toward her, the ground opens underneath it, right where Faerydae placed her golems. The Marodor tumbles heavily into the hole, breaking several of its spider legs at the bottom, some thirty feet below.

She's amazing! Archibald says to himself.

Faerydae huffs. But the Krakatorum claws its way back up and rears its head, still up and brewing out of the hole.

The creature switches its focus to Maven, still unconscious on the ground, and creeps toward her with wide-open jaws.

Sensing the imminent danger, Archibald looks to Faerydae for another spell or miracle move, but she is too far away to intervene.

Archibald has to improvise. He makes a T with his hands— one of the signs Faerydae taught him. She got it. He is ready for a diversion, his specialty since he tried getting those keys from Bartholomeo. Faerydae shakes her head and signals him to stay put, her fingers joined together and curled back. But Archibald has already made up his mind. He meets her gaze, crossing his arms on his chest—the "I care about you" sign. Daring and unafraid, he dashes behind the Krakatorum and hurls both golems and insults at the Marodor, now only a few feet away.

"Hey, chicken dragon! Hey, you giant turd!" he screams, taunting the beast.

Taking the bait, the towering monster turns its neck around.

Archibald throws one more golem at the beast just as he sees another blitz of lava gushing out of the Marodor's mouth— coming his way.

In the same breath, Faerydae lunges forward while arching her body, cartwheels with one hand on the ground, snatches a golem with the other, and throws it like a fastball as soon as she lands back on her feet, yelling, "Quiqueversio!"

In a flash, her magic stone collides midair with Archibald's, sparking an instant tornado that absorbs part of the Krakatorum's fire—but only part of it. The next second, Archibald disappears in the blast.

"Noooooo!" screams Faerydae, horrified.

Archibald's desperate move has given Maven precious time to collect her own golems. She crawls to a large oak tree nearby and hugs it, holding the golems in her hands. Her eyes are closed. She whispers something, as if talking to the tree.

When the Krakatorum turns back to her, the tree bends toward the Marodor and swats the last remaining head with a branch. Two more blows and the beast is twisting in agony, ready to give up. The tree unleashes more branches to grab the Marodor and squeeze it against its main trunk, each head and neck now firmly held prisoner in a tight armlock.

Embers are still floating in the air, and flickering flares cascade down tree trunks, reinforcing the end-of-the-world atmosphere of the scene, when Naida arrives with a handful of young fighters. Carefully extracted from the tank wreck, Rhiannon is gradually surrounded by fireflies escaping from their broken jars. She watches as the flashing creatures drift toward Willow, who is lying motionless on the ground. After forming a halo above her head, the glowworms descend and land on her blackened back, shining brighter still. Following a painful heave, Willow coughs her way back to life—not a speck of red left in her eyes. Rhiannon and her rescuers gape in awe.

On the other end of the battlefield, it's bad news. Faerydae is desperately looking for Archibald. Among burned-out trees and shrubs, the only thing she finds is a piece of breastplate armor— carbonized. Tears begin to mount in her eyes, when she hears a faint cough coming from a bush nearby.

"You're alive!" shouts Faerydae, discovering Archibald

entangled with charred creeper branches, his hair partially burned in the back and his face darkened by the Krakatorum's fire. Deflected for the most part by Wymer's armor, the blast has poked dozens of pin-sized holes through his skin. Dotting his face and hands, they are now glowing like small craters.

"This was just a bad, bad dream," Archibald mumbles, looking at his fingers sparkle in the dark, his body so numb he doesn't feel any pain.

"How do you like that blackwood bark now?" asks Faerydae, taking him in her arms.

By nightfall, Gristlemoth has switched to celebration mode. The town fared relatively well and is back to feeling safe—kind of. Yes, a handful of homes have gone up in flames. Maven has a black eye. Faerydae has bruises on the side of her face. Archibald's head looks like it was toasted on medium, and he had to trade his mum's sweatshirt, in tatters, for a medieval-style tunic. They all know it could have been much worse, though. Even Rhiannon's shattered leg seems like a small price to pay to stop the Krakatorum. The smoke has not completely cleared yet, but everyone has assembled at the Hive to enjoy the feast Wymer prepared, the tables piled high with food.

"Mmh! This Marodor is cooked just right!" he says, stirring Karl's insides from the top of a ladder.

The whole dining hall falls silent. All eyes are on Wymer, who couldn't feel more uncomfortable unless his beard was half-shaven or his flummadiddle had not risen.

"Not amusing," Karl tells him.

"I'm kidding! You know it's mostly veggies," says the chef, allowing the room to go back to loud and festive.

Maven is at a table with Archibald. Corn chowder is the soup of the day, and she is sort of the *hero* of the day. Sparing her audience no detail, she explains which golems she picked to defeat the Krakatorum Gargantus and why.

"See, when you combine Moonascendum with the Achillae rune, the Marodor will be destabilized right away," she explains, using breadcrumbs and beans to reenact the battle. "But if you add the twisting from the Inflecto rune, that's it! The beast doesn't stand a chance—doesn't stand at all, actually," she chuckles, pushing a large crumb that collapses her already shaky six-bean-high tower.

"What about the tree? How did you do that?" asks Archibald.

"I just asked him for help. You've never talked to trees before?"

"Not like that, no."

"I'll teach you if you want."

"I want to know!" says Lenora, joining them.

Archibald doesn't say no, but he has another question on his mind, gazing at the fireflies dancing in the tree-chandeliers above.

"And those, did you talk to them too?" he asks. "I heard what they did to help Willow—they saved her life."

"That was amazefooling, like nothing we've seen before. Fireflies have always been by our side, though."

"And you thank them by putting them in jars?"

"They don't mind. They want to help. Besides, we always let them go after a while. Mysterious beings, those fireflies. Almost as fascinating as dragons."

"Stop saying 'dragons'; they're not really dragons."

"You still have doubts? Look at your face!" jokes Lenora, pointing to his forehead and cheeks, which have tanned to a reddish pecan brown.

"It's just that Marodors don't . . . look like dragons."

"So tell us: what's a dragon supposed to look like?" she asks.

"You know, big nostrils, scissor-sharp teeth, flaming eyes, a snake's tongue, huge bat wings, and a spine of horns—everybody knows that."

"Have you seen one before?" asks Lenora.

"No," he admits.

"So trust me—*this* is the real thing!" she says, pointing at the beans now scattered on the table.

"You're right, though," adds Maven. "Some Marodors have all that—the bat wings, the snake's tongue, etcetera. But that's not what makes them dragons."

"What does, then?"

"The fire they spit," she answers.

"So all those monsters in the *Bestiary*—the wolf owl, the beetle skunk, or the rat raven—they're all dragons?"

"Many of them, yes," she confirms.

For Archibald, it is years of certainty, fed by books, movies, and tales from all continents, that suddenly crumble.

Two tables away, a girl has started playing a weird instrument that bears some similarity to a guitar. Another joins her with a flute and another with a harp. A bunch of girls quickly surround them, singing and swaying as one.

"Wait, is that Rhiannon?" Archibald wonders aloud, surprised to see her among the growing crowd of dancers.

"Yes," confirms Lenora. "Willow is still at the hospital, but Rhiannon is already back on her feet"—limping a little on those feet, but, incredibly, her wounds and pain seem to have all but vanished.

"How's that possible? I thought she broke her leg in the tank."

"She sure did," confirms Maven. "So many broken bones it took hours and four golems to mend them all."

"You can do that?" he exclaims, amazed.

"Of course! Do you want to know how?"

"Maybe later," says Archibald, scanning the room, obviously looking for someone.

Now Maven's feelings are truly hurt.

"Have you seen Faerydae?"

"I think I saw her step outside," says Lenora.

Archibald finds her on a terrace at the back of the dining hall. She is looking at the sky, a somber expression plaguing her face, observing the Marodors flying near the Gristlemoth perimeter. With the music playing in the background, the contrast is startling.

"Are you okay?" he asks.

"What will happen next time?" she says.

"What do you mean?"

"What if we had come back an hour later? Even just half an hour. What would we have found?"

Archibald understands. At the same time, his questions are still of the most basic kind. "Demons? Dragons? What are those things, really?" he asks. "I know you said they were born from the blood spilled on Earth, but it doesn't make sense."

"Well, the story goes that the first breeds of Marodors were just insects, feeding off that blood directly from the ground. That's why many of them still have body parts from termites, beetles, spiders, you name it."

"And you guys thought eating bug burgers would be a good idea?" jokes Archibald. "No wonder Marodors are so angry; you're eating their cousins—maybe their kids!"

Faerydae cracks a smile.

"What about the other parts?" asks Archibald on a more

serious note. "The animal and people parts."

"We're not sure. Probably a mix of humans killed in battles and animals slaughtered on Earth, all waiting here for their revenge."

"Some of them look so human. Have you thought about treating them differently?"

"What do you mean, 'differently'?"

"I mean, what's the point of capturing them and keeping them in cages forever?"

"That's what we do; that's what we're here for, to keep them under control, so they can't access the earth. Don't get me wrong; they might look human, but they're mostly animals."

"I don't think they're just animals. Actually, I don't think animals are just animals. Anyway, humans or animals, are we really that different?" Archibald wonders aloud.

"Maybe not on Earth, but in this world we are. By the way, do you think someone will get you back up there?" she asks.

"It depends. When we met, you called me an accident. What did you mean by that?"

"I don't know if you've noticed, but there aren't many boys around. Only girls were sent down here. They were the only ones in danger. Boys, not so much. So when we find one, we know for sure he was a mislimp, an accident."

"Is Wymer a . . . mislimp too?"

"One hundred percent," she confirms. "He fell asleep under the table where we had put the globe. He was drunk. We didn't see him. He got absorbed with everyone else in the room."

"So no," says Archibald.

"What do you mean, 'no'?"

"No is the answer to your question. I don't think anyone will get me back up there. Because you're right; I was an accident. I'm just like Wymer. It's not like anyone else knows how I came down here, so I doubt anyone will ever bring me back."

"Do me a favor, then," says Faerydae. "Don't say any of this to the girls. They all dream of going back up with you. It would shatter their hearts."

HUNTERS AND PREY

Pancake flipping on Shrove Tuesday is a big thing for the Finch family. That and watching the queen's speech on Christmas Day. Five days before is another ritual, this one dreaded by all: visiting Grandpa Harvey—or, as Hailee puts it, prayer day. It has nothing to do with saying grace before dinner, even though a few uttered words might not be unwise for those hoping to survive the food. Hailee's consideration is somewhat more down to earth. Before each trip, she calls upon the skies for help, wishing for a hailstorm, a tornado, a swarm of winter locusts, or just more snow—anything that would derail this annual event. With Archibald gone, she had found some solace in the certainty that the gathering would be canceled. But Grandpa Harvey insisted.

"He'll be back before Christmas," he assures, while slicing his traditionally overcooked meatloaf.

"We surely hope so, Dad," sighs Kate.

"Trust me; this kind of thing gets resolved quickly—on TV, at least," he says.

"*What* kind of thing?" asks Hailee.

"It's okay; we don't need to know," says Kate, a bit nervous.

She knows her father has declined some in the past few years. He is notorious for saying the most unpredictable—some would say inappropriate—things. Just last week, Kate had to call the local bakery to apologize on his behalf after he told the salesperson she had, quote, "the most beautiful buns."

At eighty-seven, he is still jolly, though. Tonight, he is wearing a snowman sweater with a blinking carrot nose. He has matched that with a small green elf hat on his shiny white hair—the same he's strapped around Stuart's head with a rubber band, making his cheeks all puff up as if he had a tooth infection. Kate can consider herself lucky. She got a cute reindeer hat.

"Put your branches on like your mum!" Grandpa Harvey tells Hailee.

"Not branches, Dad—they're antlers," Kate corrects nicely.

"Oh, that's what those are, huh!" he says, nodding.

"I'm good; thank you," says Hailee with a fake smile, while staring at her phone on her lap.

"Hailee, I told you a thousand times: it's very impolite to be on your phone during dinner."

"I'm not, Mum," defends Hailee. "I'm just expecting something important."

She has not heard from Oliver in two days. She is starting to wonder whether she gave him the right number or whether something terrible happened to him too.

"Have they asked you for a ransom yet?" Grandpa Harvey asks out of the blue, causing Stuart to swallow the piece of meatloaf he had been chewing for the past five minutes.

"Dad, no!" gasps Kate, dropping her fork. "Archibald was not kidnapped! Please don't say that. We don't know anything."

Hailee rolls her eyes. The truth is, nothing coming out of Grandpa Harvey's mouth can hurt her anymore, except for that spluttering, of course. Besides, if she needs a good excuse to be a no-show next year, he has just handed it to her on a platter—and it's much more enjoyable than his meatloaf.

"I'm sorry," says Grandpa Harvey. "You're right; it's too soon."

Kate can breathe, for about half a second.

"If they don't ask for money by next week, though, you should start to worry," he adds, bringing consternation back on Kate's and Stuart's faces.

Hailee checks her phone again. Still no message from Oliver.

"What about those orphanages Celestine left behind?" asks Grandpa Harvey.

"It's all good; they're well taken care of," answers Kate.

"Except for one of them where half the kids disappeared," mentions Stuart.

"What do you mean 'disappeared'?" asks Grandpa Harvey.

"Yes, what do you mean 'disappeared'?" asks Hailee, maybe seeing a link with what happened to Archibald.

"They didn't disappear—sorry—'escaped' would be more accurate," corrects Stuart. "They packed all their things and left. Nobody knows where they went. It happened around the time of Celestine's death. Maybe they got upset. They were all so close to her."

"We don't have much to do with the orphanages. She had good people taking care of them; nothing will change, really," says Kate, worried her loose cannon of a father will start talking about Archibald's adoption in front of Hailee.

"Before I forget, I have a gift for you, young lady," Grandpa Harvey tells Hailee.

All giggly, he heads to the kitchen, the second of the three rooms in his charming house.

"Great," says Stuart, eager to switch to a different topic— and leave.

"Great," cringes Kate, much less optimistic, remembering what her father bought her daughter last year. Hailee has not forgotten either.

"Another weird DVD, Grandpa?"

"What's wrong with a little history lesson?"

"The history of mobsters and killers, really?" says Kate. "Hailee had nightmares for months."

"Well, *this* will be useful," he says, excited, placing the roughly wrapped gift next to her on the table.

"Maybe I should wait until Christmas?" suggests Hailee.

"No, no, no, I want to see the look on your face," he says, grinning widely.

Hailee unwraps her gift slowly. Her parents brace for the worst.

"Surprise!" shouts Grandpa Harvey as Hailee discovers a brand-new pocket knife and mace spray kit. "For self-defense," he points out.

"That's not bad!" comments Stuart.

"Not *too* bad," whispers Kate.

"This way you won't get kidnapped like your brother. Anyone want more meatloaf?"

But Kate has gone very pale, and everyone has definitely had enough—meatloaf and all.

"Why did you guys accept his invite in the first place?" Hailee yells at her parents from the back seat of the car.

"Give him a break. He has a good heart," says Stuart.

"Just not a very sound brain," adds Kate. "I feel bad having him all alone in that tiny house."

"How could you even think that going there would be a good idea, especially without Archibald?" asks Hailee.

"Look, we all miss Arch very much," assures Stuart. "But we have to keep our spirits up, and that means living as much of a normal life as possible. Tonight was exactly about that: focusing on something else just for one evening."

"Oh, that was the point? That definitely worked, Dad!" Hailee reacts sarcastically.

Thankfully, Grandpa Harvey doesn't live too far—for the sake of everyone in the car. They are back home in fifteen minutes. They were away for less than two hours total, but it felt like eight. They are drained. Kate and Hailee head to the front door while Stuart looks for something behind one of the two winged lions guarding the entrance. From an empty flowerpot, digging through a few dead leaves, he draws out the famous ring of keys Bartholomeo carried around everywhere.

"We really have to change the locks. I mean, look at the size of this thing! We can't even take our house keys with us; it's ridiculous! Can you imagine me going to the office with this?" he says, posing with the huge, cumbersome set of skeleton keys.

"Or maybe you could do the opposite," Kate says, "and get matching keys for the car?"

"My chariot, you mean?"

Kate and Stuart share a laugh and even manage to crack a faint smile on Hailee's face.

"I don't even know what some of these open," he says, "especially these four small ones. I've tried everything."

As soon as he enters, Stuart knows there's a problem. Something seems stuck between the door and the tiled floor. It sounds like gravel. Stuart turns the lights on and sees that a marble goddess statue has fallen off its pedestal and is now strewn in pieces all over the foyer.

"Careful where you step," he warns.

"What happened?" asks Kate.

"The statue fell down."

It's more than the statue, though. Kate pushes the door wide open, revealing the full extent of the damage. Jackets and rain boots seem to have flown out of the coat closet and landed on the stairs nearby. The rugs are folded in half. Each drawer lining the side of the staircase is open, its contents scattered around and mixed with the debris from two other sculptures smashed on the floor.

"Maybe an animal snuck in?" wonders Stuart.

"And went through the drawers?" snaps Hailee.

"Maybe it was that thunder again—the same thing that happened the night Archie disappeared. Maybe he was right. Maybe this house is haunted," Kate whispers.

"Guys, I'm no Sherlock Holmes, but this was no thunder," says Hailee, pointing at dirty shoe prints on the steps and on the rugs.

"Burglars!" says Stuart, making Kate jump. "Maybe they're still here! We have to call the police."

Stuart pushes everyone outside. The only one not in a panic is Hailee. It's as though she knows who was behind this and what they were looking for.

Perhaps because of what happened to Archibald less than two weeks ago, no less than three police cars are dispatched to the Finch residence. Wearing fluorescent yellow jackets, their guns drawn, it takes eight officers nearly an hour to clear all fifty-six rooms of the house. Two things for sure: based on the footprints, there were at least two burglars, big guys with large shoe sizes, and they came in from the back by breaking a window in the kitchen.

Since the police didn't find anyone, Kate and Stuart can now go through the house to assess the damage. It's even worse than they feared. The library has been completely ransacked. Only a few books are left standing upright on the shelves. The rest are on the floor. Same thing in the kitchen and the pantry, where everything has been taken out of the cupboards. In the living room, Celestine's old china has not been spared. The cabinet it was in has been knocked down. Even the Christmas tree is lying on its side. Surprisingly, though, nothing seems to be missing.

"You're sure they didn't take anything?" asks one of the police officers. Twice.

"We still have a few things to check, but, no, I don't think they

183

did," answers Stuart.

"Some paintings, perhaps?" inquires the officer, pointing at the two empty spots on the wall in the staircase.

"No," says Stuart, "those were missing already when we moved in."

"To be honest, Mr. Finch, there are lots of break-ins and burglaries at this time of the year, especially in neighborhoods like this one. However, something here is rather unusual."

"What do you mean?" asks Kate, who just joined the conversation.

"Well, you have many valuable possessions in this house. Why would they break all those things instead of stealing them?"

"I have no idea," says Kate.

"Could this be some kind of revenge? Family or work related, perhaps?" continues the officer, taking notes.

"No," answers Stuart right away. "I mean, we've had issues with people at work, but nobody we know would do something like this."

"There's just one other possibility, then, I guess," says the officer, closing his notepad. "Based on the evidence I see here tonight, I believe that whoever those people were, they were looking for something very specific."

"For what?" asks Stuart.

"Well, *that* was the question I had for you, Mr. Finch."

Stuart shakes his head in dismay.

"Any visitors in the past few weeks who might have seemed suspicious?"

"I don't think so. Why?"

"You see, Mr. Finch, skilled burglars usually like to scout the premises before committing their misdeeds. So they come to your house first under the pretext of, let's say, offering their services to renovate your house, for example. Of course, it's a ploy to identify what they're interested in stealing."

"No, no one like that," confirms Stuart.

"There was that priest who came over yesterday," says Kate, "but I can't imagine—"

"A priest?" asks the officer.

"Yes, from the local church. He wanted to know if he could help with our son's disappearance."

"Yes, I'm aware. I'm sorry about that, Madam. Did that priest give you his name?"

"Heinrich. Yes, Mr. Heinrich, I believe it was," says Kate.

"A robber masquerading as a priest. That would be new, but you never know," says the policeman.

"He was a very nice man," assures Kate.

Upstairs, Hailee discovers her room has been vandalized as well. It's the second time in a short period that her bedroom suffers heavily due to some dramatic event. Even though she has no doubt Mr. Heinrich is behind this, Hailee can't make any sense of it.

"I have to tell the police," she mutters.

She wants to run downstairs, tell the officers everything she knows. *But what if that mysterious priest is also keeping Archibald captive?* she wonders. She has never experienced such a dilemma before. In her mind, it's a question of life or death—for Archibald, of course.

She has to make a decision fast, since she hears the officers getting ready to leave. She heads toward the stairs, when her phone suddenly rings. An unknown number is blinking on the screen. She swallows, afraid of whom it may be. Mr. Heinrich himself, perhaps? She gathers all the courage she has left in one deep breath and answers.

"Hailee?" says the familiar voice.

She relaxes her whole body in a sigh of relief, recognizing the voice right away.

"Oliver! I'm so glad; I've been waiting to hear from you."

"I'm sorry; I wanted to call you earlier."

"No worries. Listen, something happened. My house—some burglars. I think they were looking for the globe."

"What? Are you sure? Maybe they just wanted to steal stuff. There are tons of break-ins right now."

"No, listen, they didn't take anything. I have no doubt. It's that priest. That's why I gave you the globe. I knew he'd come for it."

"Hailee, this is crazy!"

"I know how it sounds—trust me. It's like one of those gangster stories from my grandpa's DVD."

"From what?"

"Never mind. Look, I don't know what it is about that globe, but there has to be something special about it to explain all this."

"I'm not sure," says Oliver, "but I think I found something."

"You did?"

"It's just weird. I have to show you. When can you meet me?"

"The police are here right now, so it's probably not the best time. What about tomorrow?"

"We should meet in a public place, with lots of people around."

"Good idea. Where?"

"St James's Park, by the blue bridge—you know where that is?"

"I'll find it. What time?"

"Noon?"

"Okay, see you there. And Oliver, be careful—who knows what that priest is capable of."

"Don't worry," he says before hanging up.

Of course, Hailee barely sleeps again, especially with her room now in shambles. She doesn't even bother putting her mattress back on the bedframe. She tosses and turns all night and wakes on the floor, groggy and full of sore muscles. She slept late but is up in time for her meeting with Oliver. In fact, she is starting to worry. It is now half past twelve, and Oliver is still a no-show.

It was easy for her to find the blue bridge. Not only is it the only bridge in St James's Park but it's, well, blue. The view of Buckingham Palace from here is just enchanting. For a second, Hailee imagines the green slime on the lake to be floating lilies as painted by Monet in the *Nymphéas*. She dreams of different circumstances in which this could be a normal date. But nothing is normal anymore, as she is reminded when Oliver arrives pale and out of breath.

"What happened?"

"Maybe I'm paranoid, but I think I was followed."

"All the way here?"

"No, I'm pretty sure I lost them. I stopped by my dad's shop earlier. It's a mess; someone went through it also."

"The globe!" reacts Hailee.

"Don't worry; they didn't find the secret room. I left the globe in there. Still no trace of my dad, though."

"I'm sorry; your mum must be so worried."

Oliver chuckles. "I've not seen my mother in a long time. To be honest, I barely remember her. She left us when I was two," he says, looking down.

"Where do you live, then? You're on your own?"

"Look, my mother is long gone; my dad is a drunk; I have not been in school in three years; I have pretty much always been on my own," says Oliver, giving Hailee a forced smile. "Now, you want to hear what I found?"

"Yes, please."

"Don't get too excited. This might be nothing."

"Tell me."

"Okay, this is it," he says, opening a binder with plastic sleeves containing a bunch of brownish old documents.

"Newspapers?" questions Hailee.

"Kind of . . . not really. This is one of the first tabloids ever printed. There are only a few copies left. I saw these years ago at the shop, but I thought of them only yesterday."

"A tabloid?" asks Hailee. "I don't understand. What does it have to do with that globe or my brother?"

"Look at the date. It's from 1519. Guess what people cared about in 1519? The same stuff that captivates them today—what rich folks are doing with their money and who dates whom. Back then, of course, there were no movie stars, no reality TV. The celebrities were the kings, queens, and princes. That's why the name of the tabloid was *Crowns*, see? Not sure if you can read this; it's in Old English and with that funky old-fashioned font."

"Wait, I thought you found out something about the globe?" says Hailee, looking confused.

"I did," says Oliver, taking one of the paper clippings delicately out of its sleeve. "Look—this is the interesting part. Like in any tabloid today, there's always some crazy story somewhere, something completely made up or hard to believe, right?"

"Right. Like the guy who married his vacuum or the woman who got abducted by aliens."

"Or that kid who got absorbed into a globe."

"Please don't make fun of that."

"I'm not," he says, opening the old tabloid to the last page. "In January of 1519," explains Oliver, "the crazy story of the month *was* about a globe. Look at the title."

"I can't really read that; what does it say?"

"'Tavern owner claims globe stole customers and best

shanker'—his best bartender, basically," translates Oliver.

"Is this a joke?"

"You tell me. The story says that the tavern owner saw, with his own eyes, I quote, eleven young girls being sucked up into a terrestrial globe, along with his shanker sleeping under the table. The story doesn't say why the shanker, who goes by the name of Wymer, was sleeping under the table."

"Does it say what happened to the globe?" asks Hailee, now starting to understand the point of this demonstration.

Oliver starts reading again: "According to the tavern owner, a mysterious woman arrived a few minutes after the incident and took the globe with her."

"This sounds completely made up!"

"Is that why you didn't want to share your story with anyone? You were afraid they'd think you made it up?"

"You're right," admits Hailee. "But, I mean, the guy owned a tavern—a bar, right? Don't you think he was just completely drunk and hallucinating?"

"Maybe, except there's one detail in here that tells me he didn't lie. It's right here," says Oliver, pointing at the middle of the article. "The tavern owner said that right before the young girls and his helper disappeared, he saw, and I'm quoting again, a tremendous flash of light, as bright as the sun, followed by a loud bang that sounded like thunder. Remind you of something?"

Hailee is speechless. The drawing in the article features that bright light coming out of a globe and radiating toward a group of girls standing in a circle around it.

"Don't get me wrong," adds Oliver. "If you hadn't told me about your brother, I'd never have taken this story seriously."

"What about now?"

"If I believe you, then I don't have a choice—I have to believe this story. And I do want to believe you."

"You think it's the same globe?"

"Possibly—this story is from 1519, four years later than the date carved on your globe."

"This is unbelievable."

"Wait," says Oliver, suddenly grabbing Hailee's arm.

"What's wrong?"

"I thought I just saw that guy," he says, trying to see through the clutter of tourists cramming the blue bridge. "Heinrich!" he shouts in the same breath.

Hailee wheels around in fear, seeing Mr. Heinrich's face clearly for the first time. He is standing at the opposite end of the bridge, his hands in his coat pockets, looking at her with a smirk on his face.

"That's him?" whispers Hailee.

Mr. Heinrich's bodyguards are already running toward them, pushing people aside bluntly.

"Let's go!" says Oliver, pulling Hailee by the cuff of her jacket, leaving the newspaper clippings behind.

They also have to make their way through dozens of people strolling the narrow paths of the park. One of their two huge pursuers has collided with the bridge guardrail and fallen into the water. But the other one, Crazy Boris, is scrambling after them.

"Stop that kid!" he keeps shouting. "He took my wallet!"

Hailee has taken the lead. Constantly looking back to check on the second henchman, Oliver doesn't see the baby stroller standing in his way. He trips over it and falls to the ground. Boris yanks him by the collar.

"You're not going nowhere!" he says with a croaky voice, dragging Oliver toward Mr. Heinrich.

"Let go of me!" screams Oliver.

"Quit jiggling or I'll break your neck."

"Oliver!" shouts Hailee, turning around to help him.

She grabs Oliver's arm and tries pulling him the other way—but she is no match against that three-hundred-pound gorilla.

Then it hits her. She remembers that gift from Grandpa Harvey. Her gut feeling told her to put the can of mace in her pocket this morning before leaving the house. She pulls it out and sprays Boris's face profusely, forcing him to let go of Oliver with a painful scream.

Hailee and Oliver run away and soon break free from the clusters of people.

"Thank you, that was amazing!" says Oliver.

"Thanks, Grandpa," she mutters.

HOW TO TAME A MARODOR

For the first time, Archibald wakes up in Gristlemoth knowing this is not a dream—although yesterday felt like a nightmare—knowing where he is—more or less—and not wanting to leave—not really. His loud yawn slowly mixes with a whining howl from Paws, the loyal and apparently comfortable pet garbage mound he slept on all night.

Archibald has not quite recovered from his encounter with the Krakatorum Gargantus. His neck is stiff, and the burn marks on his face and hands have turned into black freckles, big and small. Not to mention the smell of carbonized hair he carries around with him. At the same time, he doesn't mind those war wounds. They are much more meaningful than any medal he could have gotten and definitely something to brag about when he goes back to Cuffley.

HOW TO TAME A MARODOR

Going through Gristlemoth, he seems to be walking a little taller today. He truly feels like the knight of the village. No one is going to slap him behind the head here. He might be called a liripoop from time to time, but it's not that bad, and it still sounds better than "dweeb." Everywhere he goes, girls wave and smile at him. One of them has just rushed up to him to pin a flower onto his chest. *Wait, this might be a dream after all.*

He passes Wymer's house. The garage door is open. Only his Hérisson is there—or what's left of it, to be more precise. A few blocks down near the village entrance, a well-organized team effort is at work to fix a hut damaged by the Marodor. Burned-out beams are taken away while a newly carved double-headed owl is heaved onto the roof—all by means of golems, of course. No trace of Wymer around, though. Archibald finds him minutes later by the Marodors' pen. He is building a new cage for the Krakatorum. The existing ones were just not big enough for that Gargantus, levitating nearby for now. The new one is dramatically larger and reinforced in each corner with nails as big as heron beaks.

Proud of his contribution in capturing the colossal Marodor, Archibald can't help but also feel terrible for the beast. Its long necks are now hanging down like deflated balloons, with all four of its partially human faces seemingly fighting for the saddest face award.

Soon the Krakatorum's wails will get lost among those rising from other cages. One in particular catches Archibald's ear. It almost sounds like "Heeelp"—a long, painful, drawn-out call for help. As far as he knows, though, Marodors don't talk.

Is this like looking at clouds? he wonders, when one can pretty much make any shape or form out of those constantly morphing cotton balls. No, the sound echoes again.

"Heeelp," says the distant cry.

Archibald sets out to pinpoint it.

After a few detours, backtracking and zigzagging through the woods, he finally finds the source of that peculiar plaint. It's coming from Parnel's cage, or so he thinks, since she is now silent.

"Did you call for help?" he asks her.

Lying on the ground, she is contorting her body to try to stand up, obviously in pain.

"It's your arms, isn't it?"

Archibald gets closer to the cage. Parnel is just staring at him.

"Do you need help?" he whispers, getting even closer.

194

The next moment, Parnel throws herself at the cage, scaring Archibald so much he is knocked off his feet. She crawls back to the shadows, moaning louder now that she's probably hurt her arms further.

"I get it; you're mad," he tells her. "But I know you need help, and I'm going to give it to you, whether you want it or not!"

↑
Ν

Archibald hurries off to the Hive, to the golem workshop. Maven is there, still bragging about defeating the Krakatorum single-handedly. He takes her aside.

"I have a question for you."

"Sure," she shrugs.

"You told me you fixed Rhiannon's leg, right?"

"I did."

"How did you do it?"

"You didn't seem to care about it yesterday."

"I know; I'm sorry. I really want to know, though."

"Okay, let me show you, then," she says, taking him to a shelf where she keeps her personal golem collection.

"How many do you need?" asks Archibald.

"It's not about how many; it's about choosing the right ones!" corrects Maven.

"Okay, so which ones, then?"

"Well, it's also about how many," Maven adds, making Archibald's head spin. "When it comes to golems, you need a minimum of two. Three is definitely the magic number, but, personally, I always like to add one extra."

"I'm sorry, but we're talking about eggs or golems?" asks Archibald, semiserious.

"What? Golems, of course!" answers Maven, annoyed. "See, for Rhiannon's leg, I used Aequae ≈ as a base, then Mallemendia ✝, to facilitate healing. I love this one. It's my favorite rune."

"I thought the one with the pyramid was your favorite rune."

"Yeah, that one too. Anyway, then I picked Durare ♭, for stronger bones."

"The angry B," notes Archibald.

"Is that what you call it? You're right; it kind of looks mean. It *is* a tough one, mostly known for its hardening power. It would have worked fine, but I wanted her leg to heal fast, so I added Fulguris ⋨, to speed up the whole process."

"You talk about it like it's a recipe," says Archibald, amazed.

"Because it is. You need all the right ingredients from A to Z, starting with the right herbs, by the way."

Archibald laughs.

"I'm serious," says Maven, with a straight face.

"How does it work?"

"I just told you!"

"No, I mean the spell. How do you *activate* those powers?"

"That's the easy part. Once you have all your golems lined up, you just speak their names one after another, then you pronounce the key word."

"The magic word, you mean?"

"If you want to call it that, yes."

"I knew there was a magic word! So what is it?"

"Malenvoli. The only time you don't need it is in the tank. The cannons activate the golems directly."

"So that's it? Just the names of the golems plus the magic word?"

"Yes," confirms Maven, "and the golems will just do exactly what they've been told."

Archibald leans in close to Maven.

"Can I borrow these?" he whispers.

"For what?"

"I can't tell you, but it's for someone who needs help."

Maven hesitates. "Just have your friend come over and I'll take care of her."

"No, she can't walk; she's in really bad shape."

"Who is it? I didn't know anyone else got hurt."

"I can't really say—I'm sorry."

Maven hesitates again. "Okay," she finally says. "On one condition . . ."

"Anything you want."

It's her turn to whisper. "You have to take me with you!" she says, all excited.

"I can't; my friend is very shy."

"No, not to your friend. When you go back, you know, up there," she says, glancing up.

Archibald is embarrassed since he has no clue how, when, or even if he'll go back home.

"Okay," he finally says, without *really* lying.

Maven exults and gives him a hug.

"One more thing," says Archibald, "you'll need to write down the names of the golems for me. They're too complicated!"

"Only from great effort comes great power," says the golem master. Hard to understand for a boy whose motto has always been "Why do today what you can put off until tomorrow?"

"You know what would be easy?" he says. "Give each golem a number and replace Malenvoli with something punchier, like *boom*, for more impact. So when you read your spell, you can just say one, twelve, twenty-three, and 'boom,' instead of all that mumbo jumbo."

"That's a good idea; I'll think about it."

"Really?" he asks, proud of his find.

"Of course not!" she says, roaring with laughter.

"That's not funny," he scowls.

"What do you think? That we just made those names up? The runes get their names from plants. Don't you remember when I talked to that tree?"

He nods dismissively.

"When we spell out each formula, we do nothing more than call upon those plants to wake up the golems," she explains.

Archibald doesn't seem convinced. "Still way too complicated if you ask my opinion."

"Good, 'cause no one's asking!"

Archibald is experiencing something entirely new. He has never been this excited for anyone but himself. Just a few days ago, this kind of feeling would have been so foreign and so counter to his nature.

Parnel seems asleep when he gets back to her. He tries not to make any noise and places the four golems around her cage. Time to read the formula Maven gave him. He unfolds the piece of paper but can barely understand a word of it. As if this exercise was not complicated enough! Now he has to try to decrypt Maven's writing, made of intricate cursive letters as curvy and beautiful as they are gobbledygook to Archibald.

"Who writes like this?" he fumes, giving it a try. "Malle . . . media, Ful . . . guri, Aquea, Durera?" he says aloud, stumbling over nearly every syllable. And then in a more solemn tone, the magic word, "Malenvoli!"

Archibald waits a good half minute for the golems to light up, but nothing happens. He taps on one of them—still nothing.

Not even a spark. Maybe he made a mistake (four, in fact).

His eyes back on Maven's notes, Archibald tries again, this time more carefully:

"Mallemendia, Fulguris, Aequae, Durare . . . Malenvoli!"

The golems light up almost instantly.

"Yes!" he exults.

Parnel wakes up in a jolt. Her body starts jerking, as if hit by internal spasms.

"What did I do?" mumbles Archibald, worried.

Suddenly, the convulsions stop. Parnel collapses to the ground.

"I killed her," gasps Archibald.

Maybe he misspelled the spell and triggered a completely different outcome, but Parnel's eyes soon reopen. A few more seconds and she springs back up, now standing firmly on her arms.

"I did it! We did it!" shouts Archibald, trying to get a closer look at Parnel's arms. But, again, she rushes toward him and crashes against the cage, hissing some more.

Archibald is back on the ground. "Are you a pincher bug or a cat? I guess it will take a little more than fixing your arms."

♫

The morning after, Archibald pays a visit to Wymer. They are both sitting on the ground in his garage. Gristlemoth's number one—and only—handyman has a daunting task standing in front of him. Not quite standing, actually, since his tank has been reduced to a heap of splinters.

"How can I put this back together? It's like an impossible puzzle," complains Wymer. "I'm a repair guy, not a magician!"

"Why don't you ask Faerydae for some magic, then? Isn't there something she can do with golems?" suggests Archibald.

"No, unfortunately, this is pure engineering. Golems might be able to fix a leaky roof, but this tank is like the gout in my foot—too many moving parts. It'd be easier to build a new one!" he notes.

"A new foot?"

"I wish!" says Wymer, laughing.

"You know, if one day you do build a new tank, maybe you can tweak the design a bit."

"Oh yeah? Tweak it how?" asks Wymer, skeptical.

Archibald starts drawing something in the ground with his finger. "It's just an idea, but, see, instead of having cannons all around the tank, you could have just one bigger cannon, which means bigger golems and more power."

"Nice try, but that would never work. You could fire in only one direction," comments Wymer, shaking his head.

"Not if you put that cannon on a rotating tower. That way you could still fire from any angle, but with only one cannon to worry about and reload."

Archibald has essentially drawn a modern tank, similar to the ones you could find on battlefields nowadays. Wymer is looking at the rough sketch, scratching his head, quite impressed.

"Not bad, kid!" he exclaims. "See, that's what happens when you eat your vegetables!"

"Yuk!" objects Archibald.

"Are you hungry, by the way?"

"Not for veggies. I miss ice cream," he says, salivating.

"None of that here—sorry, son."

"I can't believe you guys don't use sugar. That's the best stuff," he laments.

"Nope, though we could get it from beets," notes Wymer.

"What do you mean?"

"Beets. You know beets?"

"Of course I know beets—I hate them. They taste like radish, celery, and eggplant mixed together: disgusting!" says Archibald, wrinkling his nose.

"Sounds like a nice stew to me. And, yes, there *is* sugar in beets; you just have to extract it. After all, we use black treacle in flummadiddle—that's sugar, kind of."

"There's sugar in flummadiddle? That thing does not taste like sugar!"

Wymer gives up. Even his broken tank is not as much of a headache.

"Go ask Naida; she'll tell you all about it."

Sugar from beets? For Archibald, that just doesn't sound right, but he still wants to get to the bottom of it.

Five minutes later, he shows up in Naida's garden. There she is, that criminal, planting more carrots.

"Don't you think we have enough of those?" he asks her.

"Carrots are so good for you!"

"What about beets?"

"They're great, too, and even better when cooked together with carrots."

Archibald's gag reflex takes over. "Is it true you can get sugar from beets?"

"Black treacle. You know, molasses? We put that in—"

"Flummadiddle, I know. But I'm talking about real sugar, you know, the good stuff."

"You don't need that; it's bad for you."

"It's *not* bad, and it's not for me. I mean, I'm not going to lie; I will probably eat some, too, but it's for someone else."

"Who's that?"

Archibald is not sure he wants to tell her. "Parnel," he finally admits.

Naida shakes her head and chuckles. "What? Are you all here?"

"What's that supposed to mean?"

"That maybe you left some brains behind in that battle! Marodors don't eat."

"Well, they have a mouth, don't they?"

"To spit fire, not to eat! Don't you think we thought about that? Trust me—we've tried everything: bell peppers, carrots, brussels sprouts, celery . . ."

It takes a lot of self-control for Archibald not to throw up, and Naida is not even done yet.

". . . cauliflower, asparagus, eggplants. I'm telling you: we tried e-ver-y-thing," she says. "Guess what? They didn't want any of it!"

"Shocker! Of course they didn't—I wouldn't want it either!" says Archibald. "And you're wrong; Marodors do eat."

"Oh yeah? So what do they eat, then?"

"Candy bars! I dropped one on the ground when that wingy whatever you call it beast was chasing me, and it ate the whole thing—I'm telling you."

"I doubt it, but, go ahead, feed 'em your . . . candy bars."

"That's the problem; I ran out."

"I'm sorry, but we don't grow those around here."

"But you know how to make sugar!"

"I guess," she admits.

"Can you show me?"

Naida thinks about it for a minute. "Okay, but only if you—"

"If I what?" he asks, even though he has a pretty good idea . . .

"If you go back up there, you have to take me with you," she whispers.

"Who told you?" he asks, though, again, he could easily guess.

"Maven. She told me about your globe."

Archibald sighs. He really doesn't want to lie—too much.

"Okay, I'll take you with me, but I'm not sure I *can* go back."

Naida smiles really big and gives him a long hug, then runs to another aisle to get some beets. She has so much energy suddenly that she pulls five large ones out of the ground in no time.

"They grow in the dirt?" says Archibald, stunned, with that familiar look of disgust back on his face.

"Of course—they're roots," says Naida.

"No wonder why they're so gross. They're like carrots."

"Once we cook them, they won't be that bad," assures Naida. She leads Archibald to Wymer's kitchen, which has four huge baskets of carrots ready to be peeled, chopped, and roasted for tonight's supper.

"What is wrong with you people? You'll all turn orange soon!" he warns.

"Take a seat—this might take awhile," says Naida. "Ready, Karla?" she asks the small cauldron sitting on the table.

"I just need a few minutes to warm up," says Karla with a yawn, obviously waking up from another nap.

Archibald never would have imagined it was so complicated to make sugar. Naida spends hours preparing the beets, cooking them, extracting their liquid through a cloth, and spreading the precious nectar on a baking tray. When she's finally done, Archibald has fallen asleep.

"Voilà!" says Naida, awakening his senses with a striped bar she has placed on a knotty birch twig.

She obviously had fun shaping this improvised lollipop in the likeness of Marodors, with multiple horns and big eyes made of raw beet. To Archibald, who has not had sugar in so long—a record five days—this honey-colored candy looks like pure gold. All it takes is one bite to trigger a meltdown with a cascading effect, starting with his eyelids, followed by his mouth, his shoulders, his belly, and all the way down to his knees, which buckle in pleasure.

"How could you live without this?" he asks Naida.

"Is it that good?"

"It is," says Karla, her handles still shivering.

"You have to try it. Did you make enough for another one?"

"I think so," she says, unveiling a tray with enough caramelized beet sugar to make a hundred more lollipops.

"I must be dreaming," says Archibald, on the verge of tears.

He places a few pieces of Naida's creation in a towel before heading out. By the time he reaches Parnel's cage, the towel is 80 percent empty, 20 percent crumbs.

"Oopsh!" he says, his mouth full.

He throws three surviving chunks inside the enclosure, near the dark corner where Parnel likes to hide. Her reaction is swift and very frog-like for an earwig Marodor. The initial sniffling quickly gives way to a frog-like leap toward the syrupy candy, which disappears in one frog-like gulp, followed by a no less frog-like burp.

But what matters most to Archibald is the purr she soon produces—the very same purr the first Marodor made when eating the Yorkie from his desk.

"Better than turnips, isn't it?" asks Archibald.

Unsurprisingly, Parnel retreats back into her favorite corner in no time. The purring doesn't subside.

"You're part cat, aren't you?" says Archibald. "You were hissing at me, and now you're purring. That's progress."

Archibald is now known in the village to spend most of his time in the Marodors' pen.

"Have you seen Archibald?" Faerydae keeps asking. She's not too worried, though. As far as she's concerned, he is busy drawing Marodors—the Krakatorum, in particular—making the *Grand Bestiary* slightly less incomplete. Besides, he still shows up every evening for dinner, though for some reason he's never that hungry anymore.

On most days, Archibald just devotes long hours to feeding Parnel and entertaining her. He loves to lie down by her cage, reading her a book he found at the Hive: *The Facetious Nights of Straparola*, a collection of fairy tales, some very strange, some fun, some scary.

"Which story do you prefer?" he asks Parnel. "The one about the Pig-King or the one about the living doll?"

Archibald is not sure Parnel can understand a word he is saying, but he doesn't mind. She has not tried to attack him in a while—that's progress! Archibald also noticed something curious: her eyes are not as glaring as they used to be. The red has dimmed down to a pale pinkish color. Maybe it has to do with all the beet sugar he's been sharing with her. Or maybe it's thanks to the jar of fireflies he opened near her cage two days ago. They've been fluttering around her since and seem to have a calming effect.

"Maybe they'll heal you, like they did with Willow," he whispers.

Today, Archibald has brought a guitar he borrowed—not stole—from Rhiannon's friend. It's not really a guitar. It ends in a strange bend resembling a crane's neck. They call it a lute. To Archibald, it doesn't make much difference. A lute or a guitar, it's all the same to him since he doesn't know how to play either one of them, anyway. He just likes to brush his hand against the cords and see Parnel react to a particular note. Each time, the expression on her face changes slightly, her neck moving up, left, or right, depending on the melody.

"Are you dancing?" asks Archibald, not expecting an answer, just enjoying the moment.

The sun is out but can't quite reach Parnel, due to the bundles of wood stacked on her cage. *If only I could move those a little*, thinks Archibald.

He leaves for a few minutes and comes back with a ladder under his arm. Wymer agreed to give it to him, wondering what he could need it for. Archibald refused to say, well aware that the foliage was placed on all the cages for a specific purpose, as a secondary shield, besides the natural umbrella of trees above, to keep the Marodors as restrained as possible, in the dark.

He sets the ladder against the cage. "You won't jump on me, will you?" he asks Parnel.

Even though she's been more peaceful lately, he knows she is still highly unpredictable. Faerydae's words are echoing in his head: "They might look human, but they're mostly animals."

Archibald has made up his mind. He shall *not* heed

Faerydae's warning. He starts up the ladder. Parnel does react, but she seems more scared than anything. Reaching the top of the cage, Archibald pushes some branches aside, allowing in some light, but not nearly enough. He decides to step on the cage itself, hopping from one wood beam to another, trying to avoid the gaps in between, his arms up like a tightrope walker.

He stops suddenly, standing right above Parnel.

What am I doing? What was I thinking? The worst fear has just settled on him. He realizes that, at any time, Parnel could jump up and catch one of his legs. Or both at once! He is sweating even more than the day William Tanner held him upside down by his underwear in the gym locker room—and that was a big sweat.

It is the peace on Parnel's face that eventually calms Archibald and encourages him to keep going. He removes more branches from the roof of her cage, creating a well of sunlight that reaches the edges of her body.

After initially folding up into a ball and covering her head, Parnel extends her neck to fully enjoy the rays of sunshine. Archibald is in awe. He gets ready to come back down, when his foot slips off the edge of the cage. He loses his balance and falls backward, letting out a shriek. His whole life flashes before his eyes. An impressive eleven years of snapshots condensed in one quick slideshow: images of his mum, his dad, Hailee (very, very briefly), that cute cat he saw at the pound—and ice cream.

The cage must be twelve feet in height. Archibald is on his way to break his neck for sure. Maybe worse. He cringes, bracing for impact. For some reason, though, this fall is taking much longer than he expected.

Maybe I already hit the ground and died instantly? he wonders.

Archibald opens his eyes, to realize he is lying in Parnel's arms—those arms he healed for her. She passed them through the cage and caught him right before he hit the ground. They are now staring at each other.

"Faerydae!" Archibald tries to scream, letting out nothing but a squeaky chirp. His tongue has dried up like a giant prune tasting of rubber. Sweat is pouring off him from head to toe. Parnel seems to be probing him, the same way a predator would before devouring its prey. Based on what he knows, Marodors don't eat humans, but Archibald has been eating so much candy since he was born that half his body must be made of sugar by now—so who knows!

"You're not going to hurt me, are you?" he asks.

What if she does? What if this is the final embrace—that hug of death Faerydae told him about?

In the village, no one could suspect what had just happened. All the girls are busy doing what they normally do: gardening, planting, schooling, carving, polishing, and witching around.

Rhiannon is talking to Wymer about ways to improve the Hérisson. The master builder is just nodding, stroking his beard. Suddenly, his eyes get bigger, and bigger, and bigger!

"Are you okay, Wymer?" asks Rhiannon.

"Ma-ma, Ma-ma—" he mumbles.

"What? Are you calling for your mother?"

"Ma-mmm . . . Marodor!" he finally blurts out.

"What are you talking about?"

Wymer points at something coming from the east, on the edge of the village. It's Parnel, standing in between two cabanas.

"Marodor on the loose!" screams Rhiannon, sowing panic throughout Gristlemoth.

Archibald is nowhere to be seen. What happened to him is a mystery. Did he get overly optimistic thinking Parnel could be tamed? More importantly, what did she do to him?

When Faerydae shows up, she can't believe her eyes.

"To your golems!" she shouts, as most people seem to be looking for shelter.

"I'll fetch some cannons just in case," says Wymer before running away, perhaps back to his pit.

Parnel seems headed straight for Faerydae. Surprisingly, though, she doesn't show any sign of anger, the way other Marodors would if they escaped from their cage. Faerydae was not born yesterday, though—definitely not. She knows looks can be deceiving. As the saying goes, don't judge a book by its cover, especially in Gristlemoth, where all book covers are essentially identical—brownish or grayish, worn, rubbed, with no title and *for sure* no pictures.

A few hearts have paused. Maven has just handed Faerydae two powerful golems that will stop Parnel in her tracks if need be. Far from flinching, Faerydae starts walking toward her former best friend, ready to confront her.

Parnel stops suddenly. She slowly turns her neck around, looking at something behind her.

"Maybe another one escaped?" murmurs Faerydae.

"Let's hope not," replies Maven, knowing such a scenario would probably mean the end of Gristlemoth.

Instead of a Marodor, something else steps out of Parnel's shadow—Archibald, drawing the loudest gasp among the girls surrounding Faerydae.

"What the heck!" says Wymer as he hurries back, straining under the weight of a cannon.

To make it perfectly clear to everyone that Parnel is not a danger anymore, Archibald places his hand on her arm. She is blinking gently, her eyes now fully back to normal—green, deep, sweet, beautiful.

Faerydae drops her golems and approaches them.

"Hello, Faerydae," says Parnel in the tenderest of voices. "I've missed you."

MALLEUS MALEFICARUM

Hailee and Oliver have not stopped running since they escaped Crazy Boris in St James's Park. In fact, they look poised to never stop, not until they reach a sea or an ocean, at least. As they round the next corner, Oliver grabs onto a lamppost for support, stooping to catch his breath.

"You think we're far enough?" asks Hailee, panting as well.

"I'm not sure, but this is it—this is my place," says Oliver, motioning to the building behind her, an apartment complex twisted like a politician, leaning left at the bottom and veering right at the top.

"Great!" says Hailee, just relieved to have found a hideout.

They look both ways, repeatedly, before stepping inside, still worried Heinrich's henchmen might be around the corner. The building is old, completely rundown, with a strong smell of mildew hanging in the air. It stings Hailee's nostrils as soon as she enters. Caught off guard, she covers her nose with the sleeve of her jacket.

"Sorry—I know it stinks in here. It's mold, among other things," says Oliver. "This place is so ancient. Holes everywhere, it's like a giant colander."

"No worries. What floor are you on?"

"The very top one. Sorry—no elevator."

"It's okay! We ran for over three miles; I think we can manage this," smiles Hailee.

"It's not that. You gotta watch where you step."

What concerns Oliver isn't the arduous climb but all the broken planks leading to his place—not counting the ones rotted due to water leaks. He was right to worry. Hailee trips and falls twice on her way up.

"I'm sorry; this is not quite like your house," he says as they reach the top floor.

"It's okay; the floors at home are not in great shape either. And at least this place's safe, right? I mean, do you think Heinrich could find us here?"

"I doubt it," says Oliver as he unlocks the door. "We moved here just a few months ago. We couldn't pay our rent in the last building. Slightly better than being on the street, but I think that's next," he predicts.

His first priority when they get in is to empty out the five large buckets that have been collecting water from leaks in the ceiling, black with mold. He doesn't look too surprised. This is something he is obviously used to.

"You can always sleep at the store," says Hailee.

"Nah, my dad can't afford the rent there anymore either," he comments. "Now that Heinrich sent his guys to wreck the whole place, I really doubt things are gonna get better."

There are only six pieces of furniture in the room: a carved dining table and two matching chairs, a sofa, a small one-person bed against the opposite wall next to a corner kitchenette, and a desk by the window—all beautiful antiques that stand out like a gold tooth in a pirate's mouth (full of cavities).

"I'm sorry," says Hailee, pausing. "I feel like this is all my fault."

"Why would it be your fault? You didn't force my dad to drink. Oh, wait, did *you* tell my mother to abandon me?"

"You know what I mean."

"Trust me—you have no reason to feel bad about anything.

This disaster started way before you showed up. Do you want a tea or something?" he asks, emptying the last bucket in the tiniest of sinks.

"If you use that water to make it, I can't wait!"

He chuckles.

"I'm okay, thanks," says Hailee, crossing the living area in nine short strides. "Wow, you've got an amazing view," she says, looking out the window.

They are obviously in the suburbs. From here they can see nearly all the way to the center of London.

"That's the only good thing about this place," says Oliver, grabbing towels to soak up water where the buckets have overflowed. "That, and the charm of living under a tin roof, of course. Freezing in winter, boiling in summer. The first five days of April are pretty enjoyable!" he jokes.

Something catches Hailee's attention—a business card in an open folder on the desk.

"Did you see this?"

"What is it?" he asks, still sponging up water.

"A business card."

"Yeah, that's my dad's desk. I usually leave it alone. He hates it when I touch his stuff."

"I think you should have a look at this," she says, showing him the card as he comes closer.

It reads "Jacob Heinrich" and has two phone numbers, one in London, one in New York.

"That's that priest's card," observes Oliver.

"Is that an hourglass?" says Hailee, rubbing her index finger on the symbol embossed on each side of Heinrich's name:

$$\boxtimes \qquad \textbf{Jacob Heinrich} \qquad \boxtimes$$

"I think it's heraldic. Pretty normal stuff. People who are into history and relics love this kind of symbol, like crosses, lions, and all that stuff. I'm actually surprised this guy is not using the swastika!"

"The Nazi symbol, you mean?"

"Exactly. That would fit him better!"

She nods. She couldn't agree more.

"Anything else in there?" asks Oliver.

Hailee pulls out another piece of paper from the folder. "Just a receipt," she says, handing it to him.

"It's from a delivery company. My dad uses them only for expensive stuff. This is for that book he sold Heinrich years ago," he explains.

"Which book?"

"It's written right here. It's just an abbreviation."

Across the receipt are two abstruse words.

"Mal Mal," reads Hailee. "What is that?"

"It stands for *Malleus Maleficarum*. I remember because Heinrich paid a fortune for it. My dad took care of a lot of debt with that money."

"Just the title sounds creepy," says Hailee. "What is it about?"

"It's in Latin. It means *The Hammer of Witches*. I don't know much about it, but I think it's about witch-hunting, you know, Middle Ages stuff."

"Fun guy, that Heinrich!"

"Right? Let's find out who he is. We have his full name now. You wanna search him on your phone?"

"Sure," she says, spelling out each syllable of his name as she types: "Ja-cob Hein-rich."

"Anything?"

"Not really," she says, scrolling down.

"What about 'Father Jacob Heinrich' or 'Jacob Heinrich priest'?

Maybe you should try that."

"Good idea," she says.

Hailee shakes her head. "Nope, nothing. Oh, wait, this is weird. What did you say that book was called?"

"*Malleus Maleficarum.*"

"That's it; there's a link to it right here."

"Really? Under Heinrich's name?"

"No, that's what's weird. It's under Jacob Sprenger. But guess what? He's a priest, one of two priests who wrote that book," says Hailee. "You want to know who the other priest is?"

"Who?"

"According to this, his name is Heinrich Kramer."

"Let me get this right," says Oliver. "The guy who's after us, his name is a combination of those two guys, Jacob Sprenger and Heinrich Kramer? That can't be a coincidence."

"I definitely think Heinrich is a freak. Look at this picture; it's a painting, actually," says Hailee, showing Oliver an image of the two priests/authors side by side. "Not only did he take their names but look at this—it seems he's also trying really hard to look like one of them."

"That's crazy! Kramer looks exactly like Heinrich! Or Heinrich looks like Kramer!"

And indeed he does. Same creepy haircut, same chiseled features, same gaunt, elongated face—and the same dark emptiness in his eyes.

"They could be twin brothers," notes Hailee.

"Does it say anything about a globe in there?"

"I don't think so. You were right, though; that book *is* about witches. It's like a disturbing step-by-step manual telling people how to find them and get rid of them. It sounds like they're talking about rats, but it's actually about people."

"The good old times," jokes Oliver.

"This gets even weirder—it's like those dolls in my grandma's library."

"What are you talking about?"

"When they caught the witches, they shaved their heads."

"Yeah, I've heard that before."

"Listen to this. Shaving a witch was meant to locate a scar or a mark that would provide undeniable proof of her pact with the devil."

"Geez, you'd better not bump your head back then."

"You're not too far off. It seems even a birthmark would qualify," says Hailee. "You want another fun fact?"

"I'm not sure," says Oliver.

"You know Sprenger, the second writer? It says here he was murdered."

"Really? By whom?"

"It doesn't say, but it seems Kramer and Sprenger didn't get along. They were fighting over who actually wrote the book."

"Are you saying Kramer had him killed?"

"I don't know."

"If that's true, then Heinrich has definitely found his mentor in Kramer. A priest, a weirdo, a killer . . . the perfect role model," says Oliver.

"It's interesting, but it doesn't tell us much about Heinrich himself," sighs Hailee.

"Or maybe it tells us everything, and we don't really know how to read it. Sometimes things are right in front of your nose and for some reason, you're just blind to them."

"Are you sure you've not been to school in years?" asks Hailee, half-serious, half-kidding. "I mean, you're smarter than most students in my class. And I'm not just talking about William Tanner."

"You know what I love about da Vinci?"

"A lot, apparently," smiles Hailee.

"He barely had a formal education. He pretty much taught himself everything. And he learned mostly by looking around, by observing nature and people. Nothing better than the school of life. I'm no da Vinci. I'm just street smart, I guess. Too bad they don't have a degree for that," he jokes, now looking at the book receipt again. "Maybe we should try something else. What about this address we have here for Heinrich?"

"What are you thinking?"

"I'm not sure. It's been four years since that book was delivered, but you never know; maybe he still lives there."

"What's the address?" asks Hailee, ready for her next search.

"44 Wilton Place, in Belgravia. Our priest is loaded. That's an expensive neighborhood."

Hailee starts searching. "Okay, directions to, no, find on map, no, for sale nearby, no, let me see . . ." she mumbles.

It starts raining again, as the trickling in the buckets indicates, getting thicker and louder. Oliver moves each of them slightly to better catch the drips.

"Wait!" exclaims Hailee.

"You found something?"

"People are sharing that address on social media."

"For what?"

"They don't say much; they're just talking about an event that's supposed to happen at that address. December 23, 6 p.m."

"Hailee, that's today! That's tonight!" shouts Oliver. "It's in a couple of hours; we can make it. I mean, we have to go, Hailee—what else do we have?"

"I'm not going to that crazy guy's house."

"Do you want to find your brother or not? Something tells me this is your best shot."

"And something tells me this is crazy," she says, showing him something on her phone. "Just look. The people talking about this event, they're saying Master Kramer himself is going to give a grand speech tonight."

"Okay, so they call him Master, big deal. Are you really surprised? I mean, look at the guy. He's probably a cult leader or something."

"You don't understand. They're going to that event to see *Kramer.*"

"So? That's his house, right?"

"No, you're missing the point," she says, frustrated. "That house is supposed to belong to *Heinrich.* Kramer is the guy he looks like from five hundred years ago!"

Oliver looks suddenly as puzzled as she does.

The night has just finished settling upon London, blanketing every rooftop, every wall, every street.

"This is crazy," says Hailee as they walk out of the Tube station.

"But exciting, right?" says Oliver.

He'd obviously managed to convince her to go to that event.

"Actually, *you* are crazy," she corrects. *And exciting*, she admits, keeping that part for herself, though.

Once on Wilton Place, they don't have to wonder long about which one of the large five-story houses is Heinrich's. The traffic is at a complete stop because of a long line of taxicabs dropping off guests at the entrance of a large courtyard. Hailee and Oliver slowly mix with the crowd made up of middle-aged men, mostly. Looking around, Oliver knows that something doesn't add up.

"No tuxedos—not even suits. This is weird," he mutters.

"Why? It's just like people going to church."

"Except this is not a church; this is Belgravia, an island for rich folks, and these are not rich folks. It doesn't make sense." Given the neighborhood, he expected Heinrich's guests to be fancier. These are just regular people, most of them wearing shabby—if not raggedy—clothes. Oliver's father could be among them. In fact, he is!

"Dad?" says Oliver, walking up to his father in line, waiting to squeeze in like the others.

"Oliver! What are you doing here?" says Mr. Doyle, shocked.

"I thought you were dead," says Oliver.

His dad looks terrible, with a shaggy beard, tousled hair, and mud stains on his pants, as if he's been drinking and sleeping outside—which wouldn't be something new.

"You've gotta go, Son."

"Dad, these people destroyed your shop!"

"What are you talking about?"

"The shop, Dad—it's been ransacked."

James Doyle keeps blinking his eyes, speechless, obviously unaware of the break-in.

"I've not been there in a few days. I was . . . busy."

"It's Heinrich, Dad. His guys did it—I know it."

"You don't know nothing! It could have been anyone."

"That guy is crazy. He's been following me."

"Mr. Heinrich is a noble man. He'll help us."

"Dad, no. You've got to trust me."

"Don't go make things worse than you did already," says Mr. Doyle, grabbing his son by the collar. "You gotta go home—now. I'll deal with you later," he says, pushing him away.

Oliver goes back to Hailee.

"What is he doing here?"

"I'm not sure."

"Oh no, not him!" sighs Hailee, spotting one of Heinrich's men posted by the gate, the one she coated with mace—Crazy Boris. "We can't go that way."

"You really thought we'd go through the front door?" smirks Oliver.

"I don't even want to know what that means."

"Follow me," he says, leading her to the house next door.

It's nearly identical to Heinrich's, except there's no guard blocking the entrance. Better yet, the courtyard gate is unlocked. Oliver pushes it open.

"Where are you going?" asks Hailee.

"Trust me," he just says, grabbing her hand.

They go in, heads down like a pair of ostriches, and head straight to the tall wall separating the two properties. Within a second, Oliver disappears into a tree. Hailee tracks his climb through the cracking of branches and the shaking of leaves.

"Oliver?" she whisper-shouts.

"Right here," he says, as he pops up at the top and crests the wall.

She hesitates for a moment but eventually follows him, taking the same improvised path. Oliver extends his hand, pulling her up for the last stretch of the escalade.

They slide down on the other side, hiding behind a hedge of trees. The darkness also helps them reach the side of Heinrich's house without being seen.

"These homes usually have some kind of basement access," mutters Oliver while looking around. "Here," he says, kneeling down to clear ivy from a small window close to the ground. One sharp hit from his elbow and the window snaps open.

"You've done this before, haven't you?"

Oliver heaves a sigh. "How do you think my dad got most of his antiques?"

"You're a robber!" Hailee gasps, covering her mouth to abort a louder reaction.

"I'm not proud of it. That's just the way I was brought up."

Hailee has a doubt suddenly. "The break-in at my house, that wasn't you, was it?"

"Don't be ridiculous; we both know who that was, and that's why we're here. So are you coming or not?"

She shakes her head, speechless.

"Okay, I'm going in. It's up to you," he says, going through the small opening, legs first, soon disappearing.

Hailee looks around and ponders one last time. "Wait for me!" she says all of a sudden, following Oliver down that creepy hole.

Hailee enters the gloom of the basement, where light filters in solely from the narrow windows squinting all around at ceiling level. She lands on a cardboard box, one of many piled up throughout the room.

"Congrats, you're officially a criminal," jokes Oliver.

"It's not funny," she groans. "And what's that smell?" she asks, groaning a bit more.

"The sewage?" he guesses. "Anyway, we gotta find the stairs."

"Over there," she says, pointing to the other side of the room.

Slowly, they wade their way through the mountains of boxes.

"I'd really like to know what's in these," says Oliver.

"I'm sure you would, but we don't have time," says Hailee, stopping suddenly. Something has caught her eye—something shining beneath the staircase.

"Wait, what is that?" she asks, squinting.

"I thought we didn't have time?"

Hailee leaps backward in horror. "Are those *eyes?*" she asks, gesturing toward one of many glass jars crammed onto four tiers of shelving.

Oliver comes closer to give his expert opinion. "Yep. Pigs' eyes," he says, reading from a half-faded yellowish label.

"That's gross!"

"Well, I guess we've found the source of that delicious smell," he says, knocking on the cork top.

"Does it say owls' feet on that one?" asks Hailee, pointing at another jar.

"It sure does. But if you think that's gross, check these out: rabbit brains, rat tails, cockroach juice, tick blood. Not your usual preserves, that's for sure!" he jokes, sorting through a sordid inventory including but not limited to beetle horns, owl legs, raven beaks, bat wings, lizard scales, moth powder, snake skin, spider legs, and toad saliva.

"This is so bizarre. Is Heinrich a priest or a sorcerer?" Hailee wonders, keeping her distance from this wall of horrors.

"What could he possibly do with these? Do you think he eats them?" asks Oliver.

"I think I'm going to be sick," she says, looking a bit like Archibald facing a plate of veggies.

"You never know with rich folks. Always looking for the next big thing," sighs Oliver.

"Whatever this is for, it's a pretty odd thing to have in your basement."

"Yes and no," he argues. "I've met people at the store who collect the weirdest things. You'd be shocked."

"I don't even want to know," she blurts out, walking away.

"Let's just go," says Oliver, starting up the stairs.

Hailee holds her breath as shadows pass beneath the door. Oliver opens it slightly. Through the narrow slit, he can see the main entrance. Some guests are still streaming in, but it seems as though most people have arrived.

He also spots another flight of narrow stairs, probably used by maids, waiters, and the hordes of staff members taking care of this enormous house.

"As soon as I get out, you follow me, okay?" he tells Hailee.

She nods, obviously paralyzed with fear.

The hallway is finally clear. Oliver runs out, then Hailee. They go up the second staircase on their tippy-toes. About halfway up, they freeze.

Someone is coming down.

They have nowhere to go.

Hailee cringes . . .

It's a waiter, carrying a pile of empty trays. "Hey, kids," he says, passing by without a thought.

Hailee and Oliver look at each other and sigh, their eyes wide. They keep climbing and soon reach the second floor. It's crowded. People are lining up at several counters, trading their jackets and scarfs for thick, chocolate-brown coats.

"This is a weird coat check," whispers Oliver. *Why would they want to wear something like that inside?* he wonders.

It's only a matter of time before someone sees the two kids who look quite out of place.

"We can't stay here," Oliver tells Hailee.

The service stairs seem to continue up at least one more floor. They rush forward as fast as they can. The next level is more peaceful. In fact, it seems completely deserted.

Oliver and Hailee advance cautiously, guided by a strange and sinister humming sound. It seems to be coming from the doors lining the hallway on their left. Oliver carefully opens one of them. It leads to a balcony, empty as well, with a view of a grand ballroom packed with people.

The coats guests picked up at the entrance are actually monks' robes with wide hoods resting on their shoulders. Everyone is wearing the same costume, making all of them blend into one another, creating an anonymous, uniform crowd. Standing in tight ranks, dozens at a time but proceeding as one, they each raise a tall candle up in the air, the only source of light in the room.

No shouting, no talking—no thinking—is emanating from this sea of brown, only that constant buzzing, disturbing and chilling.

Facing a large stage with a carved arch and multiple layers of curtains, everyone seems to be gearing up for a show, a one-man-show, obviously.

"This guy has his own theater," murmurs Oliver.

"Look, it's that hourglass logo again," says Hailee, pointing at an emblem detaching from a white circle on long banners hanging from the ceiling—the same emblem they found on Heinrich's card.

"Not quite an hourglass," Oliver notes. "Look closely: it's actually two letters facing each other."

Indeed, Hailee distinguishes a gap in the logo, splitting it vertically in two identical halves.

"Two Ms," she says.

"As in *Malleus Maleficarum*," adds Oliver. "The guy really loves that book."

The stage lights up suddenly. The main curtain is pulled back. Heinrich makes a grand entrance.

The humming stops instantly. A searchlight is tracking Heinrich's every step. He, too, is wearing a monk's robe, but his head is partially uncovered.

"My children," he begins, "I have come back again. I have come to save you!" he says, his voice echoing from speakers throughout the giant ballroom.

"This has been an extremely long and difficult journey. For the last five centuries, I have worked tirelessly to protect you," he continues, each of his words paired with grand gestures in a perfectly choreographed—and probably rehearsed—speech.

"I have been your shield and your sword. I have been your

prophet and your servant. In 1487, in the darkest of ages, I started this fight against the most wicked, vile, and maleficent enemy— witches!" he whispers in the microphone pinned to his habit. "Most of them were caught, but many escaped. Once again, they are standing in our way, plotting in the shadows, in a world unknown to most of you. That secret underworld has allowed them to disrupt the natural course of history. It has allowed them to delay the inevitable, the Apocalypse and the necessary cleansing of this Earth."

"This guy is nuts," mutters Oliver.

"Shh," says Hailee, fearing someone might hear him.

Heinrich has grabbed a silver goblet from a pedestal next to him. He takes a large sip of a viscous mixture bubbling inside, slime sharing the surface with unidentified chunks.

Nothing happens until he drops the goblet to the floor. He cringes suddenly, his face crisscrossed by painful twitches and convulsions. His entire body is soon afflicted, seeming to grow under his robe, nearly doubling in height and width within seconds. When he reopens his eyes, they are glowing white.

"I can see them . . ." he whispers, his voice trembling.

The audience is conquered and bewitched. Hailee and Oliver are speechless.

"I am watching them," continues Heinrich. "Soon I will lead you to their hideout. The witches can't get away," he says, shaking, slowly getting back to his still pretty creepy self.

"The time has come to complete our mission," murmurs Heinrich, placing his hand on a mysterious object covered with a black cloth on the table. "Today, I bring you the key to their secret world."

All eyes are now on Heinrich's hand or, more exactly, on whatever is sitting underneath it. Lost in the crowd, Mr. Doyle is grinning passively, hypnotized by Heinrich's words.

"I give you . . . the Orbatrum!" shouts the man on stage, throwing back the cloth and unveiling . . . a globe, apparently identical to Archibald's, from the lions' feet to the crank on top.

In theater, Heinrich's dramatic move would be called a deus ex machina, something that appears out of nowhere to change the outcome of a story. Sure enough, Heinrich gets the effect he counted on, triggering a gasp that reverberates throughout the audience.

The loudest reaction comes from above, though, from the balcony.

"No!" shouts Hailee, recognizing her brother's globe.

Oliver pulls her away from the balustrade, but Heinrich's bodyguards are already headed upstairs.

"We gotta go!" he yells, grabbing Hailee's hand.

They retrace their steps back down, while Heinrich's men are coming up through the grand staircase.

Seeing the main entrance unobstructed, the two intruders run outside without looking back. They soon reach the street and mix with the Christmas crowd.

"Did you see his face? And his body? Was that some special effect?" asks Oliver.

"I don't know," utters Hailee, still in shock, but for another reason. "He has my brother's globe," she says, while slaloming around pedestrians and traffic.

"How could he get it?"

"Don't you understand? It's your dad; he gave it to him!" says Hailee, angry.

"That's impossible. My dad didn't know where I put it."

"He must have found it in that room!"

"He didn't even know the store had been wrecked."

"I'm telling you: he just lied to you."

"There's no way. I stopped by this morning, and I swear, the globe was still there. We're not far. I have to go check."

"What's the point? He has the globe now," says Hailee, as they reach the Realm of Antiques.

Oliver doesn't want to say anything until he sees it—or doesn't—with his own eyes. He unlocks the door. The store is a mess, reminding Hailee of her own house following the break-in. They have to carve a path through broken lamps and upside-down furniture, their eyes riveted on the large mirror commanding the entrance to the back room.

One tap on the mirror frame and they are in. No globe in sight, though.

"What are we doing? Oliver, he has the globe. See, there's nothing here."

Oliver remains silent and walks to the circular ottoman in the middle of the room. He kneels down, detaches one of the top cushions, and pushes it aside.

"I knew it!" says Oliver when he looks inside. He slowly pulls something out and turns around to show her—it's Archibald's globe.

"That's impossible! How can it be?" says Hailee, surprised and relieved. "What was that other globe, then?"

"I have no clue. The real question is, Why would Heinrich want this globe so bad if he has one already?"

Now backstage, Heinrich has taken his monk's robe off. In pants and T-shirt, a towel on his shoulders, he seems exhausted, like an actor after a demanding performance. In fact, he is sitting in front of a Hollywood-style mirror with a twenty-bulb frame, like the ones you'd find in the dressing rooms of professional theaters.

"That was a great speech, Master," says one of his minions, the one who drives him around everywhere. A few punches on the nose have given him a bulldog profile and a twangy duck voice.

"Thank you, Edward."

While petting a snow-white cat on his lap, Heinrich is inspecting the globe he unveiled earlier to his followers. It looks exactly like Archibald's—to the last detail, it seems, including the imaginary islands, the missing American continents, and all the monsters.

"May I ask you a question, Master?"

"You may, Edward."

"I was wondering, what would those people think if they knew this globe was broken?"

"Those people don't think, Edward; they follow."

"I understand, but—"

"Soon, we'll have a new globe, all questions will be answered, all doubts will vanish, and the prophecy will be realized," assures Heinrich.

"Yes, Master," says Edward, about to leave the room.

Heinrich reaches into his jacket folded on the counter in front of him and pulls out a picture of Archibald—probably the one Kate gave him when they met.

"Find this boy. I think he has what we need," he says. "And, Edward . . ."

"Yes, Master."

"Don't forget about the grandma," he adds in a cryptic tone.

ᚾ ᚾ ᚾ

THE WORLD OF

MARE DAMNVM

GALLITERRA

KAKKER

MARE PERDITVM

MYRMECIA

urlagone serpentis

Spinkiae en

meluum

tungo

MANDRVLLA TORR

LOBVLIA

rarung

sarguna

ARACHNAGAR

Hosltor

VMBRA

THE JOURNEY TO BELIFENDOR

D eep turmoil has gripped Gristlemoth. Except for Archibald, no one quite knows how to deal with Parnel's rebirth. The whole village has assembled at the Hive to see her. She is standing in the schoolyard, in front of the chalkboard still full of drawings, warnings, and instructions. Until this morning, that is where they studied Marodors, how to identify their weaknesses, how to fight them, how to fear them. Everything they knew, everything they thought true, now seems uncertain.

"Everyone, please be quiet!" demands Faerydae, facing an overwhelming barrage of questions from many, waving their hands and shouting over one another.

"Is this really Parnel?" asks one of them.

"How do we know it's not trumpery?" asks another.

"A ruse," Faerydae translates for Archibald.

He gives her a confident nod, implying he remembered (though he didn't).

"Maybe she's like a Trojan horse, a way for the others to get in," says Naida, adding her voice to the swell of concerns.

"Why don't we let her answer for herself?" suggests Maven.

Parnel waits to speak until everyone has gone silent.

"I understand your doubts," she says, serene and peaceful. "I'm not asking you to trust me. I'm not even sure I can trust myself."

Her remark sets off more commotion.

"Put her back in her cage," screams someone.

"Lock her up," echoes another.

Even Rhiannon has doubts. "This is too risky," she says.

Parnel starts speaking again. "My friends, my sisters, I don't know if I'm fully back to myself, but I know what brought me back among you," she says, turning to Archibald. "What brought me back is kindness, attention, and care. That's what our mothers taught us. That's what I'm asking you to trust—what's in your heart."

In the crowd, it's shakers versus nodders. Many, like Naida, don't seem convinced. They are shaking their heads. Still, Parnel seems to have won over a few people ready to give her a chance. They are the ones nodding. Some of them are even tearing up.

"We have to heal more Marodors," shouts Archibald.

"What do you mean?" asks Naida.

"We know how to do it," preaches Archibald. "We know how to treat them. We can heal them all."

"The rest of them are different. They're not like Parnel; they've always been Marodors, and they've got nothing to get back to," notes one girl.

"She's right, Archibald," says Faerydae. "What worked with Parnel might not work with all Marodors."

"We don't know that; we just have to try!" he replies. "You told me yourself: we don't even know what Marodors are to begin with. What about the other girls, your sisters, all those who became Marodors while fighting them? Don't they deserve a chance to be cured? Some of them might even be here, in those cages."

"What do you know about this world?" Naida asks.

"Not much. But what do we have to lose? Why don't we uncover their cages at least?" he pleads.

"That's crackbrained!" yells Rhiannon, who has joined the shakers.

"Think about it. Why are Marodors so attracted to the lights of this place? Look at them!" says Archibald, pointing at the beasts flying around Gristlemoth. "Maybe they think the sun can heal them!"

"Marodors might be attracted to the light, but it is darkness they would bring," assures Rhiannon.

"Then let's heal the ones we have here first," he suggests.

"You can't tell us what to do!" shouts Naida.

"*We* have to decide what's good for us," agrees Rhiannon.

"I'm sorry, Rhiannon, but, as you know, only one person can make such a choice," corrects Faerydae.

Rhiannon backs down in agreement.

"Who's that?" asks Archibald.

"The queen!"

"The what?" he asks.

"Her name is Helena. We call her our queen," says Faerydae. "She is the mother of us all; she is the one who sent us here and taught us everything. If we're going to change the way we treat Marodors, she'll have to approve it first. Maybe *you* can convince her."

"Okay, let's go talk to the queen, then. Where is she?"

"That's . . . complicated," answers Faerydae.

Archibald and Faerydae have walked up to the library. From a long leather tube, she pulls out a rolled-up map and spreads it flat on a desk by the window. It is drawn on parchment paper. At the top, it reads:

THE WORLD OF LEMUREA

"It looks very much like Europe," says Archibald, discovering a continent with extremely rough and approximate coastlines yet familiar contours.

"I know. Only with time did we realize that. A very long time. It took nearly three hundred years of exploring to make this map," notes Faerydae. "In many ways, Lemurea is all but a mirror image of our old world—only, its darkest side."

Dark this world certainly is, with mountains shaped like fangs, erupting volcanoes throughout, and creatures roaming the lands and seas from Mare Monstrum in the south to Mare Damnum in the north.

"The main purpose of the map is to locate our colonies. See, each of them is symbolized by a different rune," says Faerydae, showing him signs he has become more or less accustomed to, scattered throughout the map.

"How many are there?" he asks, his eyes traveling from one bizarre name to another, from Agrestal to Marrowclaw, Beorbor, Spinkiden, Yolkenrof, and others.

"Twelve," says Faerydae.

"How come those are different?" he inquires, pointing at Tungolwald, south of a region called Myrmecia, and Arkæling, in the far eastern reaches of Lemurea, right by a vast Terra Obscuria.

"Those are marked with a flower of life turned black. It means the colony has fallen to Marodors."

"Scary. Where are we, exactly?"

"Right here, this is Gristlemoth," she says, her index pinned right at the center of Lemurea, in the land of Kakkerlakan. It matches the area Archibald selected by pressing that pin down into the globe with his pen, but he doesn't make that connection.

"How did I land here?" he laments. "I'm so far from home."

"This is where we want to go," explains Faerydae, moving her finger to the east, all the way to a city surrounded by mountains, between Gurguria and Worgonia.

"Belifendor?"

"That's where the queen lives," confirms Faerydae.

It also happens to be where the first crack in the globe was located. Archibald doesn't remember that either. He just noticed something else, though—a small detail standing between them and the queen.

"Does it say Transylvania right here?"

"Yes, the land beyond the forest. We've got to cross those mountains," she confirms.

"Vampires," murmurs Archibald.

"What was that?"

"You've never heard of vampires?"

"No, what are they?"

"Maybe it's just a legend, but I've heard they're creatures that suck the life out of you!"

"Oh, those. We call them Marodors around here," jokes Faerydae.

Archibald lets out a nervous laugh, not too sure how to feel about that. Faerydae goes back to the map.

"See, the problem is there's no other colony between us and Belifendor. The closest would be Marrowclaw, but still way off course. That means no stopping anywhere. That means more supplies to carry, more golems on our backs, more caution, and, in the end, more time. That's why the trip is so difficult."

"How long will it take?"

"The last time I went there was about thirty years ago. Back then, it took me about two weeks," says Faerydae.

A look of bewilderment grips Archibald's face. "I'm not sure what the craziest part is—that you were alive thirty years ago or that it takes two weeks to travel to another country."

"You don't understand," she says. "Not only is it far but the area in between is infested with Marodors—land Marodors, mostly."

"Like the Krakatorum?"

"Maybe not as big, but, yes, that kind. It could take less time if we don't encounter too many of them, but even in the best-case scenario, it's still a five- to six-day journey. No matter what, we can't leave right away. We have to wait until Wymer is done fixing the tank."

"Fixing the tank? You mean building a new one? It's going to take months—we can't wait that long."

"I've been here for nearly five hundred years. Trust me; I think I can wait a few weeks," says Faerydae.

"But Parnel can't! Naida wants her back in her cage until we get a decision from your queen," Archibald reminds her.

"There's no other way," assures Faerydae. "Besides, nobody wants to go. I might be able to convince Maven, but not Rhiannon."

"I thought her leg had been fixed."

"It's not her leg. She just doesn't believe in all this. I don't think she'll come."

"I will," says a trumpeting voice coming from the hallway.

Archibald and Faerydae turn around, surprised to see . . . Lenora.

"Really?" says Archibald.

"Don't get me wrong," she says. "I think this whole idea is crazy, but, hey, it suits me, right?"

"I'm sorry, Lenora, but you can't come," says Faerydae.

"Why not?"

"You know why not. And, no offense, but we need people with experience."

"No offense, but the casting is rather limited."

"Thanks, but no thanks," repeats Faerydae.

"I'm so sick of this!" shouts Lenora. "This is why I have no experience. My mother always tried to protect me, and now you're doing the same thing! It's not fair."

Faerydae takes a few seconds to think.

"You know we're not flying there, right?" she finally says.

"Unfortunately," grins Lenora.

"Okay, then!" says Faerydae, making Lenora's grin even bigger.

"Flying would definitely help," says Archibald.

"It's one thing to levitate Marodors a few inches off the ground; it's quite another to make you fly," explains Faerydae. "No golem is powerful enough for that."

"Why don't we give it a shot?" he insists.

"And you don't think we have?" answers Faerydae.

"Maybe not enough."

"Not enough, huh?" smirks Faerydae, uncovering her left shoulder. "See, this was on my twenty-third and last attempt," she says, showing a scar as long and wide as the zipper on a pair of trousers.

"Ouch!" says Archibald. "And no flying broom, right?"

Faerydae shakes her head.

"Just checking," he says, turning back to the map. "Maybe there's a shortcut somewhere."

"We know all the shortcuts; it's six days, minimum," says Faerydae.

"What if we take this river?" he asks, following the course of the Urlagone, running all the way to the Loch Tenebris, a nearly enclosed sea right by Belifendor.

"How do you propose we do that?"

"We have boats, don't we? That way, we can bring cannons with us and there's no need to deal with those land Marodors," he says, pretty proud of his idea.

"It wouldn't work," says Faerydae. "Those boats are too small—good enough for the Rhodon, but that's about it."

"The Rhodon?"

"The river going through Gristlemoth," she says. "By the way, yes, we would avoid the *land* Marodors, but then we'd have to deal with *river* Marodors."

"There are river Marodors?"

"Yes, I told you some of them swim," explains Faerydae. "And that's another problem; we know how to handle Marodors on land, but we've never fought them on water."

"I should be the one freaking out; I don't even know how to swim!"

"This is *really* crazy," smiles Lenora, even more excited now.

"It's cruising time!" exclaims Archibald.

Faerydae rolls her eyes, not too sure what she's getting into.

It's a new day in Gristlemoth—a decisive day. Wymer has abandoned his tank repair for a moment to focus on prepping the boats by the river. The Raad fish have been transferred into buckets nearby. The old canoes are ready to regain their original purpose after Wymer is done fitting them with an invention of his own.

"What are you doing?" asks Maven.

"Since you won't get any cover from the trees, I'm adding a special camouflage to the boats," he explains, stretching a blanket above the second skiff, fixing it to wooden poles at each end.

"How does it work?" asks Lenora, inspecting the canoe already on the river.

"It's simple, really. Instead of branches and leaves, we put water on there!"

"How can you put water on cloth?" asks Maven.

"Archibald painted some waves on it—he's quite an artist, actually," says Wymer, showing her the rippling patterns, green, white, and blue. "He calls it troopaloy, or something like that, pardon my French!"

"It's a trompe l'oeil," corrects Faerydae as she walks over, "and it means 'trickery of the eye.'"

"That's exactly what I said, troopaloy," repeats Wymer.

Indeed, from above, thanks to Archibald's magic, the boats now completely blend in with the water. Wymer adds his final touch—cannons, installed at both ends of each canoe.

Maven and Lenora start loading bags of food and piles of ammunition—meaning golems.

"Looks like we're ready to go," says Faerydae, helping them. "Where's Archibald?"

No one seems to know.

Archibald is with Parnel. As planned, Naida—and many others still wary of that hybrid Marodor—had her put back into her cage. Parnel didn't resist. She just looks terribly sad.

"I'm sorry," Archibald tells her through the bars. "They didn't want to see you roam around the village. They're worried."

"I understand. This is still unknown for most of us, including me. People always fear the unknown."

"Still, it's not right."

"I want you to know something. I am so thankful for everything you've done for me already."

"Hopefully, I'll have more luck with your queen. I just have to tell her what you went through and how special you are. I'm sure it will work."

"I'm not that special."

"I don't know how you were before this," says Archibald, "but I find you pretty awesome now."

"Thank you."

"And don't worry," he adds. "I made sure they'd give you all the sugar you want."

"You know, I've started eating regular food again."

"You mean carrots and stuff?"

She nods, looking almost ashamed.

"See, you're more courageous than I am. Be careful, though; I might start to believe there's something wrong with you after all!"

Parnel smiles at last. Archibald walks away, quickly swiping away a tear. He squats down by Paws, who now follows him everywhere.

"You take care of her, okay? I trust you," he tells the strange pup, who stops wagging his feathered tail, crashes to the ground, and pouts.

Thirty-plus girls have gathered by the Rhodon River to bid the four adventurers farewell. If Archibald and his comrades wanted to know how much support they had in Gristlemoth, this turnout gave them a rough idea: thirty something out of 287— just about a 10 percent approval rating. Hopefully, Archibald won't be running for mayor anytime soon.

"Where's everyone?" he asks.

"I guess they're not crazy about this whole plan," says Faerydae.

Fortunately, Wymer has a last-minute surprise to cheer them up.

"New armor for all!" he shouts, unloading his bag of treats.

"For us too?" asks Lenora.

"Of course for you too!" he says, handing her a bark body armor carved with Gristlemoth's wave logo.

"Thanks, but I don't need it. I only believe in the power of golems and runes," says Maven, a tad condescending.

"Suit yourself, or not," jokes Wymer. "Seriously, though, travelling so far without the Hérisson, you might want to reconsider."

Gathering her armor, Faerydae notices unfamiliar objects mixed with the bark body plates—some kind of deep wooden bowls with a handle and straps.

"I don't think we're going to eat much stew on this trip, Wymer. What are these bowls for?" she asks.

"They're not bowls, you silly; they're helmets. I figured after what happened with the Krakatorum, you need to protect those small skulls of yours."

"Cool!" says Archibald, the only one getting excited about that new piece of armor, pulling his hair back to fit it best on his head.

"Young knight, you're wearing it the wrong way," says Wymer, flipping the helmet around. "See, this part here is a nose guard. No need to tell you what it's for—the name speaks for itself, right?"

That's the part Faerydae confused with a bowl handle. Archibald has a hard time seeing with that narrow piece of wood hanging down the very middle of his face, from his forehead all the way to his mouth. It makes him want to go cross-eyed.

"You'll be okay," says Wymer, adjusting the helmet so he can see better. "I also carved a rune on each helmet—see, right here—and each one is different," he says, pointing right at his forehead.

"Which rune do I get?" asks Maven, now showing interest.

"No magic there, Maven. Sorry to disappoint—just a good luck charm, that's all."

But she doesn't mind and grabs a helmet with the sneakiest

rune of all, Vixeneme and its zigzagging arrow ↗. "My favorite rune!" she cries out.

"Is there one rune that's not your favorite rune?" jokes Archibald.

"Probably not," she giggles. "Which one did *you* get?"

"I'm not sure," he says, taking his helmet off. "Hey, I've seen this one before!" he notes. He just can't quite remember where. *In the fridge back home? Maybe on that pack of frozen salmon polluting my ice cream?* he wonders. It is indeed shaped somewhat like a fish: ∝. Not a bad coincidence for a helmet Archibald picked randomly, considering the journey about to begin. But that rune evokes something different in Maven, taken aback the second she sees it.

"That's weird."

"What is it?" asks Archibald.

"It's just that I've not seen this in so long. Wymer, where did you find this rune?"

"I don't know; I did it from memory. What did I do now? Am I in trouble again? Are you gonna turn me into a hairy monster? I'm afraid I've already become one on my own," he says, laughing.

"What's wrong with this rune?" Archibald asks Maven. "Is it bad luck or something?"

"No, it's one of the first runes we worked on."

"What does it do?"

"It doesn't matter anymore," she says, walking away.

"That girl is so strange sometimes," Archibald tells Wymer.

"Witches!" he shrugs.

Archibald is sharing a boat with Maven. Lenora is sharing with Faerydae. This is no random pairing. They argued about it for nearly an hour before deciding who was best at picking the golems and who would operate each cannon more effectively.

Rhiannon comes running at the last minute, conflicted by the idea of letting her companions down. But the boats have departed already and reached Gristlemoth's shimmering wall. No boulder in their way, only those swirling lights, ascending from the river itself.

"It's the water. We think it conducts the energy from the golems around," explains Maven, addressing the curious look on Archibald's face.

"Don't be scared—trust the light," Faerydae tells him as they pass through the luminous screen. It lasts no more than five seconds, but the experience is one of pure, hair-raising wonder, especially for Archibald, looking heavenward, his arms fully extended, swathed in layer after layer of ghostly drapes and electric ribbons. And he thought lying under a Christmas tree was magical!

Archibald comes out on the other side a changed person, or so he believes. Even a "Holy bejabbles" would not do this moment justice. "Now *this* is whimsifulous!" he bursts out. "I felt it go through my whole body! I feel stronger already!"

"You do look different," says Maven.

"Really?"

"Of course not!" she quips, making all her companions chuckle, except him.

The Rhodon snakes through the forest for miles, making for a calm ride. Archibald is twisting his paddle to try to catch some fish whose eyes are glowing phosphorescent green on the sandy bottom of the river. Lenora is using hers to splash everyone. Even Faerydae is laughing. This almost feels like a camping trip. They are starting to think the cannons take up too much room on the boats. Wymer's camouflage is working as planned. The Marodors flying above seem to be completely oblivious to their presence. Lenora is acting a bit strange, though. She keeps turning around each time Faerydae looks back at her.

"What's with you, Lenora?" asks Faerydae.

"Nothing, why?"

"You're hiding something from me."

"No, I'm not."

"Really? You think I'm buzzard-blind?"

"What's buzzard-blind?" Archibald asks Maven.

"Buzzard-blind—you know, squirrel minded."

Archibald doesn't get it.

"It's like chuckle-pate, but more like lourdish. Duncified, almost, but definitely more boobyish, if you know what I mean."

"I don't!"

"You know—witless, frost-brained, mossy, potato-headed?"

"Stupid," sums up Faerydae. "I'm not stupid, so Lenora, what are you hiding?"

From a pouch on her belt, Lenora produces several candy bars.

"The sugar is for Parnel and Parnel only," fumes Faerydae. "It's not good for you."

"But I like it," says Lenora.

"I do too," admits Maven, pulling a lollipop out of her bag.

"Do I need to tell you what I think?" asks Archibald, sticking one in his mouth.

"You're the worst influence on everyone, I swear," sighs Faerydae.

"Thank you!" he says proudly. "By the way, you keep saying sugar is not good for us, but how do you know if you don't try it?"

"It's just bad," she repeats.

"Says who?"

"Says me. And says the queen."

"With all due respect, the queen is wrong on this one," he says.

Soon, the peaceful Rhodon merges with the Urlagone, five

times as wide and with a much stronger current. No need for paddles anymore. From here, they will only be useful to guide the boats. Archibald realizes the Rhodon was more a stream than a river. He looks down, worried. He can't see the bottom anymore.

"How deep is this? About three feet, you think?"

"More like twenty," says Maven.

Archibald is not feeling that comfortable on the boat suddenly.

"Do you know how to swim?" he asks.

"Of course. You do, too, right?"

"Of course!" nods Archibald, gripping both sides of the skiff in fear. He might have something else to worry about, something worse than not seeing the bottom of the river. The glowing fish eyes have indeed disappeared, replaced by ferociously red glares emanating from the forest.

"Marodors!" says Lenora, the first to spot them.

"Don't worry; they can't catch us," says Archibald, emboldened to address the Marodors directly. "What's happening, guys? You're afraid of the water?" he shouts, taunting them.

"Careful," warns Maven, "some of them might be able to fly!"

"Or swim," says Lenora.

"Or both," tops Faerydae.

Archibald pipes down and puts his helmet back on.

"If we keep up this pace, we could be in Belifendor in less than two days," says Faerydae, as the boats zoom down the Urlagone, out of reach of Marodors on land and invisible to those above.

ß

Suddenly, the night seems darker and colder. Archibald is shivering. Lenora is drawing clouds from her breath, blowing them upward, adding a layer to the thick blanket of fog hovering above the river. Faerydae and Maven, steering the boats, can barely see where they're going.

"Am I dreaming?" Archibald wonders aloud.

He could swear he has just seen a church on the left bank of the river, a tall building with a cross at the top.

"That's Uvarok," says Faerydae.

"There's a church over there," he says.

"There *was* a church there, in fact, a whole city once."

Spectral in the mist, the church blends in with other ruins nearby. Nothing much is left standing. Some buildings are partially burned down, others completely flattened, covered with moss.

"Marodors," utters Archibald.

"Don't be mistaken," says Faerydae. "The devastation you see here was not caused by Marodors; it was done by men."

"I don't understand."

"Our mothers used to visit this place long before they sent us here. They told us of a world frozen in time, something resembling the earth—only, the worst parts," explains Faerydae. "The queen warned us, though. Lemurea is also a window into the future of the earth, of what it could become, if Marodors take over."

"How did your mothers come here? Before the globes, I mean."

"Secret potions, I believe, and deep meditation, allowing them to have a foot in both worlds."

"Why would anyone want to come here? Do you think London looks like this?"

"I know it does; I saw it with my own eyes."

Archibald gapes at the ruins. As if the fog was not bad enough, the current is getting even stronger, causing the boats to roll and sway, as if caught in a powerful whirlpool.

"I can't control the boat!" shouts Faerydae.

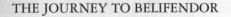

She realizes her paddle is not even touching the water anymore. The boat she shares with Lenora is being lifted off the river.

"I think we hit a tree," says Lenora. Leaning to the starboard side, she finds a giant root, woven in strips not unlike those of her braided hair.

"That's no tree," whispers Faerydae.

A large, bulging eye has just opened on those gnarled vines—inches away from Lenora's face. Almost instantly, her own eyes grow to mirror the one staring at her.

"Marodor!" screams Maven, pointing at multiple tentacles holding onto the canoe from underneath. At the end of those arms is a dark hole, ancestor of the garbage disposal, with a blend of small suckers and teeth-like splinters.

"Holy bejabbles!" exclaims Lenora.

"Just what I was thinking!" mutters Archibald, glad—and stunned—to finally hear someone else use that unique expression.

"Is that an octopus?" asks Maven.

She can't really see a face anywhere, just plenty of eyes—human eyes.

Scattered on each tentacle, they open one after another.

"Use your cannons!" shouts Faerydae.

"Aequae, Eqcelsio, Brachyamorphis," says Maven, sharing her picks with Lenora.

"She wants to turn it into ice," translates Faerydae. But Lenora's cannon has just fallen overboard and drowned. Maven herself is unable to follow through. Sucked up by the current, she can't turn the boat to adjust her fire.

Whatever breed it is, this Marodor has some smart genes. The monster is using half its tentacles to grab onto the boats while spinning the other half underwater at high speed, turning them into huge propellers. Not only does that balancing act allow the beast to move around quickly, it also feeds a tornado-like swirl that confuses its prey and disables the boats. The situation is dire.

Suddenly, a loud bang echoes through the mist. The shot came from Archibald. He literally fed the golem to the Marodor, lodging it into the creature's mouth.

"That's one out of three!" he shouts.

Faerydae is now struggling just to stand on her feet. She manages to fire the second golem, but it flies right past the beast. She turns to her paddle, hitting the Marodor where it hurts—in the eyeballs!

"Aim for the eyes!" she screams, which is not the hardest task in the world since that monster must have two hundred of them.

Archibald is pretty good at this game, wielding his paddle as if it were a sword.

"Bull's-eye!" he shouts each time he pokes one.

Maven is not bad either, but she can't avoid that wide swing from the Marodor. She is thrown off the boat. Her cannon follows. Archibald hauls her back in, rescuing her seconds before a tentacle can grab her. Shivering from the icy water but looking angrier than ever, Maven is back hitting the beast with all her strength. She might be little, but she is fierce!

Lenora has picked up another Eqcelsio golem. Since her cannon is gone, she has a different idea in mind. Climbing onto the edge of the boat, she seems to be bracing herself for a dive.

"Lenora, *no!*" yells Faerydae, doubtful of her companion's intentions.

Undaunted, Lenora jumps off and lands on one of the creature's tentacles, struggling to clamp her arms around the woodsy worm undulating under her. When she finally gets a good grip, she sticks her golem into one of the Marodor's eye sockets before letting go. She lands back in the boat—with Faerydae's body acting as a protective buffer, absorbing the shock from the harsh dismount.

"You really want to get killed!" yells Faerydae, glad nonetheless to have her back.

Even by Lemurea's standards, Lenora's move was unorthodox and daring for sure. But it paid off. Combined with Aequae, the Eqcelsio golem is already having an effect, freezing some of the water on the beast's tentacles, which get paralyzed one by one.

Already crumbling under an avalanche of paddle hits, the monster recedes back into the water with a few dozen black eyes—half-shut or blinking like stroboscopes.

Archibald and his friends can catch their breath, emerging mostly unscathed in a scene of confusion and chaos. Most of their food and provisions are floating around. Many golems are missing. Faerydae and Lenora's boat is severely damaged, suffering several leaks at the bottom. Wymer's camouflage is also gone, now leaving them vulnerable to flying beasts.

They are definitely not out of danger. About two hundred feet away, the Marodor has just resurfaced—only two eyes at first, bug eyes detaching from the gloom. Perched at the end of long antennas, they are acting as periscopes. They recess back into the submarine body as it finally emerges, massive and deceiving. It's a toad, mainly, but unlike other Marodors covered with leaves, this one looks leaf wrapped, like a stuffed appetizer. With moss, roots, and mushrooms as toppings, the beast could easily be confused with an island, if not for the two sets of jagged tusks protruding from both sides of a haunting face— part owl, part human.

Archibald and his friends realize the octopus represented only a portion of that monster—the tip of a dark iceberg. The flip side they are now facing is even more terrifying—a threat of titanic proportions, with potentially fatal consequences.

"What in the diablerie is that?" asks Lenora. "A different Marodor?"

"No, I think it's the same," says Maven.

"I've never seen anything like this," says Faerydae.

In fact, this monster is nowhere to be seen in the 182 pages of *The Grand (purposely incomplete) Bestiary of Marodors*—hence the "incomplete" part and the many pages left blank at the end. *It will surely deserve a place of choice in the book*, thinks Faerydae— only if they manage to escape that thing, of course.

Although bad news for sure, this Marodor is not entirely news to Archibald. He has the same sense of déjà-vu he had with the bear in a porcupine coat. Only this time it's not from the globe; it's from school. The beast's partially human face and his sparse mustache remind Archibald of Mrs. Richards, his math teacher.

Hopefully, this monster is not as mean, he prays.

"Let's not panic," says Faerydae, in a somewhat panicky tone.

"I thought it was frozen," says Archibald.

"Only partially. We still need Brachyamorphis and its

mutating powers to complete the spell," says Maven. "Hit it hard," she tells Archibald, handing him the key stone of the formula, carrying a rune shaped like a shackle Ω, perhaps predicting the fate of the Marodor once it is fully turned into ice. Archibald loads it quickly into his gun.

"Propellia Momentum!" Bang! His aim is perfectly in line with the target. But the golem falls short, into the water, ten feet away from the beast.

"We've got to get closer," says Lenora.

"I don't think we'll have to," notes Faerydae.

The monster is on the move again, now using the nonfrozen tentacles of its secondary body to propel itself.

Maven was right. The Marodor has been slowed down but not stopped. It is speeding up toward the boats, letting out a gurgling roar that ripples across the water. This creature is so massive it is parting the river in its wake.

Lenora hands Faerydae another magic stone.

"This is our last Brachyamorphis. Make it count!" she says.

Faerydae wastes no time.

"Propellia Momentum!" The cannon fires. The golem and the Marodor are on a collision course. Faerydae's aim was dead-on, right in the monster's face, but the golem bounces off one of its tusks.

Back on the boats, everyone knows what this means.

It's too late for Maven to come up with another spell.

Archibald exchanges a brief, panic-stricken glance with Faerydae, right before the Marodor hits her boat.

She gets the brunt of the impact. Her helmet is knocked off her head. She is projected all the way to the back, against Lenora. The front cannon flies over their heads. The monster lifts their canoe again, like a toy, with its tusks this time—and much higher. Both girls are just holding on to their seats, screaming.

"Jump!" Archibald shouts at them, seeing no other way.

It's probably the least bad solution at this point. Faerydae and Lenora look down, considering that option. They must be at least twenty feet in the air. They are hesitating. The Marodor makes the decision for them, suddenly letting go of the boat.

Released from the monster's grip, the skiff levitates in the air for a second, before plummeting like a rock.

The drop is spectacular and frightful. Maven covers her mouth. The small canoe crashes into the water and breaks in a million pieces—literally a million. Both Faerydae and Lenora seem unconscious. They're about to drown.

Archibald and Maven scramble to get close to them. They manage to draw Faerydae out of the water, then paddle toward Lenora, but the Marodor reaches her first. Its tentacles are back in force, wrapping around her tiny body. Lying side by side, Maven and Archibald are using their paddles to attack the monster. Suddenly back to life, Faerydae joins them, using Maven's helmet to punch a few eyes. But she is no match either.

The Marodor now has a strong hold on Lenora, who's still not moving, and it won't let go of her. It seems ready to settle for one prey. Using some of its tentacles as propellers again, the beast detaches from the boat and swims toward shore.

"Let's go! We have to follow them!" shouts Archibald, but neither Faerydae nor Maven seems eager to go after the beast.

Archibald can't contain himself. "What's wrong with you? We have to save her!"

"There are too many Marodors around," says Maven.

"We can't abandon her," he begs, paddling on his own.

Faerydae sits at the bottom of the canoe, shaking her head. "Maven is right. We might catch up with them, but with one cannon left and just a handful of golems, we don't stand a chance."

"Faerydae, please!" he shouts, tears welling.

"I'm sorry, Archibald; it's too late."

The Marodor has reached the bank and started crawling in the mud. Soon the creature disappears through the ruins of Uvarok, dragging Lenora behind.

THE ORBATRUM

Hailee's room has become the subject of an inquiry once more Her parents are filling in for Scotland Yard's sleuths—for now. They both look as distraught as they did the night Archibald disappeared.

"Maybe she missed her train last night," says Stuart.

"And went where?" snaps Kate. "She would have called."

Going through Hailee's nightstand drawers, Stuart finds the picture of a young man.

"Could this be something?"

"Stuart, please—it's that kid from that band!" she sighs.

"I dunno. How would I know?"

"Maybe that's the problem: we are so out of touch our kids just can't connect."

"So they just leave—that's it?" asks Stuart. "I don't watch TV, so it's my fault now," he says, visibly upset.

"I'm sorry; I'm just tired."

"It's okay; we're both exhausted," he says, switching to Hailee's desk while Kate frantically explores the pile of curled-up blankets on the mattress, which still lies on the floor.

"Maybe she stayed at a friend's house," Stuart thinks aloud.

"I called Emily's parents and Ella's parents. Nothing. Besides, Hailee doesn't do that; she would have left a note or something."

"Did you check in the kitchen?"

"Yes."

"Did you see anything on the fridge?"

"I'm not sure."

"Let's check again."

They head downstairs, when they hear the tires of a car crushing the gravel in the driveway. Hopeful, Kate rushes to the front door and swings it open quickly. She is stunned. The two inspectors in charge of Archibald's disappearance are walking up the stairs.

"What happened?" she asks right away, now imagining the worst about her daughter.

"I beg your pardon?" says one of the inspectors as they both reach the landing.

"Our daughter is missing. Do you know what happened to her?"

The two inspectors look at each other, dumbfounded. They obviously had no idea.

"Please come in," says Stuart.

The officers step into the foyer. The house is almost back to normal. The only trace of the break-in in this room is the marble statue still lying in pieces by the front door.

"Any news about Archibald?" asks Stuart, taking his wife's hand in his.

"I'm afraid not, sir," responds one officer.

"Is this regarding the break-in?"

"No, we are not in charge of that, although the cases might be related," says the inspector.

"I'm sorry—what is this regarding, then?" asks Stuart, looking even more worried now.

"I'm afraid we have more bad news," says the policeman.

Kate has placed her hand on her heart. She seems on the verge of a panic attack.

The officers exchange one more look. They seem much more careful with their words than the first time they came over.

"It's about your mother," says one of them.

"My mother?" says Stuart, both relieved and astonished.

"It's about her grave," says the inspector.

"What happened?"

The inspector clears his throat. "Someone vandalized your mother's grave," he explains.

"What?" blurts Stuart in shock.

"It happened last night, most likely," says the other officer.

"This is crazy," says Kate.

"It gets worse," adds the inspector. "They dug up your mother's coffin."

"What?" exclaims Stuart.

"They stole her body," adds the officer.

"And replaced it with sandbags," completes his colleague.

Kate gasps. Stuart is speechless.

"Have you found her?" asks Kate.

"No, Madam, I'm afraid the body is still missing."

"Who would do such a thing?" shouts Stuart.

"We don't know, sir," says one inspector.

"Although we have a theory," says the other.

"What is it?" asks Stuart. "Tell me."

"The people who did this—we think they're the same ones who broke into your house."

"How do you know?"

"We believe that perhaps what they couldn't find here, they were looking for in her coffin."

"That's crazy!" says Stuart.

"Yes, it is, sir. We agree on that point. But it's also possible," says one inspector. "Do you know of any jewelry or any possessions that would have been placed in your mother's coffin?"

"Not to my knowledge, no. My mother was very . . .

particular; she left precise instructions before her death. Bartholomeo, her butler and longtime friend, he took care of all the arrangements."

"If I may," asks the officer, "you said something about your daughter missing as well when we arrived?"

"We've not seen her since yesterday morning," notes Kate. "She didn't come back home last night."

"How old is she?"

"Thirteen."

The inspectors exchange another one of those perplexed looks.

"How was her relationship with your mother, Mr. Finch?" one of them asks.

"Not too bad, we rarely saw my mother. She was very secretive. We didn't even know she owned this house. Why are you asking?"

"Any grudge your daughter could have had against your mother?" asks the other officer.

"Are you serious?" says Stuart. "You think Hailee—"

"You never know with teenagers nowadays!" says the officer with a serious face.

"As you know," explains his colleague, "we have to explore every option."

Stuart sits on the stairs, shaking his head. *This is such an absurd theory*, he thinks. He prefers not to comment, afraid he might not be able to parse his words carefully enough.

Kate is not as diplomatic. "So let me get this straight. If I understand you correctly, we abused our son, and now our daughter is a criminal?"

Hailee wakes up on the ottoman in which Oliver hid the globe. She is lying right above the secret compartment. They obviously spent the night in the hidden back room at his dad's shop. Not a chance they would have swung by Grandma Celestine's grave.

Oliver has been up for a while. He is sitting on the other side of the large bench.

"Everything okay?" asks Hailee.

"I borrowed your phone. I hope it's okay?"

"Yes, sure. What are you looking for?"

"You remember what Heinrich called the globe?"

"His globe or this one?" she asks, pointing at the one sitting next to Oliver.

"Both, I guess. They look the same to me."

"He called it Orbator or Orbatrum, or something like that?"

"That's it—the Orbatrum. I searched it online."

"Did you find anything?"

"Nothing came up, until I found this website about the most outlandish inventions—mind-reading machines, alien detectors, that kind of thing."

"Are you serious?"

"I know, right? Between this and the tabloid story, we're definitely dealing with a *special* kind of people."

"Loonies, you mean," sums up Hailee.

"Look, I agree; it all sounds crazy, but you heard Heinrich. It's not like he made any sense either. If you believe him, he's the one who started the whole witch-hunt thing with that book five hundred years ago. Did you see his eyes after he drank from that cup? He looked possessed! And his whole body doubling in size—was that some kind of special effect or what?"

"So what are you saying?"

"What I'm saying is that pretty much everything

surrounding this globe sounds bonkers. So we might as well look into this website."

"Okay, so what does it say about that Orbatrum?"

"That's the thing," says Oliver. "It's just listed with other inventions, with no details or anything."

"So we're stuck."

"Maybe not. I called the guy behind the website—he is right here in London."

"Great! Our own nutty professor!" jokes Hailee.

"Funny you said that! The guy is not a quack, actually. He has a PhD in astrophysics from Oxford and a degree in biology from Cambridge."

"Really?"

"I'm not joking. Look, this is the guy, Professor Malcolm Brimble," he says, showing Hailee a picture on the phone.

Indeed, Professor Malcolm Brimble looks like the serious kind, a mix of Sigmund Freud and Albert Einstein—bald on top, curly on the sides, bushy above the eyes, and tufted on the chin. Not to mention the pipe that couldn't be better angled in the corner of his furry mouth.

"We're meeting him at two o'clock," says Oliver.

"What? Why don't we just ask him questions on the phone?"

"That's the problem. He wants money."

"How much?"

"Fifty pounds. I have only fourteen."

Hailee checks her pockets, pulling out a few bills. "And I have twenty-six. We're ten short."

"It should be fine," says Oliver. "It's not like the guy is starving—he's a professor!"

It's five to two. Hailee and Oliver arrive at the address Malcolm Brimble gave him in Twickenham. At 52 Heath Road, they find . . . a carpet store.

"I knew it was a scam!" says Hailee.

"Maybe he lives up there?" suggests Oliver, looking at a couple of red brick apartments above the store.

"Did he give you an apartment number?"

"No, he didn't," says Oliver, checking the names listed on four doorbells next to a staircase stuck between the carpet store and a tanning salon.

"Here!" says Oliver, showing her the printed name on the bell. "Professor Brumble."

"I thought his name was Brimble."

"Yeah, maybe I didn't read that right on his website," he says, not quite convincing Hailee. Not quite convincing himself, in fact.

He rings the bell.

"Yes?" answers a musty, old voice with a too-thick Scottish accent.

"It's Oliver; we talked on the ph—"

A loud buzzer cuts him off, unlocking the gate.

"See?" Oliver says proudly.

Hailee is doubtful. "You don't find it strange?"

"What?"

"That a renowned professor with two PhDs from Oxford and Cambridge would have nothing better to do on Christmas Eve than meet with us? That doesn't seem weird at all to you?"

"Not at all—quite the opposite, actually," says Oliver. "Think about it: the guy is a scientist. He is so into his research he doesn't care about Christmas!"

"Do you have an answer for everything?"

"Not always. I remember one day when I didn't, actually. It

was a Monday a couple years ago, I think—I was so mad," says Oliver.

"You're something else," Hailee grins.

They go up to the first floor and come face-to-face with two doors. The left one reads: "Mr. Zolthar, Psychic." The right one: "Professor Bramble."

"Is this a joke?" sighs Hailee.

Oliver shrugs again and knocks. A moment later, the tiny dot of light in the door peephole is eclipsed. Someone is looking at them.

"Fifty pounds, under the door," says the same voice with a slightly different accent—pirate-like, almost.

"The guy sounds like he's from Cornwall now," worries Hailee.

"Maybe he has a cold," says Oliver, not too concerned. He gathers their forty pounds. Each bill is yanked from the other side as soon as Oliver slides the money under the door.

"We said fifty!" complains the voice, back to the Scottish accent, now with an angry undertone.

"Sorry, Professor, that's all we have. We hope it's okay. We really need your help."

No reaction. In fact, Hailee and Oliver don't hear anything for a whole two minutes. Oliver knocks several times but gets no answer. What can they do? Call the police? Disheartened, they are about to leave when the door finally opens.

"Please come in," says a young man wearing flip-flips, frayed jeans, and a T-shirt that reads: "1N73LL1G3NC3 15 7H3 4B1L17Y 70 4D4P7 70 CH4NG3 –573PH3N H4WK1NG."

"Oh, um—hi," stammers Hailee.

"Please," says the young man, motioning for them to sit on a couch covered with blankets and bed pillows—and crumbs.

Oliver sits down right away, Hailee more reluctantly, pushing aside a sock and a cookie. This looks like a university student's apartment—the walls and bookshelves papered with Post-it notes—definitely not what they expected. They'd envisioned an antique interior; a sweatered professor seated at a rich mahogany desk with rows and rows of books behind him.

"So how can I help you?" inquires the young man, slumping his lanky body into an overstuffed recliner.

"Where's Professor . . . Brimble?" asks Hailee.

The young man doesn't answer.

"Is he getting ready in the back?" asks Oliver, pointing to a door behind him.

"Oh, no, that's the bathroom," says the young man. "And . . . I am Professor Malcolm Brimble," he says, further thickening his forced Scottish accent, arching his eyebrow into a Freudian curve.

"What? I knew it was a scam!" fumes Hailee, standing up.

"You gotta give us our money back," says Oliver, up as well.

"Relax. What did you expect? A sweatered professor, seated at a rich mahogany desk, with rows and rows of books behind him?"

"Yes!" Hailee and Oliver answer at once.

"See, that's the problem! Nobody would take me seriously if I posted my own picture, not to mention my real name."

"Which is?" asks Hailee.

"Philip Vivekenanda."

"Well, Philip," says Hailee. "If you really knew your stuff, you wouldn't need to fool people."

"Ah, yes," says Philip, shooting her a wry look. "Because names, titles, and appearances matter little in this world."

Hailee doesn't answer; Oliver nods—both admitting grudgingly that he has a point.

"Who's Professor Brimble, then?" asks Oliver.

"I made him up. I borrowed the picture from the guy next door."

"The psychic?" questions Hailee.

"He's not really a psychic. He's an actor. It was either that picture or another one of him as a dentist."

"You're such a liar!" shouts Oliver.

"Yes," says Philip, almost proudly.

"And a fraud!" adds Hailee.

"No, *that* is not true," objects Philip, visibly offended. "I *do* know my stuff. And I know a lot about the da Vinci globe."

At those words, Hailee and Oliver sit back on the sofa.

"How do you know da Vinci made it?" asks Hailee.

"I told you: I know my stuff."

"The Orbatrum?" asks Oliver.

"Yes, I might not have gone to Oxford or Cambridge *yet,* but I have studied time travel for a long time."

"Time travel?" asks Oliver.

"That's what the Orbatrum was for, I think!"

"What do you mean 'you think'?" asks Hailee.

Philip hops up from his chair to go through Post-its glued to the window frame.

"Here, Orbatrum!" he says, peeling off one of them. "It is a combination of two Latin words," he explains, squinting at his scribbles. "*Orbis*, which means 'world,' and *atrum*, which means 'dark and obscure.' To me, there is no doubt—the globe was a gateway between two worlds. Now, did it mean traveling to a different time or a different dimension? Or both? That I am not

100 percent sure of."

"How's that possible?" asks Oliver.

"How can you travel through a globe?" adds Hailee.

"Da Vinci was a genius. He studied electricity before it was called electricity. He studied clouds and thunder. Some people think he succeeded in harnessing the power of lightning and created an enormous vortex, some sort of wormhole, that could warp the limits of time and eliminate the boundaries of space."

Hailee's head is spinning. "That's what the globe does?" she mutters.

"That's what it was capable of, yes, if you believe all the legends I've read. I *do* believe them, by the way!" Philip concludes.

"Obviously," comments Oliver.

"They called it the Ark," says Philip, with poetry in his voice.

"What?" asks Hailee.

"The Orbatrum—some people referred to it as the Ark."

"Why?" asks Oliver.

"I don't really know," admits Philip. "Maybe it was like a wink, a reference to Noah's Ark. But instead of animals, it was meant to save people from some kind of catastrophe. It could have been anything. They had the bloody plague back then, so who knows?"

Hailee and Oliver exchange a deep gaze, trying to make sense of everything.

"Why would he put that time machine in a globe?" asks Oliver.

"*That's* interesting!" shouts Philip, who stands up again to grab another Post-it. "What is a vortex?" he asks, almost professorial.

Both Oliver and Hailee shake their heads.

"A vortex," says Philip, now reading from his note, "is a

region in a fluid where the flow rotates around an axis line."

Oliver and Hailee seem pretty lost.

"Don't you get it? Remember, da Vinci created a vortex to allow time travel, or multidimensional travel. So what better than a terrestrial globe to have the flow of that vortex rotate around an axis line?"

They don't have an answer—shockingly.

"Nothing! Nothing is better than a globe to achieve that. It is pure genius!"

"How does it work, exactly?" asks Oliver.

"It's a globe, man! You spin it, and then you travel," says Philip.

Hailee has an important question on her mind, probably the most crucial for her. "How do you come back?"

"You guys are pretty smart," says Philip. "Well, that is a tricky question. Most stories I have read speak of people who never came back. They were just stuck wherever or whenever it was they traveled, and the globe stayed behind."

Hailee tilts her head down. *I'll never see Arch again*, she thinks.

"But—" adds Philip, "*I* personally believe anyone traveling through that globe *could* potentially come back."

"How?" asks Hailee, her eyes regaining some hope.

"Think about it: how did you come in here?"

"We walked in?" says Oliver, hesitating for fear of sounding stupid.

"Okay, but how did you come in?"

"Through the door?" tries Oliver.

"Exactly! And which door will you use when you leave?" he now asks, looking at his watch and whispering, "Soon, I hope. This is worth much more than forty pounds."

"The same door?" says Hailee.

"The same exact door!" confirms Philip. "You'll open it from the opposite side, yes, but, still, it will be the same door."

Neither Oliver nor Hailee quite gets the analogy.

"Oh, people!" laments Philip, rolling his eyes with a loud sigh, getting up again, this time going to the bathroom.

"Man, can't you wait until we're gone?" asks Oliver.

"Would you mind closing the door at least?" adds Hailee, grossed out when she realizes her hand was sitting on that sock she pushed away earlier.

"Relax," says Philip, tossing a tube of toothpaste onto Oliver's lap.

"Open this!" he tells him.

"What?"

"Just open it," he repeats.

Oliver twists the cap of the tube to undo it.

"Now close it."

"Sorry, man. We don't have time for games," says Oliver.

"This is not a game; trust me. Go ahead—close it."

Oliver screws the cap back on.

"So?" asks Hailee.

"This, I believe, is exactly how the Orbatrum worked," says Philip.

"Powered by toothpaste?" she questions.

"No!" he snaps, annoyed. "But exactly like that cap!"

Oliver and Hailee are staring at him, dubious, waiting for more.

"You screw it counterclockwise to open the tube and clockwise to shut it."

"I don't understand," says Hailee.

"I don't either," says Oliver.

"They would have had to spin the globe the other way!" says Philip.

"What?" says Hailee. *Could it be that simple?* she wonders.

"You heard me," says Philip. "Look, I'm not sure of this, but I believe that if they wanted to come back, those traveling through the globe would have needed someone to spin it in the opposite direction—opposite to the one they picked when they left, that is."

"What if it doesn't spin, if it's broken or something?" asks Oliver.

"What do you mean?"

"Is it possible that the globe stopped spinning at one point?" he rephrases.

"Of course, it had to! Think about it: the globe couldn't just be loose and spinning freely. How could people transport it otherwise? No, there had to be some kind of locking mechanism. Da Vinci was way too smart to not have thought about that."

"So maybe it's not broken?" mutters Oliver.

"What do you mean? What's broken?"

"Nothing."

"You guys are not just smart; you're weird," notes Philip. "You're talking about that globe as if—"

It hits him suddenly. "Oh my God! You found one. You found da Vinci's globe!" he exults, his eyes wide and wild.

"Nah, we didn't," says Oliver, trying to deny it as well as he can. Hailee also shakes her head in the most overacted manner.

"It all makes sense," says Philip. "Why would you guys be asking so many questions about the Orbatrum otherwise? And why would you be willing to pay forty pounds for answers?"

Hailee rises up from the couch and gets ready to leave, heading toward the front door. Oliver follows her.

"I have to see it! Please, just a few minutes. Let me just have a look," begs Philip.

"This was so worth it; thank you!" says Hailee, as she opens the door.

"Will I get a tip, then?" Philip asks.

"We didn't lie to you; we had only forty pounds," says Oliver.

"Actually, here's a tip," says Hailee. "Stick with one name, Professor Brimbrumbramble."

Oliver nods, pointing at the tag on his front door. Philip is left with his mouth hanging open—wordless, at last.

Hailee and Oliver hurtle down the stairs. They can't wait to go back to the store and find that locking mechanism on the globe.

LA GIOCONDA

The journey to Belifendor has turned into a nightmare. Faerydae and Maven have been taking shifts, one steering the skiff, the other keeping the one surviving cannon ready—both battling exhaustion. They had to do without Archibald. Sickened by guilt, he has remained seated in the back, his head against his knees. No one on board has talked since that deceitful Marodor took Lenora.

In the last thirty-six hours, the landscape has transformed dramatically, the thickest woods morphing into the barest of valleys. In between stood a wall of high peaks that only the raging current of the Urlagone could have pierced. At one point, the mighty river shrank to a sliver, squeezed within the guts of the mountains, the bottleneck effect turning the canoe into a runaway ride. That's the only time Archibald lifted his head, unable to resist the thrill of that breakneck rollercoaster—and a bit scared of it as well.

The Urlagone has now returned to its regular width and strength, more manageable under Faerydae's paddle.

"Everyone okay?" she asks her still-traumatized crew.

"Yes," says Maven, while Archibald remains still and subdued.

"It's not your fault; there was nothing you could do," says Faerydae, trying to lift his spirit one more time.

"You know that's a lie," he says, breaking his silence.

"Lenora knew the risks; we all did," says Faerydae.

"I'm the one who created the risks!"

"Now you listen to me," yells Faerydae. "Maven here, her great-great-grandmother was a witch. She was enslaved by the Mongols, taken from China, and brought all the way to Europe just so they could use her powers in battle. Same thing with her great-grandmother, but with the Persians this time. They were after the same magic. Then it was her grandmother's turn. She refused to share her knowledge. So the Russian Cossacks made a big fire and threw her into it. If you wonder about her mother, don't; she was also burned alive. You want to know what her crime was? She used a potion of secret herbs to save her sister's life."

As Maven nods mutely, Faerydae pauses to catch her breath for a second before concluding her point. "Trust me, Archibald; you have nothing to do with this. The risks have always been there."

"I made things worse," he mumbles.

"You care about Lenora?"

"Of course I do, but—"

"Then finish what we set out to accomplish," she snaps. "That's what Lenora would have wanted. She'd never give up."

Maven takes it from here. "You know," she says, "Lenora lost her brother a few years back. One of the only boys we ever brought to Lemurea. She was devastated, but she remained strong."

"What happened to him?"

"A disease," explains Faerydae. "Even the queen couldn't save him. That's when Lenora left Belifendor for Gristlemoth."

Archibald shakes his head.

"We cannot get her back," says Faerydae, "but we can turn

our anger into strength and use it to convince the queen. You'd better make up your mind quickly."

"Why?"

"Because Belifendor is right there," she says, motioning to a dim dot on the horizon.

His eyes riveted on that tiny beacon of light and hope, Archibald wipes the tears he has been fighting off. A few seconds later, he grabs a paddle to help Faerydae. She turns around. No need to say anything. No need for sign language. The quick smile and nod they exchange are worth a thousand words.

↗
N

Belifendor is obviously more than a village. It's a city. Still a few miles away, the hole in the sky already looks as big as the one above Gristlemoth from up close. Another sky within the sky.

"Look at the size of that thing!" says Archibald, not yet blasé.

"It was our very first colony," says Faerydae. "We grew from here, but we grew here first."

"The landing was harsh," recalls Maven. "We all arrived in different parts of Lemurea. We were too scattered, vulnerable. It was a disaster. So we regrouped here. For nearly two centuries after that, Belifendor was all we knew. We pushed the city limits every year. Then we started exploring other lands."

"What about Gristlemoth? When was it created?"

"It was our third colony. It's about three hundred years old," says Faerydae, her hair blowing in the breeze, making her even more beautiful in Archibald's eyes—if that's possible.

The wind has picked up strength, though, quickly losing its charm. "SWISHHH" on the right. "WHOOSHHH" on the left.

Coming in ravening gusts, it billows through the camouflage cloth, turning it into a sail. Out of control, the boat suddenly takes off and soars in the air. In only a few seconds, it's gliding thirty feet above the river.

"So we *can* fly!" says Archibald, both excited and petrified.

"We've gotta go back down," shouts Faerydae.

Indeed, if they go any higher, they will soon walk into the lion's den—or, more exactly, fly into the Marodors' orbit.

"Let's jump in the water," suggests Maven.

"No, we can't," says Faerydae. "We're already too high." And not even quite above the river anymore.

The skiff is acting erratically, threatening to tip over any second. While Maven and Faerydae are grabbing onto each other and whatever else they can, Archibald stands up and climbs one of the poles supporting the cloth.

"What are you doing?" shouts Faerydae.

Archibald uses his paddle to cut a hole in the sail. The boat stops ascending immediately, then starts losing altitude when he tears the sail further. That second breach was a bit too bold. From a gentle glide, the skiff goes into a spinning free fall. They all let out a piercing scream before crashing, luckily on a swampy beach.

Maven and Faerydae struggle to extract themselves from the entangled cloth. A bit roughed up, they quickly forget about their latest wounds and scramble toward Archibald, seeing only his legs jutting out from deep mud.

"He's drowning!" yells Faerydae, grabbing one foot while Maven pulls on the other.

Another tug and he is out, with a rather gross suction sound.

"That was crazy!" says Faerydae, waving her hand before his eyes.

"Genius!" says Maven, clapping him on the shoulder.

"This dream's never gonna end, is it?" he mutters, spitting mud.

While Maven uses Archibald's helmet to collect water and rinse his face, Faerydae just smiles at him and sighs, relieved.

"I guess we'll continue on foot," she says, inspecting the wrecked boat.

At least they landed on the right bank of the river, on Belifendor's side.

They take cover under the long, sad branches of a weeping willow. The tree happens to have the same haircut as Archibald, a shabby-chic haystack do. As far as the eye can see, the land is covered with the same kind of tall, puffy wigs, probably grown for bald giants—naturally the main and only explanation Archibald could come up with.

Faerydae leads the way, running from one furry mound to another, seeking cover from Marodors. Many of them are flitting around Belifendor like mosquitoes drawn to a bug bulb on a hot summer night. And this bulb is bright! The city glows with the same magical lights as Gristlemoth's, but with an orange cast instead of green, radiating upward and out through swirling loops.

After trekking from the river for an hour, Archibald and his companions finally reach Belifendor's outer wall. They are dripping with sweat. Faerydae is about to blow into her horn when someone beats her to it—a girl perched on a watchtower within the city, about fifty feet above ground.

"They saw us," says Maven.

To everyone's surprise, though, a few minutes go by and nothing happens. In fact, the girl who spotted them is nowhere to be seen after disappearing down a ladder.

"I don't know what's going on," Faerydae wonders aloud.

"Why don't we call someone?" suggests Archibald.

"The horn was bad enough; shouting would only attract more Marodors," she warns.

As a reminder of the clear and present danger, one of them comes flying low to the ground and brushes the top of the trees when shooting back up. Part lion, most of his body, the paws and tail—part eagle, the wings and beak—part human, his face and front legs, this monster is a flying copy of the sphinx, the statue lying by the pyramid of Giza in Egypt.

"What is that?" asks Archibald, crouching down in fear, gazing through the branches.

"*That* is page 9 of the *Bestiary*," says Maven. "The Sphinoxis Rapatoris—one of the fastest Marodors you'll ever see."

The terrifying beast comes swooping down twice before one of Belifendor's boulders finally moves out of the way, only slightly, creating a small breach in the fence.

"One more thing before we go in," Faerydae tells Archibald.

"Don't tell me my name is Ivy again!"

"No, but keep your helmet on. Nobody knows you here; let's avoid problems until we meet with the queen."

"Fine by me."

About a hundred feet separate them from the safety of Belifendor. It is the last stretch of this perilous journey, but not the easiest by any means. In length, it's a football field of bare dirt with no tree, rock, or deep crevice to use for protection. Each nibbled yard will be a challenge.

"You've got to run and never look back," Faerydae tells Maven and Archibald. "You understand?"

They both nod. Faerydae starts the eerie countdown: "All right, three, two, one—"

They all rush through the open terrain at once, Maven first. As planned, none of them looks back or up. But Faerydae forgets to look down. They have almost made it across when she trips over a root and collapses. The Sphinoxis Rapatoris is coming back, flying toward her at full throttle, his wings swept back alongside his body for optimal velocity. Unaware of anything, Maven presses ahead.

Archibald did hear something—a loud thump. He glances back and sees Faerydae on the ground, holding her leg in pain. He turns around right away and helps her up quickly. She leans on his shoulder as they head toward the opening. The Rapatoris waits until the very last moment to unfold his wings and legs. Faerydae cringes as she hears the snap of his jaws coming together, falling just short of reaching her. The beast comes within a short lock of hair from grabbing onto her. Instead, he crashes into the boulders as Archibald and Faerydae plunge through the narrow passage.

They join Maven, who has just realized what happened. Faerydae collapses again, this time of total exhaustion. A buzzing crowd has gathered around them to get the story. This is no greeting committee but a wide display of wary faces.

"What took you so long to open the gate?" yells Faerydae.

"You Gristlemoths are so much better than us poor Belifendors," says a voice rising from the group of girls. "We figured you'd find a way in," the voice adds scornfully, triggering laughter among the locals.

"Breena! I should have known," says Faerydae, rolling her eyes.

As she slowly gets back up, Breena emerges from the crowd.

"Aye up, old friend!" she says.

They look about the same age, but there's something on Breena's face that gives her a somber appearance. It takes Archibald a few seconds and some squinting to figure it out. It's not her skin, even though it's pale as a corpse. It's her eyes, displaying almost no color, only darkness, like two dead moons.

"You haven't changed a bit, have you?" says Faerydae sarcastically.

"None of us do, remember?" sneers Breena.

"You know what I mean," says Faerydae.

Breena just smirks. "What's the reason for your visit?" she asks.

"I didn't know we needed a reason," says Faerydae. "Isn't this home forever to all of us?"

"You know what I mean," says Breena, mimicking her.

"We are here to see the queen," says Maven.

"Why?"

"*That* is something only the queen will hear."

"She's busy, you know. She might not have time."

Faerydae doesn't even bother with a comment. She just shrugs and shoulders her way through the crowd, Archibald at her heels. Maven stays behind to talk to some old friends.

"What's wrong with that girl's eyes?" whispers Archibald.

"That's just a trick she uses. Some belladonna berry juice."

Archibald looks baffled. He has never heard of belladonna berry juice. He's had lots and lots of strawberry juice, cranberry juice, and blueberry juice. He even mixed them all together once. He got an upset stomach within two minutes, but certainly nothing that would turn his eyes black.

"It must taste awful to do that to her!" he winces.

"You don't drink it. You put a few drops in your eyes. It enlarges your pupils. Very powerful. And poisonous."

"Then why would she do that?"

"To look scary. If you ask me, I don't think she needs it."

"Who is she? She sounds weird."

"Breena and I grew up here together. She always tried to compete with me for everything, especially the queen's attention. That's why she was so happy when I left. She never plays fair; she's a witch."

"Aren't you all?" Archibald wonders aloud, chuckling.

"No, Breena is a real witch. She's a guiler."

"What's that?"

"You don't know what a guiler is? A bobber, a fob, a deceptor."

"A cheat, you mean?"

"Yes, something like that, but much worse."

They stop suddenly as they hear someone shouting Faerydae's name. It's not Breena, nor is it Maven. It's another girl, running up to them with a huge grin on her big, round face.

"Finally, someone who's happy to see you!" jokes Archibald.

"Rhoswen!" shouts Faerydae, arms open wide.

They give each other a warm hug and press their foreheads together, covering each other's ears with their hands.

"It's been so long," mumbles Rhoswen, in tears.

"I know, too long," says Faerydae, crying as well. "Archibald," she says, turning to him, "this is Rhoswen."

"My name is Ivy, remember?"

"It's okay. She's my sister."

"Real sisters or BFFs?"

It's Faerydae's turn to look lost.

"You know, BFFs, best friends forever," adds Archibald.

"No, real sisters," says Faerydae, holding Rhoswen's hand.

"Well, one more boy in Belifendor!" says Rhoswen.

"What do you mean?"

"Believe it or not, we've got eighteen here now."

"What? You're pulling my leg," says Faerydae.

"No, I'm serious. They all arrived at the same time about two months ago, along with a hundred new sisters," she explains. "BFFs," she adds, winking at Archibald.

Faerydae looks around more carefully, and indeed, she spots two boys just within a twelve-cabana-and-fourteen-tree radius.

"Mislimps?" she asks.

"Nobody knows; Helena just introduced them as our new brothers."

"Is she here, the queen?" asks Archibald.

"I believe so. I'm just not sure she's available, though," says Rhoswen.

"Where could she be, anyway? Shopping?" he jokes.

Both sisters look at him with dismay.

Not only was his tone totally disrespectful but also what does "shopping" even mean?

"We have something important to tell her. I really hope she's here," says Faerydae.

"Let's go check!" says Rhoswen, bowing

and unfolding her arm, showing Archibald the way forward.

Belifendor has obviously had time to experiment with architecture—in a crude, Middle Ages sort of way. Besides the same little huts that dot Gristlemoth, the city includes a number of more elaborate dwellings up to four stories tall. Though crafted of wood and mud as well, they definitely reflect bold creativity and imagination.

Some are shaped like pyramids, with tiered gardens on one or two sides. Some are just tall, circular towers with an outside staircase swirling all the way to the crenellated, flat rooftop. Straight walls and square windows would almost make other buildings look oddly normal and boring—if they were not twisted like fusilli pasta, with each floor out of line by ninety degrees with the one underneath.

Add the winding streets, the guard towers, the narrow alleyways, and a few cabanas built in tall trees and you've built the ultimate playground. And that's not even mentioning the entanglement of rope bridges linking homes to one another.

Archibald marvels at a couple of girls running right above him.

"Must have been fun growing up here."

"It was," confirms Faerydae.

"Especially when you never really grow up," adds Rhoswen, grinning widely.

The road winds its way to Belifendor's castle. Perched on a hill, it looks very similar to the one in Gristlemoth, only larger, with many more towers and flags, featuring the colony's rune of choice, Moonascendum, the pyramid rune, in black on a yellow background. Another notable difference: the high ground confers it a much more impressive stature, as it towers over the whole city.

"Helena spends most of her time inside the Hive, so hopefully she's here today," says Rhoswen.

"Wait, I thought the Hive was Gristlemoth's castle?" questions Archibald.

"They're all Hives," explains Rhoswen. "Every colony began with one."

The castle now serves mostly as a school, just like the one in Gristlemoth. The same effervescence and excitement fill the main courtyard. Looking around for familiar faces, Faerydae bumps into a cluster of boys. She blushes red and giggles together with her sister.

"What's wrong with you? They're just boys," says Archibald, already missing being the only knight around.

Faerydae and Rhoswen exchange one more high-pitched laugh and a few whispers as they scamper into the castle. Archibald follows, visibly annoyed, trying to digest his first scoop of jealousy and its bitter aftertaste.

On the third and last floor, down a long hallway, they reach a rather simple door—not quite the entrance to a queen's palatial quarters.

"She's here," says Rhoswen.

"How do you know?" asks Archibald.

"The scarf," she says, pointing to a green piece of fabric wrapped around the knocker.

"If it was brown, it would mean the queen is away or doesn't want to be disturbed."

"We're lucky; that brown scarf can be there for months, even years sometimes," says Faerydae.

"I'll let you two handle this," says Rhoswen, hugging her sister heartily before walking away.

"We'll see you later," says Faerydae, turning back to the door, about to knock.

"Wait!" says Archibald.

"What's wrong? I thought we talked about this. Just tell her what you've done in Gristlemoth—that's it."

"It's not that. How should I call the queen? Your Highness? Your Majesty? Queen bee of this great Hive?"

"Don't worry; she's not that kind of queen," grins Faerydae. "Just call her Helena, but be respectful. And remember, you mustn't make a noise before I tell you to."

∴

287

Archibald heard what Faerydae said. Even so, he has never met a queen before. He feels overwhelmed, almost tingly. Maybe he needs more time to get ready.

It's too late. Faerydae has just knocked. He draws a deep breath and looks as though he is planning on holding it in for the whole meeting, his lips pursed.

A faint voice answers, "Come in."

Faerydae pushes the door open and steps in first. Archibald adjusts his helmet and hides behind her, tilting his head to catch a glimpse of the queen.

She has her back to them, looking out a large window, her body silhouetted against the bright lights of Belifendor.

Faerydae was right; Helena is definitely not like other queens he has seen on TV or in books. No royal gown. No satin bows or silk taffeta. No fluff. Just a simple ivory lace dress, embroidered not with pearl teardrops or crystal beads but with dried maple leaves and millet stems. No tiara or crown either, just a few daisies and seedpods woven in a beautiful headdress.

Though comfortable, the queen's quarters are also very humble. In lieu of a throne, a tufted bench is sitting in the middle of the room among layers of rugs, one of them even covering an entire wall like the tapestries at Grandma's house.

"What is this regarding?" asks the haloed figure.

"We came from Gristlemoth to see you," says Faerydae.

Helena turns around immediately. "Faerydae!" she says with much surprise and inversely little warmth in her voice. "I have not seen you in ages—what brings you here?"

"I have some important news."

"Good or bad?"

"Both, I think," she says, hesitant and confused, "but that's for you to say, my queen."

As Faerydae readies for her big announcement, the queen

walks closer to her visitors and detaches from the window glare.

Archibald squints to get a better look at her. The voice was already strangely familiar, but now he slowly recognizes her face—a face he thought never to see again.

"Grandma?" he blurts out, loud enough for both Faerydae and the queen to hear, bringing astonishment to their faces.

"What are you doing? Have you gone mad?" says Faerydae.

Startled, the queen has brought her hand to her mouth. But she can't quite hide her shock.

"Remove your helmet," she orders with a weakened voice.

Archibald complies, revealing his face.

With a loud gasp, the queen faints in an instant, folding into herself like a marionette losing its strings.

"Helena!" shouts Faerydae, rushing to help her.

"Grandma!" says Archibald, unable to move, still in shock.

Sitting on the floor next to her, Faerydae helps the queen regain consciousness, tapping her gently on the cheek.

"Helena? Are you all right?" Then turning to Archibald, "I don't know what's going on, but you'd better tell me. And fast."

"I dunno," he says, shaking his head.

The grandma he thought dead for months is right there before his eyes, possibly now half-dead, yet half-alive nonetheless.

"How is this possible?" he mumbles.

He has no idea. Doubts and questions are again gripping his mind. Did Celestine die and get reincarnated in this world? Does it mean he is dead too?

He moves closer as she slowly and painfully gets back up.

"What are you doing here, Archibald?" she asks in a weak voice.

"You know him?" exclaims Faerydae.

"I should be asking you that; you're supposed to be dead," he tells the queen.

"How did you get here?" she insists.

"The globe. I used the globe."

"How? How could you possibly know?"

"I didn't. I just found it in your library. I took the key from Bartholomeo. I unlocked the globe and got sucked into it."

"What have you done?" sighs Helena.

"Can anyone tell me what's going on? Who's Bartholomeo?" asks Faerydae. And to Archibald, "I knew you were trouble."

"No, this is all my fault," says the queen. She grabs Archibald by the shoulders. "Does anyone know? Does Bartholomeo know?"

"I'm not sure. I gave him the key back, so he probably didn't even notice I took it."

"Something else must have happened. He was supposed to bring me back a month ago."

"Wait, what do you mean *bring you back*? You knew about the globe?" asks Faerydae. "But you told us the Arks had all been destroyed."

Helena lets out another deep sigh. "I lied," she confesses. "But it was for your own good, to protect you and your sisters."

Faerydae is speechless. There is so much disappointment in those watery eyes. The queen was the only person she had always trusted, blindly, the one person she would have followed anywhere, no matter what.

"Who are you?" asks Archibald.

"Yes, who are you?" repeats Faerydae.

"I thought you were just Grandma Celestine," says Archibald. "I thought you were dead! Now you're a queen? The queen of all witches?"

"Faerydae, would you mind leaving us for a moment?" asks Helena.

"I was going to leave, anyway," says Faerydae, in the coldest tone she has ever used to address her queen. She would almost tell her to go shopping, whatever that means—something spiteful enough, hopefully.

She slams the heavy door shut on her way out.

Celestine/Queen Helena sits down on her bench, crumbling under the weight of all her lies and secrets.

"Ask," she simply says.

"I'm not sure where to start."

"I'm not sure either," she replies. "Well, my name is not Celestine; it's Helena. All of this was my idea: the colonies, bringing the girls down here . . ."

"That's impossible; you hate witches."

"What? Why would you think that?"

"The fireplace in the living room."

Helena slips a brief, furtive smile into her sigh.

"I found it at an antiques store in London. I thought to myself, 'How could someone want something so despicable in their house?'"

"That's what *I* thought."

"I bought it to make sure it would be destroyed. But then I decided to keep it, to remind myself of how dark the human spirit can be. Certain scars are there so the pain can stay alive."

"So you're a witch too?" asks Archibald.

"One of the worst, if you believe the legends. That's why the girls call me the queen. I have never quite liked that title, though."

"You're five hundred years old?"

"A bit older, actually, but who's counting?" she says with her signature smirk.

The queen walks across the room. "I have a question for you. Do you know that painting?" she asks, motioning toward a portrait on the wall behind him, near the entrance.

He doesn't need to get a closer look. He has definitely seen that woman before, seated with her arms crossed, her hair parted in the middle and a slight smile on her face. It's probably one of the most recognizable works of art in the world.

"I know this painting. It's the Mona something."

"You're right. They call it the *Mona Lisa*, but that's not what the painter called it."

"Who painted it?" Archibald asks, having no clue—surprisingly.

"A great man, a truly inspiring figure, from Italy. The same person who built the globe."

"And the tank?"

"Yes, he was very fond of animals. He imagined the tank to replace horses and elephants on the battlefield. Most of all, he designed it for us, to face the Marodors."

"I like that guy! Who was he?"

"Leonardo da Vinci. He called this painting *Happy Helena*, or *The Smiling One*—*La Gioconda* in Italian."

Archibald is stunned. His eyes travel from the queen to the painting and back, as the resemblance becomes clear. "This is you?"

"It is," she says proudly. "A few copies were made later on. One of them became rather famous. It's at the Louvre now, in Paris."

"Holy bejabbles! He must have really liked you!" Archibald exclaims.

"He sure did," utters Helena, turning her gaze to the open door leading to the next room.

"Everything okay?" asks Archibald, noticing the blank look on her face.

"Yes," she whispers, still lost in thought.

"Can I ask you something?"

"I guess," she answers, turning back to him.

"How did you fake your death? And why?"

As if she expected another question, Helena flutters her eyes, escaping a temporary torpor.

"The how part was fairly easy—a few herbs and plants did the trick. In fact, the potion worked almost too well. It put me in a deep comatose state for two full days instead of a few hours as planned. I nearly didn't wake up. Bartholomeo was so worried. I think I added too much willow bark and cloves to the mandrake. Unless it was the hemp; I'm not sure."

"But why? I don't understand."

Helena sighs heavily once more. "My time had come. After all those years, I became quite certain of one thing: men will never change. They'll continue to ravage the planet through wars, pollution, and greed, triggering one disaster after another. I have come to the conclusion that the human species is not worth saving, not on Earth at least."

"What do you mean, 'not worth saving'?" asks Archibald, almost scared.

"You know, shortly after I was born, they discovered a new continent. They called it the New World. It would later be known as America. There was so much hope, but as it turned out, it didn't take long for that New World to look awfully like the old one, shaped by violence and bloodshed. Only history will tell, but I am convinced that men have put the earth on a path of self-destruction."

"So . . . you just left?"

"I waited for five hundred years, Archibald. I didn't just make up my mind overnight. I left because I believed in something different, something better. Down here, we were given a second chance. A chance to start a new life based on simple values. No need for weapons, no need for technology we would end up using to destroy our own world, to destroy ourselves."

"But how can you build that world with only witches?"

"You're right. I cannot. That's why I started bringing in new souls, pure souls, who had suffered enough and deserved a second chance as well," says the queen. "The last time I traveled, I took many children with me. They came from one of my orphanages. They'll be happy here," she explains, looking out the window, trying to spot some of them.

"You brought orphans here? But they don't know anything about Marodors!"

"They will learn. When the girls came down here, they left their dolls behind. I told them they wouldn't be kids anymore."

Archibald surely doesn't mind that those creepy dolls stayed up in the library.

"Besides, the danger my orphans will face here is nothing compared with what they endured on Earth."

"I'm not sure about that," says Archibald, remembering his first minutes in Lemurea, chased by a nightmarish beast, let alone the surreal fights against the Krakatorum Gargantus and the river Marodor.

"At least down here, they won't have to suffer from war," she says.

"But there is a war already!" snaps Archibald. "Do you ever go out? Every colony is under siege!"

"Trust me—everything was going to be just fine. With hundreds more orphans coming here, we were going to expand all the colonies and create new ones."

"That was the plan?"

"It was," she confirms, "until you used the globe. Now I'm

afraid the elevator is broken."

"Maybe it's better that way."

"Why would you say that?"

"I don't know; sometimes I feel like an orphan, too, like I don't belong anywhere. At least here I have friends and people kind of like me."

"I'm sorry."

"Are you even my grandma, or was that just part of the lie?"

She comes close and places both her hands on Archibald's shoulders, staring deep into his eyes.

"I spent so much time with you when you were a baby," she assures him.

"I don't remember any of it. If you cared about me, why did you convince Mom and Dad to give me that stupid name? They told me, you know."

Helena smiles.

"I told you so many stories, narrated so many tales and legends, taught you so many things, big and small. Have you never wondered why you know so much?"

"Holy bejabbles . . ."

"Yes, that too."

"It was you? But how? Did you use magic on me?"

Helena closes her eyes and turns away. "It's complicated. I'm not sure you're ready for it just yet," she says, returning to the window.

"I'm tired of people telling me I'm not ready. I'm not a kid anymore—I'm the one who cured a Marodor."

"You did what?" asks Helena, frowning.

"Back in Gristlemoth. I cured a Marodor. That's what we came here to tell you," he says cheerfully.

"What are you talking about? This is nonsense—Marodors cannot be cured," says Helena, dismissive and almost angry.

"I know; I've been told. But trust me—it *can* be done. I did it."

"How?"

"I just took care of her."

"Her?"

"She was Faerydae's friend; she turned into a Marodor. I healed her wounds, spent time with her, talked to her. The sun and fireflies did the rest."

"Fireflies?"

"Yes, and sugar, but mostly . . . kindness," he adds.

"This cannot happen. I won't let it."

"But why?" questions Archibald.

"For all your wisdom, you have no idea what we are facing here. This discussion is over."

"What? How can you say that? We've come all the way here to talk to you. We risked our lives! One of our friends was taken by a Marodor. You can't just say this discussion is over."

"Who? Who was taken?"

"Her name is Lenora."

The queen is visibly shaken again. She tilts her head down and remains silent while Archibald continues his plea.

"Her dream was to fly, to fight Marodors. But if we cure them, there will be no more fighting."

"Where? Where was she taken?" asks Helena, having difficulty breathing.

"On the river, about halfway into our trip. That Marodor was really freaky. Some kind of toad and octopus mixed together."

"Isolda," mutters Helena, breathing deeply.

"Who's Isolda?"

The queen just sighs.

"Why did you have to come here? This is all your fault. I think it's time for you to leave," she says with an accusing stare.

Archibald is dismayed—but not really.

"Just when I started to think you're not so bad," he says bluntly, as he heads for the exit.

HEADS OR TAILS?

Hailee and Oliver look possessed, but the spell was of the most enchanting nature. They have been incapable of wiping grins off their faces since they talked to Philip, aka Professor Brimble.

They get off the bus a few streets away from the Realm of Antiques, race to the door, and once more make their way through the messy shop. Between a stuffed ferret and a monkey toy, both about to come alive, it seems, Oliver stops abruptly, signaling Hailee not to make another sound.

"What's wrong?" she murmurs.

Oliver points at the secret passage leading to the back room. The trick mirror is slightly open, enough for him to see the light inside. Maybe Oliver forgot to latch the door. However, the odds of him also leaving the lights on are nil.

"There's someone in there," he whispers.

Hailee's first reflex is to take a step back and freeze. Then her instinct kicks in, telling her to head back out. And run.

"Let's go!" she says, mouthing her words.

Oliver shakes his head, asking her to stay put. He will go check himself.

Since he can't hear anyone talking, there might be only one person in there—unless Heinrich's bodyguards are just waiting inside to ambush him.

Oliver takes a quick peak through the crack. He doesn't look too surprised or scared but rather embarrassed. He motions for Hailee to come over.

It's her turn to take a look.

"I can't believe this," she utters, apparently relieved.

Indeed, no monster bodyguard in there—only Oliver's father, probably drunk, apparently sound asleep, positively slouched on the ottoman at the center of the room.

Only one little problem: one of his arms is lying on the part of the circular sofa that opens up. To get to the globe, Hailee and Oliver will either have to wait or move him out of the way.

"I need your help," says Oliver, low still.

"Can't you do it yourself?"

"Sorry, teamwork."

They cross the room on tippy-toes and squat right by the ottoman. Oliver mimes instructions to Hailee. She is to lift Mr. Doyle's arm high enough for Oliver to remove the cushion cover from the secret compartment.

A painful grimace contest begins in which Oliver cringes while Hailee bites her lip during the whole procedure.

It works.

Oliver pulls out the globe gently and exchanges a smile with Hailee. She gladly lets go of his father's arm, and they are soon on their way.

Such was the plan, at least, relying upon the rather fuzzy assumption that Mr. Doyle was drunk enough to not wake up. Whether he was even asleep or faking it to discover what the kids were up to is a whole other question—irrelevant now that he turns out to be fully awake.

"Not so fast!" he shouts as he grabs onto Hailee's leg.

She screams.

"Dad, no!" shouts Oliver.

Mr. Doyle stands up quickly to get a better hold of Hailee. She doesn't even try to fight him. She is scared to death.

"Give me the globe, Son."

Oliver shakes his head, to say no, of course, but also in disbelief. He hates that feeling of having been played.

"I can't believe I was sleeping on it this whole time," says Mr. Doyle.

"Dad, let her go," pleads Oliver.

"I can't do that, Son. That globe is a lifesaver for me."

"You don't understand; we need it."

"Well, I need it more!"

"Maybe we can give it to you later, when we're done with it," suggests Oliver.

Mr. Doyle lets out an intimidating laugh. "You're funny, but I don't have time for this. Give it to me! I will hurt her—you know that."

"I know you will," says Oliver, reading the insanity on his dad's face and the anguish on Hailee's.

He places the globe on the floor at his feet, but instead of backing off, he grabs one of the crossbows from the wall. It's loaded.

"Here's our hero!" cracks up Mr. Doyle. "What are you gonna do with that, huh, Robin Hood?"

Oliver clears his throat and takes aim at his father, right between the eyes.

"Careful now, you wouldn't wanna hurt your friend here, would you?" warns Mr. Doyle, hiding behind his shivering prey.

"Ready, Hailee?" asks Oliver.

But neither she nor his dad have a clue as to what he has in mind.

Oliver winks at her and, in the blink of that eye, changes his aim to the left by about three feet. Now in his sight: a rope, holding a full body suit of armor straight up against the wall.

Oliver looses the arrow.

The rope is shattered instantly. All that target practice pays off at last. Suddenly unbalanced, the medieval armor wobbles for an instant before keeling over.

Caught by surprise, Mr. Doyle lets go of Hailee to shield himself, but he gets trapped under the heavy armor. Oliver and Hailee dash to the street with the globe, back on the run.

H

It is the night before Christmas. The sidewalks are crowded, the cobblestones freshly coated in frost. Yet it is highly possible our young fugitives just set a new world record for the two-thousand-meter steeplechase. In 5 minutes and 31 seconds, they leaped over two benches and six piles of snow of varying heights. A true feat, especially with the multiple bends they take left and right—all to get out of reach of the Realm of Antiques madman.

They find refuge among the shadows of a dingy pub, the Three-Legged Trout. They pick a corner table not for privacy but in a bid to avoid the waiter's gaze, since they don't have any money left to share even a hot cocoa (which is not on the menu, anyway).

Oliver unveils the Orbatrum, smothered in his jacket to protect it from the snow. They've been waiting for this moment for hours.

"Do we even know what to look for?" asks Hailee.

"That guy Philip, he talked about some kind of locking mechanism."

"Like a keyhole?"

"It's funny—the first time I looked at it, I thought this thing, up here, was some kind of key," he says, putting his hand on the crank. "I turned it as far as I could, but it ended up getting stuck. I hope I didn't break anything."

"What about this, right here?" asks Hailee, trying to stick

303

her finger in the dent on the globe.

"I doubt it; that just looks like a crack."

Hailee still tries to stick a straw into it.

"What are you doing?" asks Oliver, worried.

"I don't know. Maybe it *is* broken. Or maybe Philip made this whole thing up."

"It's possible, but for some reason, I don't think he did," says Oliver, running his hands over the globe's surface and on the meridian at the same time. "Wait! There's something here."

He flips the globe over, uncovering the keyhole underneath.

"That's it!" exclaims Hailee.

"Look at that pin going into the globe."

"Is that why the globe doesn't spin?"

"Probably, but without the key it's useless."

"Why don't we just break that pin, then?" suggests Hailee.

"I can't imagine it could be so easy. We don't know what it's connected to. It would probably disable the globe for good," notes Oliver. "We can't risk that."

"What do we do, then?"

"We don't really have a choice—we have to find the key."

"We've come so far. I can't believe this," sighs Hailee.

"I'm afraid we've reached a dead-end. That key could literally be anywhere—at your house, at my dad's shop, or maybe it fell off when we were running with the globe."

"Wait," mumbles Hailee, as though she had suddenly tuned the whole world out. "Could those be?" she mumbles again.

"Please tell me. I'm dying here!"

"My dad, he mentioned some keys a few days ago. He couldn't figure out what they were for."

"Keys? There are several? It doesn't make sense; we need only one."

"I don't know; your guess is as good as mine. That's the only lead we've got, though, unless you have a better idea. I just don't want to go back to your dad's shop."

"Where are those keys?"

"At my house. My parents always leave them there—that's what my dad was complaining about, that they're too big and awkward to carry around."

"This is made for a small key," he notes.

"Yes, and I think some of them *are* small."

"It's a long shot, but who knows?" says Oliver.

By the time the train brings Oliver and Hailee to Cuffley, it is dark out. The snow packed on the driveway is brightening up the night, showing the path to the house, itself shrouded in darkness.

"Seems like no one's home," says Hailee, surprised.

"Where could they be? It's Christmas Eve."

"My brother is gone, and I didn't come back home last night. I'm not sure they're up for a big celebration, and they're probably freaking out. I feel bad, actually."

"How are we going to get in?"

"I told you—that's the good thing about those keys. My parents always leave them here," explains Hailee, digging through the pot behind one of the lion sculptures. "Got 'em!" she shouts, dangling the keys.

She uses the largest one to open the front door and inspects the four little ones as soon as they get in.

"These are the weirdest keys," she notes, her eyes darting from the old man and his majestic beard, to the cobweb, the hand, and the moth, each standing out as a rather incongruous appendage.

"I'll let you choose," says Oliver.

"All right, but we can't do this here," says Hailee.

"Where, then? It's not like we have an instruction manual."

"Maybe where it was when Arch was . . . taken."

Hailee leads Oliver upstairs to her bedroom. "Right over there," she says, showing him the area where Archibald's desk used to be, and drags a chair right to that spot. Oliver sets the globe on top.

"Key, please," he asks, like a surgeon requesting a scalpel.

"Which one?"

"Let's try them all," he says with a shrug.

Hailee picks at random the only key Archibald didn't, the one ending in a cobweb. While Oliver tilts the globe, she gets ready to insert it into the keyhole—but stops suddenly.

"Are you seeing what I'm seeing?" she asks, stupefied.

"It's like it's melting!" says Oliver, stunned as well.

The cobweb of iron is coming apart before their widening eyes, some threads separating from the rest and, indeed, melting into one another to form a different shape—a seven-pointed star.

"A heptagram," says Oliver. "Some call it the elven star or the faery star, associated with witchcraft."

"That's a good sign, I guess?" asks Hailee with a gulp and a cringe.

"It's okay. You can do this," says Oliver, gently holding her hand and guiding the key into the lock, where it spins and spins like a spoon in jelly.

"Nothing's catching—they don't match up," sighs Hailee, removing the key. Its star pattern briefly turns into a spider before reverting to a labyrinth of woven threads—solid and still again.

"You sure don't see that every day," says Oliver.

"Let's try this one," says Hailee, grabbing the hand-shaped key. "Fingers crossed."

"Not quite," she whispers, as the hand forms a fist, then a

pointing finger, and finally a claw.

Hailee slides it into the keyhole without another thought, closing her eyes, to reopen them seconds later at the sound of an awakening rattlesnake—a mechanical rattling, that is.

The pin is out. Oliver is as amazed as she is. They both step away from the Orbatrum.

"What now?" he asks.

"As you said, there's no instruction manual."

"I have to admit: I'm a little freaked out."

"I don't blame you."

Hailee approaches the globe again. Oliver takes his position on the other side.

"Remember Philip's theory. If we follow it, to reverse your brother's travel, we just have to spin the globe in the opposite direction," he says.

"I get it, but the opposite of *which* direction?"

"That's the problem," says Oliver. "We don't know which way Archibald chose to begin with."

"So we're supposed to guess?"

"Kind of. As long as it's an educated guess."

"Educated guess? That sounds like 'crash landing' or 'only choice'—one of those bizarre word combos that doesn't make sense."

"You're almost exactly right," jokes Oliver.

Hailee smiles. "Okay, it's funny, but I'm not following."

"If you look around, so much in life is based on patterns," he says.

"What do you mean?"

"Habits—things people do automatically without putting much thought into it. You know, like shaking hands or putting their socks on. We just have to ask ourselves: what would most people do? *I* think most people would spin it like this," he says, slicing the air with his right hand, counterclockwise, the same way a tennis player would to give a wicked effect to a ball. "That means we have to do it the other way."

"Are you sure about this?"

"Of course not. Again, it's just an educated guess."

"We can't base our decision on that."

"What else, then? We'll never be sure, Hailee. We just have to try," he says, switching hands and getting ready to spin the globe.

"Wait!" she yells. "Not Archibald. You're right; most people would probably spin it that way," she says, mimicking his slicing motion. "Most people, but not my brother."

"Why is that?"

"Because Archibald is a lefty."

A rather scary thought occurs to Hailee. "Oh my God. If we're wrong, wherever Arch went, we're going," she says, triggering a long silence.

"Only one way to know," says Oliver, reaching for the globe again.

"No," Hailee stops him. "He's my brother. *I* have to do it."

"Are you sure?"

"Yes, I'm sure. Besides, if anything goes wrong, at least you can get *me* back."

"What if I get sucked up with you?"

"I was in the room when it happened," recalls Hailee. "The globe absorbed everything around it, but not me. I was obviously far enough away, right there by the bed. I think as long as you stay that far away from me, you'll be fine."

Oliver grabs her hand and kisses it lightly. "For luck," he says.

Hailee leans in close, twines her arms around his neck, and gives him the same gentle kiss—on the lips.

Dazed, Oliver steps back—all the way to her bed.

Hailee turns back to the Orbatrum, gazing intensely into its glow. She extends her arm above it. Her pointer finger starts swirling, alternating between clockwise and counterclockwise, as if mixing an invisible batch of whipped cream.

"Eeny, meeny, miny, moe. Arch, tell me which way to go!" she whispers.

THE DAY THE FISH RUNE DIED

Was the trip to Belifendor just utterly pointless? Archibald s starting to wonder. Who would blame him, looking back at what it took to get here? Fighting that two-sided river Marodor was a feat for the books—and not just the *Grand Bestiary*. For most people, that encounter alone would have made a change of heart legitimate and a U-turn a no-brainer. But Archibald didn't stop there. He'd braved the waters of the Urlagone, survived a two-hundred-foot drop from the sky in a boat turned airborne, and won a sprint against flying sphinxes.

Worst of all, he lost a friend along the way.

Convincing the queen to cure Marodors sounded like a noble endeavor. The end goal was great enough to justify the worst hardship and the most painful sacrifice. Now, exiting his meeting with Helena, Archibald is left with more doubts than certainties.

Faerydae is waiting for him, sitting on the floor, her back against the wall. She doesn't seem too happy.

"You two had a lot to talk about, didn't you?" she says with a dose of sarcasm, two spoons of resentment, and a pinch of anger.

"Too much for one day, that's for sure," responds Archibald.

"I bet it helps you both speak the same language, though."

"What's that?"

"I don't know—whatever tongue liars speak."

"I'm not a liar."

"Maybe, but *she* surely is," says Faerydae, standing up to make her point more forcefully. "The queen of lies!" she adds, turning to the door.

"Shh," whispers Archibald, a silencing finger on his lips, worried Helena will hear.

"Don't shush me! What is she going to do? Turn me into a saddle-goose? I'm already a big one just for believing her."

"Maybe she didn't lie—maybe she just wanted to protect you like she said."

"Did she brainwash you too?" she shouts. "Don't you understand that she's been lying to us for five hundred years? She was going back and forth this whole time and abandoned us here whenever she felt like it."

Archibald walks away, motioning for Faerydae to come along.

"I don't want to be insulting, but couldn't you figure that out before? I mean, she put that scarf on her door, and you guys would leave her alone for months, right?"

"Yes—we respected her wishes."

"I get that, but didn't you ever wonder what she was doing in there, how she could even survive?"

"Of course not. She's a witch, she's the queen; we figured she found a way . . . somehow."

"And what about the fact that she got older and you guys didn't? You never found that odd?"

"That's a good point, but, again, she's the queen! I thought that kind of logic didn't apply to her."

"I see. I guess being a queen is pretty convenient, huh? It kind of explains things that would make literally no sense otherwise."

"Are you saying I'm unguileful?"

"No, I would never say that—"

"Good."

"I would never say that," he clarifies, "only because I have no clue what that word means!"

"You know—plain-hearted, naive!"

"Oh, that's what it means. Then, yes, I would say that."

Faerydae pouts the way Archibald used to just fifteen days ago, before this adventure changed him radically, before he became a

313

man—about a quarter of one, but a man in the making
nonetheless.

"What now?"

"Now I need to sleep. I've barely closed my eyes since we left
Gristlemoth," she says. "We should head to my sister's place."

"You're going to tell her?"

"About Helena, you mean?"

Archibald nods.

"I'm not sure," says Faerydae.

Since Belifendor doesn't seem to believe in street names or
house numbers, Rhoswen's address would be rather fun to spell
out. Someone asking for directions might describe it as "the house
brushing the clouds, perched on the tall sequoia by the golem
shop, between branches 33 and 36" (out of 47). There are indeed
two other cabanas built up and down that giant tree, on branches
9 and 21, respectively.

"Yes, my sister lives at the very top."

"Where's the elevator?" asks Archibald, quite seriously,
expecting some kind of gadget to drop down and sweep them off
their feet.

"E-le-va-tor?" questions Faerydae. "Let me guess—you're
talking about a giant slingshot! No, wait—a catapult, maybe?
Something that would throw us all the way up there in one big
swing?"

"Not . . . quite. You were close, though."

"That's a good idea; I'll keep it in mind. In the meantime,
come this way," she says with a smile, showing him, well, the
hard way.

First, they have to access the pyramid house next door, which happens to be a library, then walk out to one of its tiered gardens. Only from there can they cross over to Rhoswen's sequoia on a suspended bridge. Then comes the trickier part: climb a ladder to cabana number 2, cross a second bridge going from the north branches to the south branches, and, finally, go up another— much taller—ladder straight to the top.

"Don't look down," says Faerydae, which Archibald didn't— until now. Doesn't he always do what he's not supposed to? Needless to say, he regrets it right away, hugging the ladder like he would his pillow on a thundery night.

They are so high up that the wind is blowing ten times as hard, making it that much more difficult for Archibald to scrabble up the last few steps.

If Faerydae was tired before this obstacle course, she is now completely worn out. She almost feels relieved that her sister is not home. As soon as they arrive, she crashes onto her bed and falls asleep almost instantly.

"You cured a Marodor?" is the question—more of a shout, really—that shakes Faerydae out of her dreams five hours later.

Rhoswen is back, lounging on the floor with Archibald among piles of blankets. Obviously, the two have been talking.

"I can't believe it! I never thought it would be possible," she says.

Faerydae sits up on the bed, wiping the sleep from her eyes. "Did you tell her everything?" she asks Archibald.

"Pretty much."

"Why would you do that?"

"You told me not to lie anymore!"

Faerydae shrugs her shoulders and shakes her head in dismay.

"I know about the globe," says Rhoswen. "It's so exciting!"

"What about the queen?" asks Faerydae, a bit worried.

"What *about* the queen?"

Archibald and Faerydae look at each other, wondering how to answer that.

"You've got to tell her what you did with that Marodor," says Rhoswen.

Archibald and Faerydae look at each other once more.

"Wait, that's why you came to Belifendor, isn't it?" realizes Rhoswen. "You came to tell the queen about it."

Faerydae nods.

"Are we going to try it here?" asks Rhoswen, staring eagerly at her sister.

"Don't ask *me*. I'm not that close to the queen, like some people, right, Archibald?"

He just rolls his eyes.

"What did she say?" insists Rhoswen.

"She didn't have an answer yet. She said she'd think about it, but she didn't seem too convinced."

"That's impossible—how could she think that?"

"She was pretty upset about Lenora getting caught," Archibald informs them.

"You told her?!" erupts Faerydae.

"Yes, why?"

"I don't think we'll get anything out of her now," sighs Faerydae.

"We have to find a solution," says her sister. "We can't continue to capture Marodors and put them in cages—we'll be running out of space soon."

"How many do you have here?" asks Archibald.

"I don't know exactly. Maybe three hundred."

"What? That's crazy!"

Rhoswen goes to the window. "Let me show you," she says.

Archibald looks out and takes in the dizzying view. It is simply breathtaking. Remove the Marodors flying in the background and you'll have a place of unspeakable wonders, the most idyllic postcard panorama of rooftops, treetops, and hilltops— not to forget golemtops and their runes that read like a giant alphabet carved on those imposing boulders surrounding the city.

Rhoswen points toward the area beyond the castle, a blanket of green with a few holes here and there.

"That forest spans from one side of Belifendor to the other."

"All that is the Marodors' pen?" asks Archibald, stunned.

"All of it," says Rhoswen, sorry to confirm.

"Belifendor is turning into a prison," laments Faerydae. "The rivalry between colonies has only made it worse."

"What rivalry?" asks Archibald.

"This hunt for Marodors has pitted us against one another for centuries. It's Belifendors versus Gristlemoths or Marrowclaws versus Nifequods. Pick your team. We all try to outdo each other by capturing more beasts," explains Faerydae.

"This can't work for much longer," says Rhoswen.

"What's going on over there?" Archibald wonders aloud, focusing on a large open square they crossed earlier, at the foot of the castle. Preparations are being made for something, with a wooden structure erected right in the middle of that square.

"It's strange—I didn't hear about this," says Rhoswen.

"Let's go check!" suggests Faerydae, heading to the door.

"Couldn't you live on the first floor?" whines Archibald, cringing at the idea of using those perilous ladders again.

Getting closer to the mysterious wooden structure doesn't quite make it less mysterious. Braced to scaffolding made out of bamboo, what resembles a totem pole is being anchored to the ground by two additional legs at the base. The weird-looking tripod gets even more suspicious when Faerydae spots Breena nearby. Her old friend seems to be supervising the construction.

"What's going on, Breena?" she inquires.

"Oh, you're still here? I thought you left already."

"What's all this for?"

"Queen's orders."

"What orders?" asks Archibald.

"That I cannot say," replies Breena with that default look on her face—malicious.

Before Faerydae can ask another question, Helena arrives, flanked by four young men—obviously some of the orphans she brought here with her a few months ago.

"Can you tell us what's going on?" Archibald asks her.

"Do you know the meaning of that rune?" she asks, pointing at the helmet Archibald is holding.

"The fish rune?"

"Yes, the *fish rune*," she says, smiling.

"I'm not sure. I asked Maven, but she didn't remember."

"Oh, no, Maven remembered—trust me," replies the queen. "She just couldn't talk about it."

"Why?"

"She worked on that rune, along with me and a few others. That was many years ago. We called it Hesperialis."

"I've never heard of it," says Faerydae.

It even seems to come as a surprise to Breena, who frowns.

"What was it for?" asks Archibald.

"A better question would be, *Whom* was it for? And, *Where* was it for?" says Helena.

"I don't understand," he says.

"It was not made for use in Lemurea," she says, looking up. "It was designed to be used on Earth, on people."

"You can't use runes on people!" exclaims Faerydae. "It's too risky!"

"That's why Hesperialis took so long to craft. The goal was not to hurt people but to change them, to make them better humans—or just humane. The idea was to use it on a few and make those few the vanguard for a wider change, disciples of a new ideal, our ideal, which would spread, to eventually vanquish greed and violence. And who knows—stop the wars, maybe."

"I don't understand," says Faerydae. "How could Maven believe in this? She didn't even know you had a globe, did she?"

"No, I never told her. She just trusted me to find a way back."

"You deceived her too?" accuses Faerydae.

"That's one way of looking at it. I just wanted to keep her dedicated and focused," replies the queen.

"You've played us all," sighs Faerydae.

"As I told you before, it was for—"

"Our own good? Is that the best you can come up with?"

"Silence!" shouts Helena. "There is no point arguing this any further. Hesperialis was a dream and a dream only. That's why I had that fish *rune* drawn on my casket. Remember?" she tells Archibald. "I wanted it buried, forever. That idea was naive. It would never have worked."

"How do you know?" asks Archibald.

"Because I know people, Archibald. Mankind has repeated the same mistakes over and over for centuries, never learning from them. I have come to believe that people don't *want* to change their ways. Therefore, they don't deserve that rune; they don't deserve to be saved. Anyway, this debate is now closed. It's time for plan B."

"What's plan B?" asks Faerydae, fearing the worst.

"Hesperialis was not the only rune I worked on. There always was another option involving a rather *different* scenario."

"What was that?" asks Archibald.

"Kill all Marodors," says Helena, cold.

"What?" he exclaims.

"How?" asks Faerydae.

"I thought they *couldn't* be killed," says Rhoswen.

"I made another rune," reveals the queen, "a unique rune, so powerful it doesn't need to be combined with any other. I never thought I would use it, even though deep inside I was afraid I'd have to. By coming here, Archibald, by closing the door on us, you left me with no choice."

"But there's another solution," insists Archibald. "I told you: Marodors can be cured."

"It's too late. I had my doubts, but now that they took my daughter, it's over. The Marodors have to go."

Archibald is startled. It takes him awhile to understand.

"Lenora? Lenora was her daughter?" he asks Faerydae.

"I thought you knew," she responds.

The queen points her finger at Faerydae like a prosecutor would.

"I trusted you to protect her."

"I'm sorry; I failed you."

"If we don't do anything, you'll be next, Archibald," warns the queen. "Complete eradication is now the sole option moving forward. And it starts tonight, right here," she says, gesturing toward the strange-looking totem.

"You can't do that!" Archibald exclaims.

While Rhoswen is speechless, next to her, Breena can barely contain her joy.

"It is I who will decide. I won't let you disrupt my plans again," says the queen.

"What if it doesn't work?" worries Faerydae. "What if trying to kill them ends up creating more Marodors? It could even make them stronger, maybe strong enough to access the earth!"

"That's a risk I am willing to take," the queen says calmly.

"Why rush into this? Let's talk about it," implores Faerydae.

Helena turns to the four young orphans behind her, and to one of them in particular, his hair so short he looks bald.

"Theo, please make sure they don't cause any problems," she asks him before walking away.

"Please don't do this," pleads Archibald as Theo, nearly a head taller than him, comes standing in his way.

"Don't make me hurt you," warns the tough guy.

The others have grabbed onto Faerydae. Rhoswen wants to intervene, but her sister motions for her to stay put.

"Do you wish to follow them?" Breena asks her.

Rhoswen shakes her head. "I'm loyal to the queen," she assures, quite convincingly.

"Good girl," says Breena. "Do me a favor, though: make sure you stay home tonight."

"What's going to happen to them?"

"A little time in jail has never killed anyone," answers Breena.

Rhoswen looks very concerned as her sister and Archibald are escorted away.

"Those Gristlemoths," mocks Breena, "a bunch of idealists."

It's the second time in two weeks that Archibald is thrown in jail. One more and his reputation as a teacher's pet and a wimp might be history, making way for a new boy in town—a *bad* boy.

He's already starting to act like one. He yelled at the guards when they threw him and Faerydae into this cell. He even pushed one of them. Yes, it was a girl, but at least he resisted. Even better, Archibald kicked the door a few times, before realizing it was there to stay—probably made of that same unyielding blackwood Wymer built his tank with.

For the last three hours, Archibald has been inspecting every square inch of the cell. Looking for weak points or flaws, he finally turned his attention to the two metal bars anchored into the tiny window. Archibald is now digging into the dried mud around them, using one of the dead batteries he kept in his pocket. At this pace—a quarter of a teaspoon of powdery mud removed in fifteen minutes—it would take him days of nonstop grating to clear a path out.

"I've seen this in a movie," he mumbles.

"I'm not sure what you're talking about or what it is you're trying to accomplish, but you should stop," says Faerydae, seated on the opposite side of the room.

"We have to do something. We can't let her kill that Marodor!"

"There's nothing we can do. Trust me—I've been in here before."

"You have?"

"Four times," she says, running her fingers into a series of tally marks etched into the wall.

Based on that count, Faerydae spent at least twenty-five days locked up in this cell.

"What happened to your 'door unlocked' concept? You

know, the whole 'it's not a prison, just a time to reflect'?"

"It's different here."

"So what did you do to end up here so much?"

Faerydae looks embarrassed. She definitely regrets mentioning that detail about her past. "Let's just say that Helena doesn't like to be challenged."

"Wait, you were thrown in jail because you disagreed with her? The queen's a meanie, huh?"

"It was pointless. After the third argument, I gave up. That's when I left to create Gristlemoth."

"So what did you do the fourth time?"

"What do you mean?"

"You said you were sent here four times, so three because of those fights with the queen and once for . . . what?"

"Oh, that was nothing, really."

"For what?" insists Archibald.

"Nothing," says Faerydae, looking even more embarrassed.

"You . . . stole something, didn't you?" says Archibald with a "gotcha" kind of grin.

Faerydae shakes her head but struggles to offer a strong denial.

"You did!" shouts Archibald, realizing he might be right.

"Fine. Yes, but only once. And it wasn't really stealing. I just couldn't find my own herbs, and I really needed to finish that potion I was working on."

"Let me guess: you *borrowed* those herbs?" he says, cracking up.

"Not funny," says Faerydae, smiling, admitting it kind of is.

Archibald's laughter is interrupted by the sound of horns reverberating all the way to the prison cell.

"What was that? Someone at the gate?"

"No, three horns at once—that's the signal for some kind of

ceremony. I think the killing is about to begin."

Archibald stops digging, anger accelerating the flow of blood to his brain, fueling the search for a way out. He looks up and gets an idea.

"If you step on my shoulders, maybe you can squeeze between those beams," he suggests, pointing out the narrow openings in the ceiling.

"What do you think I am, a cat? Not even a squirrel could fit through that!"

"Maybe the beams can move a little—that's our only chance."

"Okay, fine. I'll try."

Archibald puts his back against the wall and braces for Faerydae to step onto his cupped hands. She takes a few steps back to get a good run-up, when the door suddenly rumbles—a jolt as violent as it is brief.

"Was that a knock?" he asks.

"From what? A twenty-foot giant?" Faerydae replies. Archibald's idea exactly.

Another tremor hits, but this time it's not only the door but the entire room that vibrates with it. Archibald and Faerydae hold on to each other, nearly losing their balance. The door is about to come off its hinges, but the doorframe itself suddenly detaches from the walls around it and collapses flat onto the ground.

Emerging from a cloud of dust, Maven steps in, coughing and spitting, holding two golems she used to knock down the door.

"I was just trying to unlock it," she says, looking sorry.

"Maven!" rejoices Archibald.

"How did you know we were here?" asks Faerydae.

"Everybody knows! But your sister told me what happened.

She couldn't come—Breena had her followed."

"Give me some golems; I might need them," says Faerydae.

Maven hands her one.

"Do you have more?"

"No, but I know where to get some."

"We don't have time; we've got to hurry," says Faerydae, leading the way as they run out of the crumbling prison.

When they reach the execution area, the night has already fallen on Belifendor. The darkness about to prevail, however, will have far longer-lasting effects. Large fires have been lit all around the square, flames leaping high in the sky from several pyres. Packing the streets, peeking through windows or standing on rooftops, countless onlookers are gearing up for an event most don't know anything about.

A cortege shows up in the distance. The image is surreal. A Marodor is levitating above ground, gliding through the crowd. Kept at bay by four guards armed with golems, the beast looks dead already, its body and expression seemingly frozen. Chosen to star in this grand premier, the unlucky creature is paraded through the city like a war trophy. The final stop is near the totem built in a hurry this afternoon—more of a gibbet, it turns out. The monster is tied roughly to the pole with heavy chains, on a short leash.

"That Marodor is so small," notes Archibald.

"It's a young one," says Faerydae. "Helena is not sure her new rune will work; that's why she didn't pick a full-grown."

We're still talking about a rather healthy baby, probably nearing fifteen hundred pounds. Compared with his two- to ten-ton relatives, this Marodor is definitely a lightweight—and a casting error. Not the ideal specimen for a queen trying to convince her people that an entire species must be wiped out. This little one probably hasn't even made it into the *(purposely incomplete) Bestiary of Marodors*—perhaps as a footnote.

The usual circus aggregate of countless animals, this creature doesn't resemble any in particular. From behind, just based on the brown fur and long hind feet, one might think of a rabbit. That's if one can look past the scaled armadillo tail, of course. Pan 180 degrees to its wide beak and an eagle or hawk is what comes to mind—only, an eagle or hawk with fluffy ears, horns sticking out of its neck, bug-like eyes, and a torso resting on human arms. Not much of a bird in the end, especially with only one wing left—that of a giant insect, apparently. Veined and transparent, it blends in with the long, white hair flowing among leaves on the monster's back, which is curved like a hyena's. From afar, the whiskers curled on either side of its face could look like tusks, but up close, that funny mustache is the one feature that makes the Marodor slightly less nightmarish.

Released from the spell of subduing golems, the Marodor has regained some of its wild spirit, roaring and growling again. A chill spreads through the crowd but quickly fades away. The queen has just appeared on the second-floor balcony of a house facing the square. Her dress is different than earlier; this one is studded with dried corn husks whose twisted ends jut out like spikes on a suit of armor.

"This is a historic day—the beginning of a new chapter in our fantastic journey," she says in a somber voice. "When we arrived here, the hope was always to return to a better world. A world that would not only accept us but also be guided by new values: tolerance, love, and compassion. Unfortunately, after all these years, we have to come to terms with our reality. There is no way back. Our future is here. The path we're about to take will help us secure that future."

Archibald, Faerydae, and Maven worm their way through the silent crowd, getting closer to the soon-to-be-slayed Marodor.

"The time has come to eliminate the remnants from the Old World," says Helena, continuing her sales pitch, now raising her voice. "Marodors do not belong here. We have been struggling with those demons for centuries, even though we had nothing to do with their birth. Today, we say enough. Today, we part ways with the beasts. Only with a new rune can we lighten our burden, a rune powerful enough to kill all Marodors!"

The queen's final words cause the crowd to erupt. Some are shocked and afraid—others hopeful. The queen raises her hand to silence them, and all fall rapt.

"I give you . . . Venomurtis!"

In her hand, a golem, held high for everyone to see.

Scattered throughout the square, Breena and the queen's loyal orphans show the crowd more golems bearing the same rune—a single line intersecting a rough diamond-shaped carving. But to all, it reads like an ominous eye—⧫.

"Now what?" Archibald asks Faerydae.

"I don't know," she says, looking around frantically in search of a strategy.

Helena raises her voice further as she nears the height of her speech.

"We cannot do anything for the Old World, but we can save this one, our new world, a more perfect world."

That's Archibald's cue. He breaks from the throng and runs to stand between the queen and the Marodor.

"She's lying to you!" he shouts to the crowd, pointing

dramatically at the queen. Then addressing her directly: "If this world is so perfect, why do people want to leave?"

"Who? Who wants to leave?" she thunders, casting a fiery gaze on the audience.

Her tone makes an impression. Scattered booing erupts, aimed at Archibald. But just in his vicinity, there are also some Belifendors—a few, visibly shaken—who seem tempted to raise their hands. At the same time, who would dare challenge the queen? In the end, no one does.

Faerydae manages to join Archibald, but Maven is caught by one of the boys under Breena's command.

"What if they do want to leave? Are you going to throw everyone in jail?" asks Faerydae.

"There's no leaving anymore. This is the only way."

"Who are you to decide who will be saved?" asks Archibald.

"Everyone will be saved," she assures him.

"Here, maybe. But what about Mom and Dad? What about Hailee?" he says.

"I can do nothing for them," says Helena, her voice broken.

"Look around," says Faerydae. "Doesn't it remind you of something? The hellish fires, the crowds incited to violence—fear feeding extremism. This is what you saved us from! This is why we escaped!"

"You can't understand. You have not seen what I have seen. You don't know what these beasts are made of," says Helena. "I won't let anyone stand in my way."

"This is not the queen I used to love and respect," says Faerydae, tears welling in her eyes.

"Proceed," Helena tells Breena.

Faerydae and Archibald move back, their arms spread wide as though to shield the Marodor. They are only a few feet away from the beast, getting dangerously close.

Breena moves toward them, holding two Venomurtis golems.

"They're in the way," she tells the queen.

"Proceed!" repeats Helena.

Breena gets even closer.

"You don't have to do this," pleads Faerydae, armed with one regular golem, useless as an unloaded gun.

Breena freezes. "I can't do this. What if I kill them?" she tells Helena.

"These golems will do them no harm," says Helena.

"Are you sure?"

"You don't trust your queen? Perhaps I should have Theo take care of this instead?"

Seeing him step forward with no doubt on his face, Breena tightens her mouth and clenches her teeth. She turns back to Archibald and Faerydae, takes a large breath, and extends her arms.

"Please don't!" calls Faerydae, rushing toward her old rival.

Breena seems ready to activate the golems. Just before she speaks the fateful words, a halo of white light appears on the ground, right under Archibald's feet.

Faerydae whips around to see the bright ring of undulating light slowly growing around Archibald, who is frozen in fear.

"What's happening?" utters Breena, wondering whether the golems might have acted on their own. After all, no one quite knows how the new rune works.

"What is this?!" echoes Archibald, gazing down at his feet, now covered in a blurry veil.

"It can't be . . ." gasps Helena.

"I can't see my legs anymore!" shouts Archibald.

Indeed, part of his body seems to have vanished, as though he was slowly sinking into a pond of fog.

After stabilizing and hovering at ground level for a few seconds, the halo erupts, forming a glowing ball that tears through the sky.

No golem could ever release such power.

Total pandemonium breaks out on the square. Those who have not yet fled are looking desperately for cover, when suddenly hundreds of screams are silenced by a loud suction sound that fades into the sky, along with the column of light.

The commotion is over. It has given way to an eerie silence. Archibald is squatting in a fetal position, his head bowed forward onto his arms. Once free of the high-pitched whistling in his ears, he straightens up drowsily.

For several seconds, up is down and vice versa.

The blur from the blinding beam of light slowly dissipates, and a familiar silhouette comes into focus. Only a few feet away from Archibald, facing him, is the one responsible for the "big bang" that just happened—Hailee, seated on the floor, palms down, mouth and eyes wide open. Behind her, Oliver is the only one standing, though he looks just as bowled over as she does.

Instinctively, Archibald swivels his head, peering around feverishly. But there's no Marodor in sight, no burning pyres, no Queen Helena, no Faerydae . . . only his old bedroom. Struggling to believe he is back home, he pats his body to make sure it's in one piece. Hailee can sigh, relieved she didn't send herself to who-knows-where.

"Uh . . . hi?" she mutters tenderly, taking notice of his shabby outfit and the strange helmet he is holding. She is dying to hug him—something she can't remember ever doing before.

But their family reunion will have to wait, cut short as it is by
a loud bang just above them, followed by a galloping sound.
They all glance up, tracking the rumbling as it travels
from one end of the roof to the other, then stops abruptly,
the room plunged into silence once more.
"Was that thunder again?" whispers Hailee with
fear back in her voice.
All three are left glancing nervously at each
other, even more questions filling their heads—
and for Archibald, a weird hunch.
At his feet, the globe is lying sideways
on the floor in the middle of a fresh set of
burn marks. Spark and trigger of this
carefully engineered chaos, the
magical device swallows back the
last remnants of the formidable
energy just released. A
feeble glow travels its
surface, bolts of slow-
moving lightning
strikes that come
dying into their
maker's
initials
—LDV.

To be continued . . .

AFTERWORD

It was 1539
when Swedish writer Olaus Magnus
created an incredible map
haunted by the strangest beasts
called the "Carta Marina."

At a time when science was in its infancy,
the unknown represented an endless source of fear, rumor, and
legend. Imaginations were free to run as wild as the beasts
lurking in the surrounding darkness.

While werewolves, griffins, manticores,
bonnacons, leucrotas, and basilisks
were believed to roam the thickest of forests,
under Olaus Magnus's pencil, the oceans gave birth to a new
breed of monsters, from sea serpents to owl-sharks and
pig-whales.

The "Carta Marina" also happens to be the main source of
inspiration for the adventures of Archibald Finch. As an homage
to Magnus, several of his monsters were included in the map of
Lemurea on pages 232–233. The other creatures on the map were
drawn by Flemish poet Jacob van Maerlant around 1270, for *Der
Naturen bloeme (The Flower of Nature),* an encyclopedia and bestiary
written in verse.

Listen up! Enjoy *Archibald Finch and the Lost Witches* in audio, available wherever audiobooks are sold.

Andrews McMeel Publishing
a division of Andrews McMeel Universal
1130 Walnut Street, Kansas City, Missouri 64106

www.andrewsmcmeel.com
www.archibaldfinch.com
www.zinakostich.com

21 22 23 24 25 SDB 10 9 8 7 6 5 4 3 2 1

ISBN: 978-1-5248-6772-0

Library of Congress Control Number: 2021936663

Editor: Melissa R. Zahorsky
Art Director: Michel Guyon and Tiffany Meairs
Production Editor: Elizabeth A. Garcia
Production Manager: Chuck Harper

Made by:
King Yip (Dongguan) Printing & Packaging Factory Ltd.
Address and location of production:
Daning Administrative District, Humen Town
Dongguan Guangdong, China 523930
1st Printing — 6/21/21